PRAISE FOR

PERILOUS PACIFIC

AND THE TARA SHORES THRILLERS

"FBI agent Tara Shores is back in Chesler's latest pulse-pounding techno-thriller, *Treacherous Tropics*, an intelligent page-turner that will keep you reading late into the night!"

—**JEREMY ROBINSON**, author of *Threshold*

"Chesler melds science and adventure with the brilliant command of the late Crichton. *Treacherous Tropics* takes readers on a Hawaiian journey they won't soon forget."

—**DOUGLAS CORLEONE**, author of *Night on Fire*

"Great scientific concepts that are based in reality, especially the secret messages encoded in DNA.... Vivid setting in Hawaiian islands with lots of local color and local detail. Good pacing will keep you reading to the end. FBI agent Tara Shores is one cool, competent chick."

—**SCIENCETHRILLERS.COM**

"Rick Chesler's biotech thriller *Treacherous Tropics* is a pulse-pounder of the highest order!"

—**WEEKLY EBOOK READER**

"The lush Hawaiian setting is conveyed in a way that immerses the reader in the story. There's a strong scientific element to the plot, but is handled in a way that keeps the book accessible. *Treacherous Tropics* is an exciting techno/science thriller in the spirit of Michael Crichton."

—**MEGALITH REVIEWS**

"Chesler really had me with all the clever science experiments, fast-paced chase scenes, gun action and original twists and turns. I need a crowbar to pry myself away."

—**THENOVELBLOG.COM**

"*Deadly Depths* is a fast-paced thriller that is one third deep-sea adventure, one third FBI sleuthing, and one third awesome. A superb novel and killer concept."

—**JEREMY ROBINSON**, *New York Times* bestselling author of *Infinite*, *Project Nemesis*, and *Island 731*

"A whale of a tale by author Rick Chesler involving modern-day pirates, media moguls, and a sexy federal agent."

—**STEVE ALTEN**, *New York Times* bestselling author of *MEG*

PERILOUS PACIFIC

ALSO BY RICK CHESLER

TARA SHORES THRILLERS

Deadly Depths

Treacherous Tropics

OMEGA FILES ADVENTURES

Atlantis Gold

Ark Found

Golden One

Cross Found

JURASSIC DEAD SERIES (WITH DAVID SAKMYSTER)

Jurassic Dead

Jurassic Dead 2

Jurassic Dead 3

OUTCAST OPS SERIES

Game of Drones (with Rick Jones)

The Poseidon Initiative

African Firestorm (with Craig Reed, Jr.)

Red Ice (with Craig Reed, Jr.)

Watch List (with Craig Reed, Jr.)

DANE MADDOCK ORIGINS (WITH DAVID WOOD)

The Tomb

Treasure of the Dead

Amber

Electra

Splashdown

OGMIOS TEAM ORIGINS (WITH STEVEN SAVILE)

Lucifer's Machine

STANDALONE TITLES

DMZ

The Tank

The Flat

The Yeti

Landing Party

Sawfish

Hotel Megladon

Luna

Blood Harbor

PERILOUS PACIFIC

A TARA SHORES THRILLER

RICK CHESLER

KEYLIGHT BOOKS
AN IMPRINT OF TURNER PUBLISHING

For my wife, Tabbatha Chesler, who loves the sun.

KEYLIGHT BOOKS
AN IMPRINT OF TURNER PUBLISHING COMPANY
Nashville, Tennessee
www.turnerpublishing.com

Perilous Pacific: A Tara Shores Thriller
Originally published as Solar Island in 2012

Cover design by JD&J Design
Book design by William Ruoto

Library of Congress Cataloging-in-Publication Data
Names: Chesler, Rick, author.
Title: Perilous pacific / Rick Chesler.
Other titles: Solar Island
Description: Nashville, Tennessee : Keylight Books, an imprint of Turner Publishing Company, 2024. | Series: A Tara Shores thriller
Identifiers: LCCN 2024052585 (print) | LCCN 2024052586 (ebook) | ISBN 9798887980607 (paperback) | ISBN 9798887980614 (hardcover) | ISBN 9798887980621 (epub)
Subjects: LCGFT: Thrillers (Fiction). | Novels.
Classification: LCC PS3603.H4848 S65 2024 (print) | LCC PS3603.H4848 (ebook) | DDC 813/.6--dc23/eng/20241119
LC record available at https://lccn.loc.gov/2024052585
LC ebook record available at https://lccn.loc.gov/2024052586

Printed in the United States of America

LIGHTNER ENTERPRISES

SOLAR ISLAND

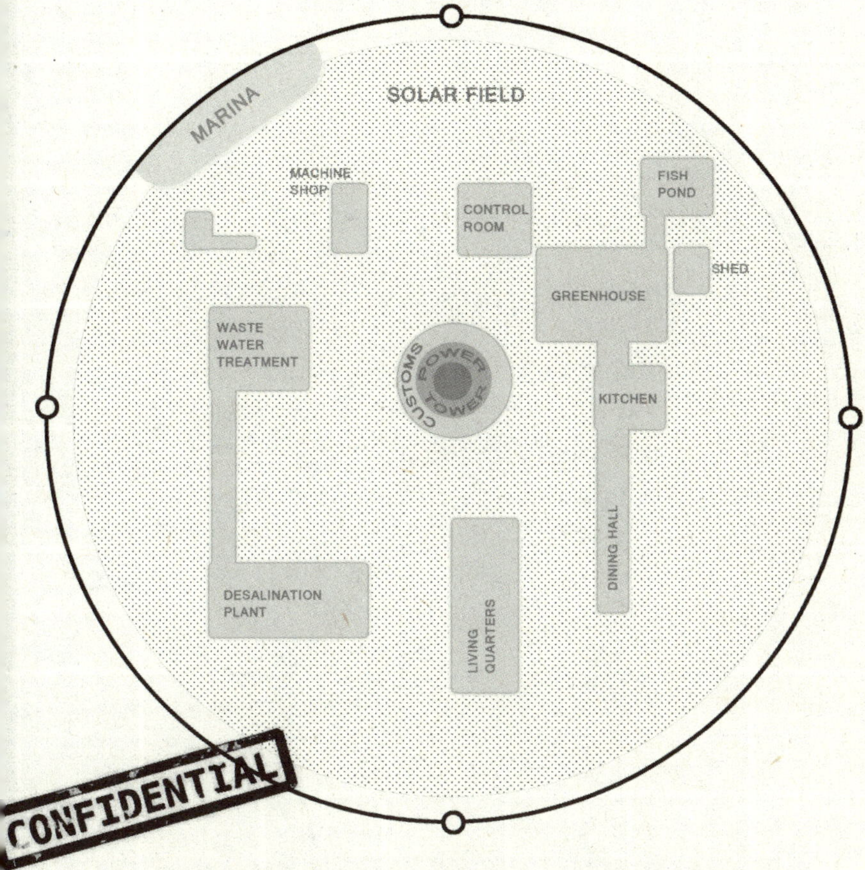

WARNING: Corporate map only, not for distribution

Lightner Enterprises, Inc.

If I had to choose a religion, the sun as the universal giver of life would be my god. —Napoleon Bonaparte

If it's worth doing, it's worth overdoing. —Ayn Rand

ONE

Pacific Ocean, southeast of Japan, 8:30 a.m., local time

"It won't hurt that much. Let's just get this over with so we can leave this godforsaken island, all right?"

Bernard Riley didn't answer, but continued to study the stencil he held in his hands.

His associate, Robert Benson, was losing patience with his stall tactics. "Bernie?"

The two men stood huddled together, eyes alert for unseen observers. The tropical sun glared from the open blue sky, transforming the surrounding sea into a glittering jewel—a jewel with a floating island as its only flaw. The sole purpose of this sprawling artificial construction was, ostensibly, to control a tiny fraction of that radiant energy—to harness a timeless force.

Riley looked up from the stencil. "This would be a lot easier with a Sharpie. No luck?"

"I asked around a bit—discreetly—but I didn't want to push it too hard. With Lightner allowing monitored emails, there's no need for letter-writing; and with the computerized automation, what's there to write down for work? Nobody's got a pen. If there are any on this island, they're locked up tighter than Fort Knox."

Riley let out a sigh as he looked up at the sky. "Man, I still say Lightner must be paranoid not to allow frickin' pens."

Benson stared at him for a few seconds before speaking. "It's not paranoia, Bernie, if they really *are* out to get you. If we did have access to a pen or a marker, we'd have used it already in a way he doesn't want. This place is worth a thousand fortunes.

Remember that. That's why we're going to these extremes." He gestured to the stencil once more.

"You mean that's why *I'm* going to these extremes."

Robert's reply dripped sarcasm. "Oh, okay. So I didn't spend like a hundred hours cutting away on that damn stencil? And that was somebody else in those off-limits areas, committing those designs to memory so I could transcribe them later to the stencil, and check and recheck them every time I went back? Because that's funny—maybe I'm coming down with a little case of island fever—but I thought that was me!" His voice had begun escalating in volume, prompting Bernard to glance around skittishly, as if they might have been overheard.

"As long as you think it'll work, Robert. If Lightner catches us—"

"Don't worry, it'll work! We've got the schematic and we've got the formula represented on the stencil. The hard part's over. Now all you need to do is get some sun for a few hours."

"This is really going to hurt, isn't it? How come you can't do this part?"

Robert exhaled sharply. "We've been over this! You've got the day off. I have to be at my station in sixty minutes. That's not enough time to let the stencil set."

"You mean burn."

They both knew *set* was a euphemism.

At length, Robert clapped him on the shoulder. "You look like you could use some color anyway."

Bernard looked up from the stencil. "You know damn well that after twenty minutes, I'll be as red as a lobster."

"Use the sunscreen on your arms, legs, and neck so it's not obvious you've been tanning. Stick to the plan."

Benson removed his polo shirt. The ubiquitous garment bore the Solar Island logo: a circular raft of solar panels on shimmering blue water reflecting back a blazing ball of light. He tossed the shirt on the "ground," as residents of Solar Island were used to calling it, even though it was functionally and materially closer to a ship's deck. Now clad only in a pair of khaki shorts and sunglasses, Bernard shoved the intricate stencil into Robert's hands.

"Tape it on."

Robert looked at the stencil to make sure he had it aligned properly. Its convoluted cutouts had been painstakingly done by hand with a precision blade during several sessions over the course of two tension-fraught months. During this time, the two men had maintained a near-constant state of risk in order to access a secure area of the island that was normally off limits to them.

And now that gamble was about to pay dividends.

Solar Island's Power Storage Center was the most critical piece of technology aboard the facility. The solar collectors, although a new design with increased efficiency compared to the clunky panels in use since the 1970s, were useless without the ability to store the power they generated until it could be transferred to paying customers. The capacity to retain the power produced by the panels for nights and cloudy days had long been alternative power's weak point. But the owner of Solar Island had made great strides in this problem area.

Many in the energy industry were eager to talk with Dr. Jacob Lightner about the technology employed in his so-called "pilot project"—and specifically his method for energy storage—but thus far he had not returned any calls, becoming something of a hermit on his private island of industry.

Robert Benson and Bernard Riley, however, had decided that their technician salaries were worth risking for what would amount to a stunning jackpot were the technology to be known by the right people. One night, they had stolen into the power storage center, pried the panels open, and identified the unique proprietary circuit boards that made it all possible. On subsequent visits, they had taken note of chemical labels and digital diagnostics displays until they were able to reverse engineer the process back to what little they had already been privy to, based on their legitimate access privileges. All the while, they left no trace of their activity, mentioned it to no one.

The job would have been relatively simple had it not been for Dr. Lightner's extraordinary security measures. They had signed the standard noncompete clauses and nondisclosure agreements when taking their jobs, but Lightner refused to depend solely on legal measures to safeguard his work. After all, for one thing, those documents were only binding in the United States, and Jacob Lightner had declared Solar Island an independent sovereign nation.

Lightner posited that when afloat in international waters, the island was not officially part of any existing nation. While this position wasn't strictly supported by maritime law and no other country had yet formally recognized Lightner's attempts at nationalization, Solar Island had been designated an area of special sovereignty by the United Nations.

Port visits by Solar Island were few and far between. "Foreign visitors," as Lightner referred to anyone who didn't live and work on Solar Island, were also rare; when they did occur, tough security measures were implemented. Employees who left the isle were frisked by security guards who weren't merely going through the motions, even after they had passed through metal detectors. No media-storage devices of any kind were allowed on or off the island without Lightner's direct approval. That meant no laptops, cell phones, cameras, or magnetic disks of any kind. And Lightner further extended his definition of "media storage" to include paper: no books, magazines, journals, newspapers, love letters, or Post-it notes were allowed on the island without first being screened by security officers, perhaps even by Lightner himself—a lengthy and inconvenient process that seemed specifically designed to discourage anyone from even bothering to try. Writing implements were even scarcer.

Lightner was aware that his engineering designs, as well as the precise layout of the island, could be sketched. Both represented proprietary secrets of immeasurable value. In a world where gasoline prices seemed to be rising exponentially, proven alternative-energy designs were in high demand, and Solar Island's technology was reputedly the Holy Grail. Lightner guarded his secrets fiercely.

Nevertheless, Bernard Riley and Robert Benson, during the course of many late-night brainstorming sessions in which they had discussed their career options at Solar Island, had devised a way to export a complex design of one of the most sought-after alternative-energy solutions in the world.

"Let's get this rodeo started: Tape it on!" Bernard prompted.

"Stand up straight; don't move," Robert said. He slapped the manila stencil, an insert removed from a binder used to store machine manuals, on Bernard's bare back. Then Robert used a roll of waterproof medical adhesive tape, taken from one of the many first aid kits stationed around the industrial island, to attach the stencil firmly in place on Bernard's back.

"Okay, it's on; but be careful, don't move too fast. Lie down right here."

With careful, guarded movements to avoid dislodging the stencil now affixed to his back, Bernard eased himself first to his knees, then to a prone position on a beach towel that he had laid on the deck.

Robert consulted his watch. Analog. Lightner disallowed any digital timepieces, for fear that they might have other capabilities.

"I have 8:43. What do you have?"

"Same."

"Okay. I've got to get going to my station. At 3:00 I'll take a break and meet you in your quarters to remove the stencil. Here's some water." Robert set a 2-liter plastic bottle next to Bernard on the ground.

"Gee. Where's my iPod, a trashy novel, and a margarita?"

"Sorry, Bernie. You gotta stay focused. You need to listen for anyone coming and, at the very least, roll onto your back if you can't hide. But there's no reason for anyone to come by."

With a heavy sigh, Bernard Riley settled down for a six-hour bake in the merciless tropical sun.

3:09 p.m. Bernard Riley's quarters on Solar Island

Bernard peeled off the shirt he had worn for the trip back to his quarters. He appraised himself in front of the mirror in his small bathroom. His face was fine, but his ears had gotten a little too much sun, he decided, even with the application of fifty-factor sunscreen. Not too bad, though. He turned to look at his back, where the stencil was still affixed.

He winced sharply with the effort. His burnt skin sent jolts of pain with the movement. It was difficult to get a good look over his shoulder, but he was shocked by what he could see. The area immediately surrounding the stencil was an irregular ring of vibrant red. He touched it gingerly in one place, and instantly a white spot formed before fading back to red.

A soft knock came at the door, and Bernard jumped. He listened for the agreed-upon coded knock: three sets of three. A few seconds after the third set, Bernard opened the door a crack. It was Robert Benson. Alone. Bernard let him in.

"How'd it go?" Robert asked in a soft voice. Bernard shut the door behind him and locked it before answering.

"Didn't see or hear anybody the entire time. Good thing this place is so huge. And so automated."

"Turn around; let me see."

He spun Bernard around so that his back was facing him. "Looks good so far," he said. "I'm going to take it off."

"Take it easy when you do. Hurts like a mother."

Robert started to peel the upper strip of tape from Bernard's back. The skin was bright red above the tape.

"Aw, crap!" Bernard whispered.

Then Robert ripped the tape strip off in one swift, powerful motion. Bernard didn't scream, but let out a rasping exhalation. Robert let the tape drop to the floor.

Over the next few minutes he ripped away the rest of the tape from Bernard's back until the stencil was stuck in place only by his day's worth of sweat. Robert slowly peeled away the template, letting it drop to the floor as it separated from Bernard's back.

"Make sure you cut the stencil into little pieces before you throw it overboard," he said. Then he gazed in wonder at his associate's back.

Robert had harbored doubts that the sunburned image transfer would have sufficient clarity to render the complex schematic serviceable, but the sharpness of detail spread across Bernard's back was unmistakable. The regularity with which hundreds of electrical components were represented on the canvas of Bernard's back was very nearly as good as the stencil itself. The chemical equations, too, had been equally well portrayed. Imperfections aside, he figured that experts would later be able to infer any unreadable sections.

The overall effect was that of some kind of extensive tribal tattoo, he thought.

So mesmerized was he by the abstract beauty of it that he hadn't heard Bernard asking him how it had come out. Robert reached a hand out to touch the fire-engine red representations of flow lines and multiple arrays of capacitors, transistors, integrated circuits, diodes, photodiodes, and thermistors.

"That hurts!" Bernard spun around. "Don't touch me again! What the hell?"

Robert backed up a step. He was almost a foot shorter than the bearish Bernard, which was another reason he thought Bernard should be the one to wear the schematic. "Sorry. But it worked fantastically, Bernie! It's a vivid picture."

"It's vivid, all right. I'll be sleeping on my stomach for a week."

The sunburn was horrendous. In a few days, his skin would start to peel, destroying the delicate imprint; but that would be enough time to accomplish their mission.

"Stay in your room tonight. Don't talk to anyone. Tomorrow in Okinawa we'll go our separate ways off the shore boat. I'll meet up with you tomorrow night at eight in the lobby bar of the Miyako Hotel, where we'll toast to our future. To unlimited possibilities!"

"And sunscreen."

Next day, 8:15 a.m., local time

Robert Benson finished dressing and hurried out of his quarters. In fifteen minutes he was scheduled to board the small boat that would take those with shore leave from the island to Okinawa.

Once on Okinawa, he'd meet Bernard, and there they would begin the process of transferring the design to a more permanent and usable form. Robert planned to purchase a laptop in Naha, the Japanese prefecture's capital city.

Even without their clandestine goal, he was aware that he hadn't set foot off their floating home for nearly eight months, and so the chance for shore leave was that much more desirable.

Stepping onto the perimeter jogging track, which featured pull-up bars, rings, or some other kind of exercise apparatus placed at regular intervals, Robert could immediately see that something was wrong. The land visible in the distance should have been the looming coastline of Okinawa, no more than three miles away. He should be able to see a shore dotted with buildings. Instead, he could barely make out the dim outline of a landform that was probably fifty miles away.

Robert increased his pace on the jogging track. This was not good. Solar Island was an enormous structure that moved at a near-glacial pace. Even if wind and current favored their course, and Lightner ordered full speed ahead with Solar Island's twin tugboats, they would not blow away from Okinawa. *We must have been heading away from the coast all night to be this far away now. Probably even with the tugs pulling us.*

He hurried to the shore-leave staging area, where a small crowd was gathered. Normally there would have been a line of employees waiting to get through the security check before boarding the launch. Instead, there was a disorganized, nervous huddle. A machine-shop technician walked toward Robert, shaking his head on the way past. "Shore leave canceled. We're stuck on the panel."

Robert slouched as the news hit him. "The panel" was their nickname for Solar Island, much as residents of Hawaii sometimes referred to their home as "the rock," a reference to the isolation of living on an oceanic island.

We're stuck on the panel.

The phrase echoed around Robert's brain as he approached the staging area.

Then he heard a message being broadcast over the loudspeaker system. Dr. Lightner's rich bass voice boomed out over the decks in a neutral tone: "Attention, all personnel: Shore leave has been canceled due to logistical considerations. Talks with Okinawa officials will proceed via teleconference in lieu of an in-person meeting. You will be notified of future shore-leave plans. Also, please now direct your attention to the community monitor screens for an urgent message. Thank you for your understanding and cooperation."

Robert was flabbergasted. Shore leave canceled? The energy talks relegated to video conference? What the hell was going on?

Regardless, his plans for the schematic had been ruined. He had to find Bernie right away.

Then he passed under the first community monitor, a massive LCD screen suspended from support struts that held up an awning covering this part of the deck.

Red type scrolled across the LCD:

"ATTENTION ALL HANDS."

The message underneath:

"URGENT: Missing Employee. Possibly Man Overboard within last 24 hours. Report any info about this employee's recent whereabouts to Operations immediately!"

There was a scanned photograph underneath. It was Bernard Riley's Solar Island ID-card photo.

TWO

Three days later
FBI Field Office, Honolulu, Hawaii

Assistant Special Agent in Charge Tara Shores walked over to a computer workstation occupied by a young man, who looked up from his screen on her approach.

"Agent Marconi, got a minute?" Tara asked with the barest hint of a smile. Hers was an angular, attractive face framed by stylishly cropped black hair. Although Tara was not much older than Special Agent in Training Dillon Marconi, she knew that her trainee's respect for her was immense. Her exploits within the agency were legendary, her experience reputed to be beyond her years.

"Of course! What's up?"

"I just received an email from Internal because no one else knows what to do with it. It came in from outside, to the public Bureau tipster email address."

Dillon raised an eyebrow. "What's the tip?"

"It's best if you just listen to it." Tara took a seat next to him and tapped on a keyboard. Dillon sat up straighter in his chair.

"Okay," he said, watching intently as Tara brought up an email account on the screen. She pointed at the monitor. "This one. 'Subject: New song.'" She clicked the mouse, and the email message opened. Both of them read in silence:

Son, not much to do here on Solar Island during my down time, so I indulge in my hobby of making electronic music. Let me know what you think of this latest piece.

Dad

"Sound file attached," Dillon said.

"Yeah, Internal says IT scanned it and it's not a virus or any kind of malware."

Tara opened the sound file, and the computer speakers pulsed with a series of low-frequency hums and vibrations. It was vaguely musical, in the most abstract sense, owing to a machine-like cadence that contained rhythm and structure. But it was only a low drone that varied slightly in pitch and volume, punctuated occasionally by a low hissing noise.

"If this is what passes for Top 40 these days, I'm sticking to jazz," Dillon said, shaking his head.

"Maybe people who use those white-noise recordings to sleep would like it."

After a few more seconds, the audio file ended.

"Doesn't mean anything to me," Dillon admitted. "Let's check who sent it."

"Right," Tara said, expanding the message headers.

"It's been anonymized," Dillon noted, leaning forward to squint at the technical information displayed on screen. "The file originated from an anonymous email account that routed it all over the world through a small army of proxy servers before it ended up here. And it looks as though it was written *to* someone else and forwarded to us by that second party."

Tara pressed the play button for the sound file again. "Let's go back to the recording." The indistinct rumbling noises played again in the background. "What do you think it is?"

Dillon shrugged, twirling a pen in his fingers. "It's garbled noise. How do we know it isn't from some wacko sending in random stuff to the FBI, and it doesn't mean anything at all?"

Tara sat for a moment in silence, staring at the screen. "I guess we could submit it to Audio Analysis to see what they make of it."

"Sure," Dillon said, starting to type. "But first let me try playing it backward, see if it has any Satanic messages encoded into it."

"I think that only works with rock music, but not a bad idea. Try it."

Dillon clicked some buttons on the screen, and the sonic presence began playing in reverse. "Doesn't sound too much different," he said.

Tara nodded. "Gives me an idea, though. Let's *look* at it."

Dillon shot her a quizzical glance.

"We should take a look at the spectrum analyzer. You know, that screen on your computer that shows the waveforms when audio plays."

Dillon nodded and pressed play on the audio program, this time bringing up the visual waveform view.

"Change it to spectral display," Tara said. He did as she asked. The sonic pattern appeared on the screen as a series of neon yellow spikes and valleys marching from left to right while the audio played out. Dillon shrugged. "Doesn't look too—"

Suddenly, the cadence of the sound changed, alternately increasing in pitch and then bottoming out in a low, almost subsonic rumble, only to climb again. The waveforms changed with it, taking the form of distinct peaks. Tara smiled ever so slightly.

"I see several groupings of spikes," Dillon said, cocking his head to one side while he looked at the waveform, which continued to visually represent the progressing audio track.

"Yeah, two in the first and now this next cluster has five," Tara said, scrambling for a pen and paper. She jotted down numbers as the graphical depictions of the sounds appeared on screen. They watched in bewildered silence as a parade of spikes and valleys traveled from left to right across Dillon's monitor.

"They do look deliberately formed," Dillon said, as the last series of spikes scrolled past.

"Somebody tweaked this odd sound recording so that, visually, the graph of its waveforms produced a series of peaks with breaks in between. Two peaks, then flat, then five peaks, then flat, then seven...with ten groupings of peaks in all."

"Phone number?"

"My thoughts exactly," Tara said, removing a cell phone from her pocket. She entered the ten digits derived from the spectrum analyzer into her phone and showed Dillon the screen.

She dialed the number.

THREE

"Shouldn't we record it?" Dillon asked.

"I *am* recording it—voice memo," Tara said.

"You don't even need the audio lab, do you, Agent Shores?"

She set the phone to speaker mode as it began to ring. "If this turns out to be anything other than a prank, Audio will have to confirm everything. But they're booked solid right now, so let's just see what we get."

Dillon rolled closer to Tara in his chair, leaning forward to hear. After the fourth ring, a prerecorded message played:

"Listen carefully, please. My name is Chris Tenner, and I'm not dead. I've been living and working on Solar Island, and I'm in terrible danger. There's a madman on the loose here. Please send help!"

Then the recording ended. There was no opportunity to leave a message.

"Solar Island?" The junior agent pondered the name aloud while he started to perform an Internet search.

"Chris Tenner...." Tara called up a database on her computer. "I'll search for Tenner's name in DIVS," she said. The FBI's Data Integration and Visualization System extracted information from hundreds of sources simultaneously from a single interface.

Dillon looked over at Tara's monitor and groaned as the search returned hundreds of results. "Pretty common name," he said.

"In the message, he emphasizes that he's *not* dead, though; so let's filter the results to show only those Chris Tenners who are also deceased."

Dillon nodded and turned back to his own workstation as Tara refined her database search. "That's better," she said upon viewing the truncated list. "A lot of these have been dead for a long time, over twenty years," she pointed out.

Tara clicked on an entry to expand it. "This Chris Tenner died three years ago in a windsurfing accident," she said.

"Does he have a son?" Dillon asked, thinking aloud while he searched the Web for any reference to Solar Island.

"No, but listen to this," Tara said, pointing at her screen: "He worked as a solar-panel-installation technician in Arizona for over a decade."

She and Dillon met each other's gaze and held it before Tara turned back to the computer.

"According to this, he doesn't have a son! He has an estranged wife..." she traced her finger down the screen as she scanned the database record "...but no children, none listed on his tax returns. Here's his obituary: only his ex-wife is mentioned as surviving him."

A moment of silence ensued as the two considered this, then Dillon brought his screen to Tara's attention.

"The basics on Solar Island: Artificial floating island constructed to support a solar-energy platform. Launched over a year ago in the South Pacific after the component parts were towed there on a barge that left from San Diego. *Privately owned* facility," he added with a raised eyebrow, before continuing. "The operation is the brainchild of one Dr. Jacob Lightner: alternative-energy pioneer and entrepreneur. Somewhat of a maverick, it looks like, according to these business-news reports."

Dillon clicked on a few more hyperlinks with Tara looking over his shoulder. One of the sites led to a newspaper headline reading "Alt-Energy Guru Shuns Innovation Award," while others opened straightforward accounts of the island's purpose.

"I'll say," Tara said. "Looks like the island just floats out there on the ocean—hasn't made landfall in over a year. Stations itself a mile or so offshore from small, mostly third-world island nations who want to buy energy. Sits there for a few weeks or months, and then off they go, floating around for who knows how long until they approach another shore for energy transfer."

Dillon nodded and clicked open a recent news article. "But the stakes appear to be rising. There were energy talks scheduled between the prime minister of Japan and Dr. Lightner for last week, supposedly to pursue the possibility of Solar Island remaining parked off Japan for an entire year to provide power while they recover from their nuclear-energy–plant meltdowns. Japan says that Lightner canceled the talks because they, Japan, wouldn't enter into trade talks with North Korea, of all places. And that's about all that's known about Solar Island."

Tara watched as Dillon silently digested what they had just learned. "Let's back up a bit, for my benefit," Dillon said, holding up a hand. "If this guy needs help so bad, why wouldn't he just call us? Why the subterfuge?"

Tara pointed to Dillon's monitor. "Because he's on Solar Island and thinks his outgoing communications are monitored. By whom, I'm not sure. But a lot of advanced planning went into this. Think about it: he had to first create the fake son's email account. Set that account up to forward the 'Hi, son, check out my music' message to us that could be received at any time. He created the sound file to visually represent the phone number, figuring that whoever was monitoring him wouldn't pick up on it, but that we would. And then he had the phone line set up with the customized outgoing message."

"It is elaborate," Dillon concurred.

"Those are the actions of a man scared for his life."

"A dead man scared for his life," Dillon corrected.

FOUR

Tara held her fist poised a few inches from the door of her supervisor, Daniel Ozakawa, Special Agent in Charge of the Honolulu Field Office. "Let me do most of the talking," Tara told Dillon before allowing her knuckles to make contact. He nodded at the same time they heard the voice within tell them to come in.

The room was sparsely appointed for someone ranked as high as Ozakawa—just a plain, government-issue gray metal desk that had to be at least fifty years old, two faux-leather guest chairs in front of the desk, and a few framed certificates and awards on the wall. The sole window had its shades drawn, but Tara knew that it looked out on a thick landscape of carefully manicured palms and ferns that shrouded the Federal Building.

Ozakawa nodded at Tara as she and Dillon sat in the guest seats. "Agent Shores, and who's this?" he asked, nodding toward Dillon but looking at Tara.

"This is Agent in Training Dillon Marconi, sir. He's working with me on something interesting that just came up, which is what I called you about."

"Right, right!" Ozakawa said, enthusiasm seeming to grip him even as he took a seat behind his desk. "You must be doing all right, Dillon, to have Agent Shores want you to assist her on a case." Dillon started to reply some sort of thanks, but Ozakawa steamrolled right over it, eyes focused intently on Tara while he silenced his ringing desk phone by sending the incoming call to voicemail.

"Connected to Solar Island, you said?"

Tara nodded. She quickly recapped the email, sound file, and voice mail, using her cell phone to play the recorded message for Ozakawa.

"I must say, that's good timing, Shores," her boss said, tossing aside folders and loose sheets of paper on his desk until he dangled one from between two pinched fingers for inspection.

"How's that, sir?" Tara asked.

"The Central Intelligence Agency, of all places, has been bugging me for the past few months to find some kind of excuse to investigate Solar Island for any reason. At the same time, they warned me to keep very tight-lipped about it, which I've done. Trust me when I say that you two have by far the lowest pay grades of everyone who's in the loop on this." Tara and Dillon exchanged a quick glance before Ozakawa went on.

"CIA analysts have growing concerns over Dr. Lightner's increasing political power in the South Pacific. They claim he's been withholding energy from nations whose ideologies he disagrees with, while granting favorable contracts to those who bend to his will. Basically, the CIA thinks that his is the kind of half-assed statecraft that could start a war. Some of those island nations are in serious trouble without that energy, and he knows it."

Tara spoke up. "So the CIA thinks Lightner is using his energy as a bargaining chip to sway negotiations in his favor?"

Her supervisor nodded.

"How would the FBI have any jurisdiction there?" Tara asked, motioning for Dillon to open the folder he was carrying. Dillon pulled out some printouts and selected one to read.

"According to the UN," he read, "Solar Island is an area of special sovereignty, a designation that conveys a certain degree of independence while falling short of granting full-fledged nation status."

"A status Lightner wishes to upgrade?" Tara asked, aiming the question at Ozakawa.

Ozakawa nodded. "The CIA's been monitoring his activities closely for the past three months. I can tell you right now that they're going to want to use Tenner's call for help as an excuse to infiltrate Lightner's floating kingdom," he said.

"I would anticipate some pushback on jurisdiction," Tara said; "but, sovereign entity or not, Lightner's got no leg to stand on, legally.

Although the island was assembled in the South Pacific, its component pieces were taken there on a barge that departed from a U.S. port. And many of its employees are U.S. citizens," she added.

Ozakawa nodded in appreciation. "But really," he said, "not much is known about Solar Island. Right?"

Dillon looked up from his hastily assembled file. It seemed like Ozakawa already knew more about Solar Island than what Dillon had managed to put together. He nodded. "Correct. There have been a number of dry business pieces listed under international energy deals, but never so much as a photograph. No one from the media's ever been there—which is unusual, considering that it's pretty interesting: a gigantic floating island that at least a dozen people—none of the reports I read can pin down the number—have been living on for over a year now."

"Let me tell you something else that's unusual," Ozakawa said. "Until now, we've seen Solar Island transfer power from the island to small villages by means of an electrical cable that they run from the facility, underwater, across shallow reefs and up the shore to a local station. Nothing really groundbreaking or new there, just standard electrical-power transfer. Except that the floating island itself, of course, is unique to Lightner. Still, all that, while advanced, is technology that is understandable to experts. But this...."

He clicked his mouse and swiveled his computer monitor around so they could see the color image it displayed. It was a nighttime shot, the sky and sea almost black with the exception of Solar Island itself, which blazed with light, as did a village a half mile away on shore.

"A CIA bird took this shot four months ago off Papua New Guinea. Time stamp shows two a.m., local time. That seem odd to you?"

Tara nodded. "Solar power at night?" she asked. "I guess they have battery storage?"

"Bingo, Shores. But the problem is that known battery-storage technology for solar isn't capable of providing that kind of power all night long." He clicked the mouse and scrolled through a series of images, each looking about the same but time-stamped at fifteen-minute intervals until the last one showed dawn breaking over the island.

"Solar power that can run all night?" Dillon asked, unable to hide the incredulity in his voice.

"I suspect *that's* the reason for the CIA's interest," Ozakawa said. "They want to know if it's the real deal—or some kind of hoax to appear more powerful than they really are."

Tara's face lit up, a gleam lighting in her eyes that almost frightened Dillon in its intensity. "You said no one from the media's been there yet. I think it's time for an exclusive."

"Exclusive what?" Dillon asked the question, but both men looked at her expectantly.

Tara smiled. "Report. An exclusive report on Solar Island, by a respected national news magazine."

Ozakawa waved a hand dismissively. "Well, I suppose we could request *Time* or *Business Week* or one of them to do a piece on it, but how is that really going to help us? We don't just need gee-whiz facts about how the place operates and a-day-in-the-life kind of stuff with accompanying photos: we need to assess the veracity of this emergency call. We need to go there."

Tara held up a finger. "You're on the right track, sir. But if we go there, whoever's behind the supposed sinister happenings on Solar Island will be tipped off. You heard how scared Mr. Tenner sounded in that recording. Whatever's going on, he's living there with it—in his words, he's *'been living and working'* there, and he suspects someone of something terrible."

"If a reporter won't help, and we don't want to send someone from the Bureau, then what can we do?" Ozakawa queried.

Tara leaned forward in her chair. "We send a reporter to Solar Island with permission from the owner."

Ozakawa threw his hands up. "I thought you just said—"

"The reporter will be me."

"You?" Ozakawa managed.

"In order to gain entrance onto Solar Island, I will work undercover as a reporter doing a piece for a national news magazine. Dillon will get me the cooperation of one of the major ones so that I have some legitimate press credentials—ID, business cards with the real logo, a number to call at the magazine's actual office with a manager who will play along and back me up, that sort of thing."

Dillon cleared his throat. Setting up undercover work was not usually entrusted to such inexperienced agents. It bolstered his confidence that Tara was willing to place such a large amount of trust in him. He nodded confidently as Ozakawa's gaze fell on him for a moment before turning back to Tara.

"Now, Agent Shores, what if we go through all that trouble—set up this elaborate cover, send you all the way out there—wherever *there* even is, right now—and it all turns out to be just some practical joke?"

"First of all, doubtful, because faking one's own death is a serious crime. Chris Tenner was supposed to have died in a windsurfing accident off San Francisco—his board washed up on a beach, but his body was never recovered. Great white shark attack, some said. Doesn't matter. An obituary ran. And now he pops up working on Solar Island? No way he'd out himself for anything trivial."

"I see," Ozakawa said.

"However," Tara continued, "if I am wrong and it turns out that no federal crimes have been committed on Solar Island, then I guess I might have to get a job as a real reporter after all. Right, boss?"

Ozakawa and Dillon laughed along with her, and then the Special Agent in Charge grew serious. "Speaking of which, do you even know anything about being a reporter? Presumably you'd need to act the part."

Tara put on a doubting face. "How hard can it be? Walk around with a little notepad asking questions...that's what I already do!"

Ozakawa frowned. Tara pressed on.

"Seriously, I was an investigative reporter for my college newspaper back in the day. My best piece was a thing about sorority hazing where I went undercover as a pledge." The two men traded glances. Tara continued. "And get your minds out of the gutter. It was a serious exposé that won a journalism award."

Ozakawa still looked unconvinced. "And then there's the photography," he said. "Can you do that?"

Tara grinned mischievously. "Fortunately, I won't need to worry about that."

"Why's that?"

"I'm taking a photographer with me."

"Oh? Who?"

Tara tilted her head toward Dillon, whose face went from mildly amused to highly concerned in a matter of seconds. Ozakawa said nothing, merely stroked the stubble on his chin while he seemed to consider the pair of Special Agents in front of him. Tara continued before he could say anything.

"Don't worry: I'll take a refresher course on reporting while Dillon forms the partnership with a magazine."

At this, she turned to Marconi and said, "Let me know as soon as you have something."

Then she turned back to Ozakawa, tense. If he was going to deny the Solar Island visit, he'd tell Dillon not to bother.

Dillon nodded and said, "What if Solar Island doesn't agree to the reporter coming? Maybe only a telephone or videoconference interview?"

Ozakawa tilted his head and raised his eyebrows, looking at Tara for an answer.

"I've thought of that. Tell them it will be a *cover* story on the importance of alternative energy in the South Pacific and how Solar Island is seen as a ray of hope. Like that wordplay? Reporter, see! Also offer ten thousand dollars in compensation for their hospitality."

"Is that enough money to lure him?" Ozakawa asked. "He must have access to substantial funds to have built Solar Island."

Tara held up a finger. "This is interesting. From what we've been able to gather so far, he's not ultra-wealthy, although he's certainly well-off. His personal wealth is estimated at somewhere around five million dollars, mostly due to when he made millions after selling a design for electric-power plants with adjacent algae ponds that would use the CO_2 emitted from the facility to make biodiesel."

Dillon cut in. "He also scored some profits from selling traditional solar energy start-ups."

Tara nodded. "That's right. But the buzz in the renewable-energy industry is that he built this thing on a shoestring, relatively speaking."

Ozakawa leaned forward on his desk, nodding. "The CIA says that if Solar Island had been built by the Department of Energy, the budget would have been north of a hundred million. And this Dr. Lightner did it for five," he finished, shaking his head.

Dillon considered this for a moment. "So, he's resourceful."

Tara nodded. "You can think of Lightner as having the intellectual discipline of a world-class scientific investigator combined with the lifestyle flexibility of a multimillionaire."

"Must be nice," Ozakawa said. "So, back to the ten thousand...."

Tara said, "It seems that in addition to his personal funds, Dr. Lightner was given significant financial support from many small sources. Five thousand from the Cook Islands government here, $7,500 from Indonesia there; all told, he may have dozens of these 'angel investors' all over the South Pacific and Southeast Asian regions. So he won't necessarily turn his nose up at ten grand for letting a reporter onto Solar Island for a day or two. Any more money than that would be suspicious for a magazine, but less than that and he might decide it's not worth the hassle."

Ozakawa's face took on a serious expression. "I don't think I need to tell you, Agent Shores, that the CIA's involvement here represents a unique opportunity for us."

Tara smiled. It was a rare collaboration for two agencies that were often considered rivals. But, differences aside, they both knew that for her to be selected for field work in a CIA matter was a high honor indeed.

"Are they concerned that Solar Island's unknown battery technology could fall into the wrong hands?"

Ozakawa slowly nodded, as if in deep thought. "That, and they're a little worried about his interest in North Korea."

Dillon took advantage of the temporary lull in conversation. "You have a couple of recent high-profile cases, though, Agent Shores. The DNA thing here in the islands, the whale thing in California...."

"Don't remind me."

"Sorry. My point is that you've had your picture all over the news. What if someone from Solar Island recognizes you?"

Tara wondered the same thing, but found herself unable to give a good answer.

FIVE

Next day. Honolulu FBI Field Office

Dillon Marconi looked at his computer's clock: almost 11:00 a.m. He'd been working the phones and email since five and finally had something to show for it, but where was Agent Shores?

He looked up from his desk in time to see a woman sashaying in his direction, passing between rows of cubicles; but the blonde, shoulder-length hair told him it wasn't Tara.

Dillon was dialing Shores's mobile phone when a shadow crossed his desk. Looking up, he was surprised to see the blonde standing next to him, smiling. He was even more surprised when he finally recognized her. He let the receiver drop back into its cradle.

"Agent Shores?"

Tara frowned. "You recognized me."

"Not from across the room, I didn't. You look good as a blonde! Is that a wig?"

"Thanks," she said, pulling on the ends of her hair, which was a few inches longer than normal. "Nope, it's my real hair dyed, plus extensions. Cost a fortune on such short notice. If the taxpayers only knew...."

"I've got a disguise myself, though not nearly as good as yours," he said, reaching into a desk drawer and pulling out a beige photographer's vest, festooned with pockets. "I got you a gig as a reporter for *National Reader* magazine—"

"Good work!"

"—and I got approval from Dr. Lightner himself for you to visit Solar Island for three days!"

"Excellent. I'll let Ozakawa know. When do we leave?"

Four hours later. Honolulu International Airport

Tara Shores and Dillon Marconi settled into their business class seats for the eight-hour flight to the island of Guam, a U.S. territory far to the west of Hawaii, south of Japan and east of the Philippines, surrounded by the deepest water in the ocean.

Dillon checked his laptop screen one last time before obeying a flight attendant's command to stow the machine for takeoff. "You must have some pull, Agent Shores," he said, shutting the computer off, "because not only is our helicopter already confirmed for liftoff at first light tomorrow, but we've also got an FBI pilot assigned to fly what is normally a charter helicopter for hire."

"Perfect. No one will meet the pilot, but an aviation buff might recognize an FBI aircraft. Lightner will be used to seeing these charter helos."

And with that, Tara pulled a blanket over her shoulders, adjusted a pillow, and did her best to sleep.

SIX

Guam. 5:15 a.m., local time

Tara and Dillon climbed into the waiting Sikorsky S-61R through the open bay door. The long-range helicopter sported a crisp white paint job, with the logo of a regional air-charter company emblazoned on the fuselage.

After walking through the length of what could be described as a school bus with rotors, first Dillon and then Tara slid into the first row of seats, Tara taking the window. In the cockpit, their pilot was busy throwing switches on the aircraft's control panel. Tara and Dillon donned headphones with internal intercoms and voice-activated lip mics.

"How are you, Special Agent Shores?" the pilot said into his own headset without taking his eyes off the dash. "It's been, what, about a year now since we last worked together?"

Tara shot Dillon a pained look. Despite her disguise, the pilot had recognized her with barely a glance. But she recovered quickly. "They told me I'd be getting a top pilot for this assignment, Rob. What are you doing here?"

"I think I like you better as a brunette, Shores," the pilot said, "but I'm glad to see you haven't lost your sense of humor," he finished, turning to look at her.

"You two know each other?" Dillon asked.

Tara nodded. "Dillon Marconi, Rob Tanner. Rob's been with the FBI for a while now, and has flown me in and out of danger on more than a few occasions."

She called into the cockpit. "I hope they didn't banish you to Guam from Hawaii on my account after the whole *Tropic Sequence* affair," Tara said. She fastened her lap belt and motioned for Dillon to do the same.

Rob shook his head. "Island-hopping in a storm wasn't the brightest thing I've ever done, but nobody ended up getting killed and you got your man on that one, Shores. They actually promoted me to come to Guam. I'm a big fish in a small pond out here."

"Looks like a pretty big pond to me," Dillon interjected, waving a hand at the spread of blue ocean they could see even while still on the tarmac.

Rob nodded. "You got that right, pal. The Mariana Trench isn't far from here. Deepest, wildest ocean on the planet all around." They heard a double-thump on the side of the craft and looked out to see an aviation mechanic giving Rob a thumbs-up.

Rob addressed Tara. "We're ready for liftoff. With a full fuel tank like we've got now, this old girl's got almost a thousand-mile range. You've got the updated coordinates?"

Tara nodded and handed Rob a computer printout. "Solar Island's position as of four hours ago."

Rob scowled as he eyeballed the paper. "This is 350 miles away in the middle of a huge patch of water. No refuel capabilities on the island itself, so it's just barely makeable."

Tara grinned. "I heard the word 'makeable,' Rob," she said. "Let's do it."

Dillon leaned forward to look at Rob. "Why is it just barely makeable if we have a thousand-mile range and it's only 350 miles away? Seven-hundred-mile round trip?"

Rob looked away from Dillon to enter the coordinate information into a guidance system on the control panel. "Rule of thirds. I don't use more than one third of my fuel tank to get there. That leaves one third to get back and one third in reserve—just in case—and believe me, with the stuff your boss here gets assigned to, 'just in case' isn't that remote a possibility. If you've ever done any cave-diving, it's the same concept there, too, but with air supply. We're a little under a third here, but—"

"On the way back you'll have a lighter load because Dillon and I won't be with you, which ought to gain you some mpg's," Tara said. Dillon appeared impressed.

"I wish you hadn't said that, Shores. That was my ace in the hole." Rob knocked on the aircraft's ceiling three times.

Tara rolled her eyes. "Why are you pilots all so superstitious?"

"When you make a living flying something that can't glide if an engine fails, you'd be a little wacky too. Here's your printout back," he said, handing Tara the coordinates. "Where'd you get that from, anyway?"

"Courtesy of a CIA eye in the sky."

Rob looked at Tara from under raised eyebrows at the mention of the intelligence agency. "I won't even ask," he said, taking the collective control into his hands.

Tara shifted in her seat again, envious of Dillon, who'd somehow managed to sleep the last two hours. After all the monotonous flying over endless water, she couldn't blame him. But in the distance, something man-made now marred the natural expanse. Tara turned toward a floating object and saw it flash once in the sun. She shoved Dillon awake, while Rob gradually reduced their craft's altitude.

"Dillon, wake up," Tara said.

"Sorry. Where are we?" Dillon asked.

"Solar Island. Get ready."

SEVEN

"Solar Island, this is Ranger One approaching for drop-off, over." Rob frowned as he put down the transmitter and eyed the target quickly approaching ahead. "So far, they aren't much for communication."

From an altitude of two hundred feet and a distance of a quarter mile, Tara and Dillon also stared, transfixed, at the artificial monstrosity.

"It's huge!" Dillon said, holding his hand to shade his eyes, even with sunglasses on. "That's got to be, what, a mile wide?"

"Yeah. And mostly all solar panels. The only prominent building I can see is that tower in the middle. See that?"

Dillon raised a pair of Nikon marine binoculars to his eyes. "Yes. And I do see a couple of other structures, but they're low-lying. There's some kind of track or road that goes around the perimeter, and...wow!"

"What?" Tara asked.

Dillon focused the binoculars. "Looks like they have a little harbor...I see a few boats in a cutaway portion of the island. It's a raised platform, too—the top part that supports the panels is maybe two stories above the water. Damn," he finished, lowering the binoculars and closing his eyes.

"Reflection?"

He nodded, blinking rapidly. "Remind me not to look at a square mile's worth of solar panels under tropical sunlight with binoculars again."

Tara clapped Dillon on the shoulder, then cast her eyes to the cockpit. "No word from them yet?" Tara asked Rob.

"I'll do a flyover, see if that gets their attention," Rob

announced, banking the craft into a low turn around the perimeter of the circular island.

An island where none should be.

That's what came to Tara's mind as she took in their destination while the island grew larger in front of her.

"It's floating, right? It's not fixed in position like an oil platform?" Rob asked, marveling at the peculiar structure. Next to Tara, Dillon was busy snapping photographs, already assuming the role he would play once they landed.

Tara nodded, and turned her head sharply away as a bevy of sunbeams reflected off the sea of solar collectors that the drifting platform supported. "Correct."

Dillon pointed at the island. "There's white smoke coming from it."

"Must have to do with the power plant," Tara said. "Probably steam vapor being vented off."

Rob interrupted, "If nobody responds pretty soon, I'm afraid we might have to turn—"

Then the radio crackled to life with a voice, no accent. In much of the South Pacific, Australian, New Zealand, or various Pacific Islander accents were the norm, but this one sounded American, possibly West Coast.

"Roger, Ranger One, this is Solar Island. You are here to drop off the reporter Amanda Greystone, yes?"

Tara gave Dillon a knowing look. She knew that he'd put a lot of work into developing her cover and that, should anyone from Solar Island bother to Google Amanda Greystone, they'd find a slew of well-placed news articles with her byline.

Rob nodded as he spoke into his headset. "Copy that, Solar Island. Ms. Greystone," he said, giving Tara a wink as he did so, "as well as her photographer, Aaron Crosby, are with me. I am low on fuel for the return trip to Guam and will need to begin my approach to the helipad now if we're going to do this, over."

"Copy that, Ranger One, but I'm afraid we have a problem."

The words had a stun-gun effect on all three of the helicopter's inhabitants. They all focused on the radio. Rob aimed their craft for the structure at the center of the island. Atop that tower was fixed a circular platform with a red "H" painted on it.

"WARNING, RANGER ONE!" The three of them jumped in their seats as the radio's staticky hiss assaulted their ears.

Rob reached for the radio's volume knob. The message continued. "You have not yet received permission to land. You are in violation of Solar Island airspace. As an independent nation, we are ordering you to move beyond our perimeter immediately and await further instructions. DO IT NOW!"

Rob mouthed *What the—*? at Tara.

Below, a lone figure walked out onto the helipad, aiming a rifle at the helicopter. The radio crackled again.

"Only the reporter has been granted a visa to stay on Solar Island. Not a photographer. No one else will be permitted entry."

Tara's eyes narrowed as she spoke into her headset mic. "This is Amanda Greystone, from the *National Reader*. I was told that I would be able to do journalism on Solar Island per the terms of our agreement with you. Journalism includes photography. Photography means HAVING A PHOTOGRAPHER WITH ME!"

Tara yelled the last part of the sentence at the top of her lungs. She was surprised to discover that it wasn't all an act. She was angry at this Dr. Lightner, if that was who was behind this decision, for deceiving her. Getting her to come all this way, knowing that another person had also made the journey, and then casually denying them a chance to even enter Solar Island "airspace."

But there was something more, she knew. Something a shade more ominous. She had not planned to go this deep undercover alone. Ozakawa would never allow it. He'd tell her to abort the operation.

Dr. Lightner, or whoever was acting as the voice of Solar Island, came back over the radio.

"We are sorry for any misunderstanding, but the journalism contract has only one signature on it, Ms. Greystone, and that is yours. No one but you will be permitted to land. If these terms are unacceptable, then you are free to go. Perhaps we can negotiate a tour with a photographer at some future date."

Rob tapped his instrument panel. "Fuel's over one-third, Shores, and now I'm bringing back at least one more passenger than we planned for. I gotta get this bucket back to Guam. Let's go." He started to bank their craft away from Solar Island, but then Tara put her arm on his.

"I'll go alone."

"How about I jump out with you, Rob takes off and leaves us both. What could they do?" Dillon asked, adjusting his photographer's vest.

Tara shook her head. "It is private property. They have a right to not allow anyone entry. It'd be hard to establish a good working relationship with them if they're mad at us for forcing ourselves on them. They'd just clam up and not show us anything until a chopper came back for us."

"Not that there's much to see on this place anyway," Rob noted. "Bunch of solar panels."

"Bunch of solar panels where people live," Dillon pointed out, squinting against the panels' glare as Rob centered the helicopter over the helipad.

"And possibly die," Tara added, reminding them of their visit's serious nature.

"You sure you want to go through with this?" Dillon said to Tara as the red "H" of the heliport grew beneath them. "We could go back to Guam and renegotiate."

"Give me one of your digital cameras, a small one. I can get a few snapshots."

Dillon reached into one of the myriad pockets of his vest and handed Tara a slim point-and-shoot. She tucked it into the small backpack she would be taking along as her only luggage.

"Touchdown!" Rob declared as the helicopter's skids made contact with the helipad. Outside, they could see no one. Whoever had been standing there with the rifle had disappeared.

Tara grabbed Dillon by the shoulder and turned him in her direction. "Maintain your post in Guam. Do some more research, dig deeper, see what you can find out about this operation. I'll call in by the sat-phone every night for updates."

Dillon nodded. "You got it, Agent Shores."

"Let's *go*, Shores," Rob said, eyeing his fuel gauge. Dillon shoved the door open, and a gust of warm air swirled inside.

A lone figure—a man dressed in white and apparently unarmed—could now be seen coming over the top of a ladder. He emerged onto the edge of the helipad and waved.

Tara moved to the doorway. Dillon grabbed her arm and looked into her eyes. "Watch yourself."

Tara merely nodded in return and jumped from the craft. No sooner had her sneakered feet touched the scorching surface than the helicopter had taken off behind her, buffeting her in hot, forceful airstreams.

She was on her own.

EIGHT

"Welcome to Solar Island!"

Even as she heard the voice, it was hard for Tara to take her eyes off the surreal view, unchanging through all 360 degrees. From her perch atop the helipad, it was clear that she was standing at the highest point of the man-made island. She judged it to be perhaps forty feet above sea level. Below them stretched a sea of solar collectors for about a half mile in all directions to the edge of the floating structure. Beyond that, the deep blue of the Pacific reached to the ends of the Earth while, above it all, Rob's helicopter was making a beeline for distant Guam.

Tara collected herself and turned to face the man, who she could see wore loose-fitting white pants and a button-down white shirt. White sandals were strapped to his feet, and he wore a white wide-brimmed hat. A stylized golden sun hung around his neck on a gold chain. She marveled at his skin, which was even paler than her own. For someone who lived in the South Pacific, Tara thought, on a solar-energy facility, no less, he sure managed to avoid the sun himself.

Tara turned to her greeter and extended her hand. "Thank you, Mister...?"

She knew him to be Jacob Lightner from the hastily assembled case file, but she had a part to play. She found the kaleidoscopic array of sunbursts flashing off the solar equipment behind the man to be disorienting. She pulled her sunglasses tighter against her head and narrowed her eyes, in spite of the UV protective lenses.

"Lightner," the man said, pumping Tara's hand enthusiastically. "Doctor Jacob Lightner. And you must be Amanda Greystone."

"That's me, sir," Tara said, remembering to assume the demeanor of an up-and-coming reporter rather than that of a veteran special agent.

"I think you're the first blonde ever to visit our island," Dr. Lightner said, looking directly at her recently dyed locks. Tara stiffened under his visual appraisal. Was he toying with her? Could he have learned her true identity?

He continued: "As you were informed, I'll need to see your identification. Just a formality."

Tara remembered to put on an air of irritability as she pretended to impatiently root around in her backpack for her ID. She handed him a New York driver's license made for her by the FBI, along with her press credentials from the magazine, which she wore around her neck on a lanyard.

"Very well. Thank you," he said, handing them back to her. "And now it's time to head down. But before we do, this is a good place to give you a brief overview of our island."

Tara frowned. "Before we do that, I'd like to know who's in charge of your little welcome committee. What was that stunt with the rifle all about, and not letting us land? The chopper is low on fuel."

Lightner's face took on an expression of surprise. "I do apologize for the warning, ma'am, but—and this is part of my introduction to you—Solar Island is privately owned as well as being its own independent nation. I say who is allowed to land here and when."

Tara was too interested in what Lightner had to say to be angry. She pulled a reporter's notepad and a pen from her backpack and pretended to take notes for her article, rather than for her FBI case. She noticed that Dr. Lightner's eyes lingered on her pen while she wrote.

"According to my research, you are indeed classified by the United Nations as an 'area of special sovereignty,' meaning you do not fall under the auspices of any existing nation; but the UN and all but a handful of South Pacific island nations stop short of officially granting you nation status." She could hear only the tropical breeze whistling past her ears. She looked up to see Lightner staring at her notepad intently.

"I see you've done your research already. Are you sure you even need the tour?"

Tara warned herself to tread carefully. The reporter cover was a clever way of allowing her to ask questions and to have a reason to snoop around; but should her questioning grow too pointed, Lightner's guard would be raised.

She leveled a stare at Solar Island's creator. "I don't do fluff pieces, Dr. Lightner. I came here to do an in-depth article on a unique alternative-energy solution that we believe our national readership will find of interest. To that end, I've done some preliminary work, but I need to see the facility for myself. Which reminds me, my boss will be none too pleased to find out that you denied access to my photographer."

"You've been given seventy-two hours, Miss Greystone. Even for a facility as large as Solar Island, at roughly five hundred acres, you should have plenty of time. The core idea of this place is simple: to harness the sun's energy, to deliver it where it's most needed, and to prove the concept that life on a permanent sea-based installation—*seasteading*, some call it—is a viable response to overcrowding on land, vanishing resources, and a good old-fashioned sense of adventure."

Lightner appeared pleased with his delivery of what Tara knew was no doubt a carefully prepared spiel. She merely held up her ring finger where a diamond-studded wedding band sparkled hectically in the equatorial sunlight. Lightner appeared confused. Tara was pleased.

"It's Mrs. Greystone," she said curtly, shaking the ring hand at him ever so slightly.

Easy, girl! She wanted to play the part of a sassy reporter used to getting her way but had to be careful not to actually anger Lightner, or her investigation would be stonewalled. Tara herself was single, which made the ring a little uncomfortable for her, but it was great cover. Great *tradecraft*, Tara corrected herself. She'd had time for a quick briefing with the CIA agents interested in Lightner, and some of the espionage-speak had rubbed off on her.

"My apologies, Mrs. Greystone. Come, why don't we get down off this god-awful helipad. I fear I'm beginning to burn already!"

Lightner headed for a ladder at the edge of the pad. Tara poked her arm and noticed the white imprint of her fingertip. *Less than five minutes here and I'm already sunburned.*

She trotted to catch up to Lightner, who was already climbing down the ladder. "C'mon," he said, removing a hand from the rungs to wave at her; "let's get you through customs so we can begin our tour."

NINE

Still wearing her backpack, Tara climbed down the ladder after Lightner. As they descended the tower underneath the helipad, she could feel a rumbling coming from within its walls. Some kind of machinery was at work inside. Once they reached the base of the tower, Tara could see a floor below; but, looking out over the rest of the island, she realized that it was actually the roof of the one-story building underneath them.

Below her, Dr. Lightner stepped off the ladder onto the roof and used a key on an unmarked metal trapdoor set into it. He beckoned Tara to follow him down a spiral staircase leading into a windowless, circular room.

"I'm sorry our customs entrance isn't more convenient," Lightner called up to her; "but, as you'll see, space is at a premium on Solar Island and we sometimes find it necessary to improvise."

Winding her way down the tight spiral stairs left Tara feeling a little dizzy. When she reached the bottom, she took a moment to catch her breath and looked around the room. A lighted sign reading "CUSTOMS (HELIPORT)" hung prominently overhead, while a single-bar turnstile led to an X-ray machine staffed by a tall Black man with a broad nose and short Afro. Tara judged him to be of South Pacific origin.

"Right this way, please," Lightner said, passing through the turnstile. Tara wondered why they needed it when there were only three people in the room, including her; but the turnstile was set into a wall, making it the only easy entrance into the room from the staircase. Bewildered, Tara turned sideways to squeeze through it and walked up to the man at the X-ray machine. He wore a uniform of sorts, a shirt with the letters SI embroidered on the chest, over a logo of a circular raft of mirrors reflecting back a blazing ball of light. A name tag pinned to his shirt read "Darrien."

"Good morning, ma'am, and welcome to Solar Island. Please place your effects on the conveyor." He extended a hand in the direction of the moving black belt, a smaller version of those typically seen in airport security settings. Tara looked at Lightner, raising her eyebrows.

"Really? You're serious?" She couldn't suppress a laugh, but then immediately regretted it as she saw Lightner's eyes narrow almost imperceptibly before he reassumed his island-host demeanor.

She took off her backpack and tossed it onto the conveyor. Watching it slide toward the X-rays, she realized that, in a real customs search, what she carried in her bag would never make it through without her FBI badge. She was glad she hadn't brought her badge, though. She'd considered hiding it in her pack in case its powers of persuasion should come in handy but had decided against it at the last minute. Correctly decided, Tara thought, casting a nervous glance at the X-ray monitor. She hadn't expected this at all.

While Darrien attended to the X-ray machine, Dr. Lightner waved her toward the rectangular frame of what she now recognized as a metal detector. "Please remove your shoes, jewelry, sunglasses, and any metal objects from your pockets, put them in the tray, and then step through."

"I've got a metal plate in my head from my war days," Tara said. "It always sets these things off."

"Is that so?" Lightner asked.

"Kidding. That line never works. Do you get a lot of visitors here?" Tara asked as she slipped out of her sandals and followed Lightner's orders.

"Not a lot, no, but we need to maintain strict security protocols because the proprietary technology that gives us our competitive advantage needs to be protected. That's it, just put it all in the tray and slide it down, thank you."

The siren and flashing red light made Tara jump. She damn near screamed, it was so unexpectedly loud. She looked over to Darrien and saw his features wrinkled with a concentration that soon gave way to concern. She watched as he waved at his boss, and Lightner walked behind the X-ray machine.

Darrien picked up Tara's backpack and started to open it while Lightner looked on.

"Now, wait just a minute!" Tara had to force herself to remain calm. As an FBI agent, she'd been in numerous situations requiring her to keep her wits about her, but this was so out of the blue. She was supposed to be a reporter, though, an average citizen, so she allowed herself to act out a bit.

"Put my bag down! I wasn't told I would be subjected to any personal-property searches. What is this?"

Dr. Lightner nodded, and Darrien set her bag back down. The island host assumed a caring expression. "Why, Mrs. Greystone, I thought I had made it clear. Solar Island is its own country. Just like when you enter any other country, you expect to have your bags searched at customs. It's no different here."

"You're not a real country, you're just an area of special sovereignty," Tara said. She was surprised at the acerbity of her tone. *It's not just part of my cover. This guy is really making me mad!*

Dr. Lightner frowned at her but quickly recovered his jovial tone. "Be that as it may, our customs policies are not flexible." He pointed to a large painted sign on the wall, much like those in entry ports the world over, proclaiming that all persons entering the nation of Solar Island must consent to a search of their belongings and person.

"It is nothing personal directed toward you, ma'am," Lightner continued. "Everyone who comes to this island when it lies in international waters is subject to the same procedures. Even our employees, when they return to work." Darrien nodded in agreement.

"You should have told me in advance," Tara said.

Lightner shook his head. "We don't like to disclose our security measures. We're a small nation—defenseless, really—and the element of surprise is all we have. Also, I must tell you, you recall that the agreement you signed stipulated that you will not write about anything we ask you not to. Your article must be approved by me personally prior to publication. I must ask you not to mention our customs station in your article."

Tara hoped she had some acting skills as she pretended to go livid. "What? I fly halfway around the world out to the middle of nowhere, and now you tell me I can't write about what I came here for?"

"Mrs. Greystone, you said you came here to write about our energy-production facilities. That's fine. I'm only asking you not to divulge our security measures. Please be reasonable. We have gone out of our way to accommodate you. In fact, you're the first reporter we've ever consented to have on board for an overnight stay." Darrien nodded solemnly in confirmation.

Tara opened her mouth to protest, but Lightner interrupted.

"Your options are simple: Comply with our customs regulations and go on with your tour, or else you are free to wait here for pickup transportation and return to Guam or wherever you'd like. The decision is yours."

Tara decided that she had put on a sufficient show of resistance for a reporter. As an FBI agent, she was already gathering a gold mine of information and was itching to be let onto the island. The atmosphere of secrecy was even higher than she'd expected. She let out an exaggerated sigh. She rubbed her forehead, then waved her hand dismissively.

"Fine. Knock yourselves out," she said.

Darrien waited, his hands poised over her backpack's zipper. Dr. Lightner nodded to him. "It's okay: open it," he said.

Darrien removed items rapidly from the bag and set them aside. Dr. Lightner looked on as Tara's digital camera, clothing, laptop, satellite phone, reporter's notepads, pens, and routine personal effects were piled onto a plastic tray.

Lightner immediately reached for the pens and pulled them from the tray, nodding at Darrien, who promptly held a plastic baggie open. "Which one do you want?" he asked Tara.

"Pardon?" she said.

"You can only have one pen while working on the island. The rest will be kept here and returned to you on your departure. We control the amount of writing utensils on our island because they can be used to record sensitive information."

"Wow. What kind of information?"

"Mostly the proprietary technological variety," Lightner said, nodding as Darrien sealed the plastic bag of pens and placed it out of sight somewhere underneath the counter. He handed one back to Tara. "Please listen: If you are to lose or misplace this writing instrument—a BIC medium-point black-ink pen—for more than ten minutes, I need you to inform me—and only me—immediately. Is that understood?"

Tara nodded.

"I require a verbal response."

Tara wondered if this entire encounter was being videotaped.

"Yes, Dr. Lightner, I understand that I need to keep an eye on my pen and will let you know if I can't find it." The strict property control reminded Tara of the times she'd gone into prisons for inmate interviews.

Lightner nodded, and Darrien handed him a sundries bag before turning back to continue rooting through Tara's backpack.

Lightner quickly examined the electronic items, even inspecting a tiny flashlight attached to her keychain, before setting them aside, uninterested. He unzipped the sundry bag while Tara looked on, pulling out a Swiss Army knife. It was a newer rectangular-shaped design in an untraditional lemon-yellow color, but it still featured the expected assortment of blades and tools. He unfolded its main blade and peered at Tara over the tip. "Do you always carry one of these?"

"Most of the time. Why? Are you scared I might take over your country with it?"

Lightner guffawed, turning to see if Darrien shared his mirth, but the employee's face wore a serious expression as he pulled something else out of the backpack. "Don't worry about it," Lightner said, folding the knife and putting it back in the bag.

Then Darrien handed him a handgun. Tara didn't have to act like she was nervous. She was. The gun was a pocket pistol, only a few inches long, but it was real enough.

"I see you're a derringer fan," Lightner said.

Tara nodded. "I'm a woman traveling alone around the world. It makes me feel a little safer."

"It's a nice piece," Lightner said, lining the sights up with his eye. "Simple but effective. Definitely an effeminate-looking weapon if there ever was such a thing," he added with a smirk. "How did you get it to Guam from the mainland? This doesn't look like something you could buy on Guam."

The firearm was of modern manufacture but decorated to look like similar pieces from the 1800s with imprinted flourishes and intricate patterns. In fact, it was part of Tara's personal gun collection, but she thought it would make the perfect weapon for this trip, on account of its small size and the fact that they were indeed popular with women.

"I brought it with me. Declared it and brought it tagged and disassembled in checked luggage."

Lightner turned over the dainty sidearm in his hands again before declaring, "I'm sorry, firearms of any kind are not allowed onto Solar Island." He pointed to a sign like the ones in all major airports, a handgun in a red circle with a slash through it. "You'll be able to pick it up when you leave."

He handed it back to Darrien, who placed it in a plastic bag and began filling out a form.

"Fine," Tara said. She wasn't happy about it, but what could she do? She pretended to read the customs signage as, from her peripheral vision, she watched Darrien seal the bag and drop it into a drawer beneath the counter.

"Very well," Lightner said, beaming now. "Do you have a passport?"

Tara was glad she'd had a bogus one made. She produced it for Lightner, adding "I already showed you my ID on the helipad, and no one mentioned that I would need a passport to board—is that the right word?—Solar Island."

"U.S. citizens are permitted to *enter* Solar Island without a passport, but many do have passports anyway. Reason I ask is because we'll stamp it for you. Kind of a unique memento of your stay here."

"Sure, why not?" Tara said, handing the false document over to Darrien, who promptly found a blank page and brought a rubber stamp down with enough force that it produced an echo in the room. He handed the passport back to Tara, who took a look at Amanda Greystone's new stamp.

A circular ball of fire set in orange ink bore the letters SI.

"Now you're official!" Lightner said, smiling intensely.

"Great. Can we start the tour now, please?"

"We're almost ready. Just a few more formalities. If you'll step right this way, please." Lightner walked down to the end of the counter and opened a metal cabinet. Racks of electronics and computer equipment waited inside.

"While I get this ready, Darrien is going to fingerprint you."

Sure enough, the islander set an ink pad out on the counter in front of Tara and asked her to press her fingers on it.

She ignored the request and turned to Lightner. "This is going way too far! I respect your security concerns, but this is more invasive than it needs to be. I'm not moving in, for Christ's sake, I'm here for seventy-two hours. Fingerprints?"

Lightner was unapologetic. "Again, you have the option of refusing and waiting here for return transportation."

Tara closed her eyes briefly before facing Darrien once more. She nodded her assent. He then asked her to roll her fingers onto a fingerprint card, the top portion of which, Tara noticed, had already been filled out with her cover information. Tara had taken fingerprints of suspects countless times, but she pretended to be irked at the ink smudges left on her fingertips once the process was complete. Darrien handed her a handkerchief.

The fingerprinting didn't concern Tara too much since, as an FBI agent, although her prints were on file, they were highly secure. *If they ever bothered to run them against a database at all,* she thought. It could just be for show; they'd file the card away and forget about it.

"I'm ready for you," Lightner announced. She looked down the counter and saw that he had swung out some piece of equipment at the end of a hinged arm. Tara was trying to figure out what it was when Lightner waved her over.

"Biometrics doesn't take long; let's get this over with," he said.

"Biometrics?" Tara repeated, pretending she didn't know what the word meant, in order to buy herself some time while her mind raced to figure out the implications for her cover.

"Let's start with a retinal scan," Lightner said, beckoning her to sit down on a stool in front of the contraption he'd just unfolded.

"This seems incredibly intrusive. Isn't this a violation of individual privacy rights?"

Jacob Lightner recoiled from the silver orb at the end of the articulated arm. "How can there be a violation of rights, my dear, when the nation of Solar Island establishes its own laws? One of those laws is that all visitors and immigrants alike must undergo fingerprinting and biometrics processing. If they refuse, then they are immediately deported or refused entry. Are you refusing?"

Tara took a deep breath. The biometrics made her uncomfortable. How secure was her legitimate biometric data? If Lightner was able to make a match....

"Sit down and put your right eye up to the scanner, please."

"What is this device?" Tara asked.

"It's just a video camera that will capture your iris pattern. Please sit still for three...two...one...got it, thank you." Lightner put the eye reader away and produced what looked to Tara like a microphone, attached by a cord to one of the consoles inside the cabinet.

Tara looked at Lightner expectantly.

"Time for voice recognition. You're going to speak into the microphone while we make a recording of your voice. We'll do a quick check of the levels first."

The use of sound-recording equipment made Tara wonder if this could have anything to do with how the electronic-music file was created. "State your name, please," Lightner ordered.

Tara cleared her throat and said "Amanda Greystone."

"Okay, great. Now repeat after me: I, Amanda Greystone, hereby state that I am who I say I am and that I do not harbor malicious intentions toward Solar Island or any of its inhabitants."

Tara stared at Lightner, hoping her expression conveyed that she thought this security measure was ridiculous.

"Go on, then," Lightner said. Tara put her lips up to the mic and recited the requested line. She wondered if the recording was only for vocal-quality information, or if it had a behavioral component as well—analysis of speech patterns, perhaps even a lie detector. The biometrics made her nervous, but she hoped that her short stay combined with the security inherent to her true profession would prevent Lightner and his team from making an identification while she was still on the island. Still, she had certainly not anticipated security measures this stringent, and she kicked herself for letting her guard down. *Should have done more research....*

"And that'll do it for biometrics," Lightner announced.

"Can we *please* get to the tour now?"

"Of course," Lightner said, starting to walk toward an orange-lit sign marked "EXIT." Then he stopped and turned so unexpectedly that Tara nearly bumped into him. "One final word of warning. Once we step outside of our customs facility, most of Solar Island is a rather industrial environment. We're an energy-production facility, not a Club Med. So act accordingly. Heads up, safety first. Watch your step, heed all posted signs, and, if you have any questions, never hesitate to ask either myself or any of my staff."

"Understood," Tara said, nodding.

Lightner seemed pleased. "This way, please," he said. "Our ride is waiting just outside."

TEN

Dr. Lightner climbed into a white golf cart and beckoned Tara to follow. The vehicle was parked at the beginning of a marked track that led off between arrays of some kind of solar panels, the likes of which Tara was unfamiliar with. She walked around the cart and climbed in beside Lightner, who waved an arm across the sea of mirrored collectors that stretched out before them.

"At first I thought this problem to be analytically intractable," he said; "but after a while it occurred to me." He paused as if expecting the reporter to speak. After a few moments the silence became awkward, and so Tara filled it.

"What problem, and what occurred to you?" she asked.

"The dual problem of the physics of energy combined with the logistical hurdles of delivering that energy to where it is most needed."

"So, what occurred to you?" Tara asked again, pulling her sunglasses a little tighter around her eyes in response to the intense bursts of light careening off the panels around her.

"I'll tell you about it on the way to your quarters," he said. "You must feel like freshening up. As you'll find out, the accommodations on Solar Island are basic—we don't have as many buildings as you might think, based on our size," he continued as if reading her mind, "since the lion's share of our space is dedicated to the solar farm. So you'll have to get used to being outside much of the time during your stay here. But you will have air-conditioned sleeping quarters, solar-powered, naturally—everything is on our island—and I think you'll find that our chef serves quite hearty and satisfying meals."

"That sounds wonderful," Tara said, meaning it. "I appreciate the offer of my quarters, sir, but if you don't mind I'd like to proceed with the tour. This island is incredible." She looked down a row of solar collectors the length of a football field. "It's amazing how there's almost no sense of motion, like there is on a ship."

Lightner nodded as he pressed the start button on the electric cart. "We've got too much surface area to feel anything but the largest waves. No need to worry about seasickness."

Tara was glad for that. She would never be truly comfortable around water, her parents having drowned in a car accident when she was a child, with her also being in the car. She had recently solved a pair of high-profile cases that required her to go to sea, though, and now found herself on the ocean once more in pursuit of the truth. She was glad that the island was large enough not to impart a sense of motion.

"What if there's a storm?"

Lightner put the cart into gear, and they began to roll across the white island surface between a pair of painted green lines. "A typical squall or thunderstorm has no noticeable effect on the island; however, the four sectional pods that comprise the island's base are designed to separate under extreme stress, such as a major hurricane—or tropical cyclone, as they're known in this part of the world.

"Each pod is fitted with a GPS locator coupled to a simple propulsion system that will allow them to find each other after they are separated. Haven't had to use that functionality yet, and I hope we never do, but it worked well in the testing phase."

They threaded their way between two rows of solar apparatuses. Tara was glad for the shade, although a few piercing shafts of light still found their way through to them. The heat was noticeable now, too, Tara thought, peeling her sundress from a shoulder. Although living in Hawaii had acclimated her to tropical weather, at home she was usually in her air-conditioned office, car, or condo.

"How much did Solar Island cost to build, Dr. Lightner?"

"About seventeen million dollars, including the alternative-energy technology infrastructure such as the solar collectors and power-generation station. We also have a few wind turbines, as you'll see, and the buildings and communications technology, as well as our modest vehicle fleet. The actual floating structure itself cost much less," he finished, pulling the cart to a halt underneath a gigantic solar collector.

"And how was it all paid for?" Tara asked, conspicuously holding her reporter's notebook in her lap, pen poised. She wanted him to know that she was intent on collecting the story behind the financing of Solar Island. She was interested to see if he would tell her not to take notes, or even refuse to answer financial questions.

"I started it with personal funds made as a result of my solar-energy and other engineering patents, and the rest has come from investors around the world. Renewable energy is the hallmark of the future. Are you familiar with peak oil?"

Tara rested her pen as Lightner negotiated a curve with the cart. "Yes," she said: "the idea that we've used all the easy-to-get oil, and that what's left is increasingly difficult and expensive to obtain."

Lightner nodded. "Essentially, yes. The rate at which we can extract petroleum out of the Earth is now slowing and will never again reach the peak rate, which occurred around 1970. The U.S. would like nothing more than to break its addiction to foreign oil. To that aim, increasingly exotic and desperate methods of capturing fossil fuels are being put to the test, sometimes with alarming results. Shale oil, tar sands, fracking, deep-water drilling. As the price of a barrel of oil marches inexorably higher, any petroleum deposit that was once too expensive to bother extracting has now become cost-effective."

"Do you see those methods as a threat to renewable energy?"

"Not at all. Those methods are risky. Look at the Gulf of Mexico oil spill of 2010. That was caused by drilling for oil in very deep water, the risks of which were known. And don't even get me started on the fracking, unless you enjoy natural-gas explosions and triggering earthquakes."

"Solar Island seems well positioned—literally—to capitalize on those fears!" Tara exclaimed as they emerged on the track that ran from between the collectors to the perimeter of the platform.

The island's surface was twenty feet above the waves, and they now had a commanding view of the sun-drenched Pacific. Looking to the right or left gave a view of the solar farm.

Lightner turned and looked at her while he drove. "They're not *fears.* They are *realities,*" Lightner said as he pulled the cart to a stop. "Yes, we are well positioned for that *reality.* Here, let me show you something that illustrates my point."

Lightner stepped out of the cart and walked around to the end of an elongated curved mirror, beckoning for Tara to follow. She went to him and saw him pointing at a Plexiglas cube on a stand. Inside the cube was a red gas can. A bronze plate affixed to the front of the cube bore the words "LEGACY FUEL."

Lightner grinned as he stared at the display. "This here was the last gasoline ever used on Solar Island. We used to have some power tools and emergency generators that required it, especially during the construction phase, but they have since been superseded by the more efficient methods we specialize in here."

"So it's a reminder of your mission?"

"Precisely! When solar and other renewables achieve critical mass, the world will turn its back on hydrocarbons just as we have done here." He pointed to the container. "It's still half full. One day we just didn't need it anymore, and we never looked back. The change will come that suddenly."

Tara raised her eyebrows as she stared at the *faux* relic. She found it hard to believe that it would be possible to completely replace gasoline with anything else any time soon, not that she felt comfortable voicing that opinion to Lightner.

"Anyhow," Lightner said as he began walking back to the cart, "getting back to our positioning for the inevitable shift from an oil-based economy to one based on the so-called green energy, look around you at our solar farm."

Tara made a show of turning her head right, left, and back again as they continued walking back to the cart.

Lightner continued talking as they took off in the cart again. "We're near the equator; and, what's more, the collection arrays themselves have a capability known in the industry as *tracking*, which means that they are motorized such that they tilt automatically to follow the sun's position in the sky for maximum radiation exposure. Even better, the entire surface upon which the collection apparatus, and ourselves, sit is a suspended disc—actually, there are four discs, one for each pod—that rotate in order to face the collectors toward the sun. They're computer-controlled."

"Kind of like tanning at the beach and how people get up and move every so often to line themselves up with the sun as it moves through the sky."

"Exactly! At any given time, all of these collectors are slowly, almost imperceptibly, moving to follow the sun's progress through the sky. If you've ever been to one of those revolving rooftop restaurants, it's kind of like that. They're slow-moving enough that you don't actually notice the motion; but if you watch a fixed point, you'll see that it's gone after a few minutes."

Tara tried but failed to detect the platform's motion. She looked back at her notepad. "And these other investors besides yourself, who are they?"

Lightner stared out across the sea as he spoke. "I have a few venture-capital sources from Silicon Valley back in the States—the dot-com crowd thinks alternative energy is 'sexy'—but it's mostly governments of Pacific Island nations who recognize that fossil fuels will never be a viable solution for them. Why should they depend on the whims of distant nations to provide them energy when they're bombarded with free energy every day?" He raised his hands to the sun in a triumphant gesture. "Infinite power!"

Tara waited for him to lower his arms and then continued. "But in the case of Solar Island, they're depending on you for their energy, instead of oil. They don't have millions to invest in solar-energy infrastructure as you do, not to mention the space in many cases. Are they trading one dependency for another?"

She was presenting the CIA's case. How would he react?

"Solar Island is more of a proof of concept than anything else. You can think of it as a large-scale demonstration project. A big part of our usefulness is our mobility. When we float near a particular coastline, if they are in need of energy, we can arrange to have them tow us close to shore. After a major storm or cyclone, we are always in demand. And while they don't have land area, they do have access to the ocean. I'm literally lighting the way for them.

"In the near future," he continued, "I expect we won't be the only artificial island floating around out here. And another possibility is that I could moor several energy islands together into a small archipelago."

Tara studied him closely. He appeared genuinely convinced by what he was saying. It wasn't an act or polished public-relations spiel. She decided not to push the political aspects just yet.

"You say you have to be towed. Solar Island can't move itself where you want to go, like a ship?" she asked, changing tack.

"We do have thrusters capable of moving us very slowly if the winds and currents are not significant, but Solar Island was designed to float passively, not to be directed like a ship. Think permanent facility as opposed to means of transportation."

"And what exactly are we floating on?" Solar Island certainly felt stable enough; but knowing that someone had built it, as opposed to it being a natural island, made her nervous.

"The base of the island is made up of a carbon-fiber–reinforced plastic shell filled with marine polyurethane foam. The foam provides the buoyancy; the carbon shell protects it and provides strength and rigidity."

"We're pretty high up," Tara observed, taking in the view of the waves below.

"The support pods, as we call them—there are four of them—are eighteen feet high. Then on top of that are the circular platforms and their rotation apparatuses overlaying the four pods—the deck, as we call it."

"What's the deck made of?"

"It's got a stainless steel framework overlaid with marine-grade plywood and a finished surface, like an epoxy. It supports all our solar-collection arrays as well as our buildings, which are themselves simple plywood structures. Come on, I'll show you some more."

Lightner put the cart in gear, and they rolled along an empty perimeter track.

"How many people live on Solar Island?" So far she'd only seen two, Jacob Lightner and Darrien from customs.

"About two dozen," Lightner said. "We're highly automated overall. I'll show you the Control Center."

He took a fork in the path that led away from the island's edge. Ahead on the left, two dark-skinned women could be seen wiping down solar collectors with rags. As the cart drew near, they turned and gave cheery waves. Lightner returned the wave but did not slow the cart as he drove past.

Tara turned around to snap a picture of them with the digital camera Dillon had given her. Jacob stopped the cart and grabbed the arm holding the camera, lowering it. "Please, you can take pictures of the facilities, but no people. It's rude."

Tara glared at him. "Speaking of rude," she said, taking his wrist and lifting it off her arm. "And what's the problem, anyway? They work here. I'm doing an article on what it's like to live and work on Solar Island. Why don't I just ask them whether they mind or not?" She looked at the women, who had once again busied themselves wiping the vast fields of mirrored surfaces.

"They don't speak English. They're from Tonga. We stopped there once for an energy sale, and a few of them came out to visit. When they found out that we would be drifting past some of their more remote islands, they asked if they could ride along in exchange for doing some work along the way. We have some collectors with automated washers, to dilute the salt buildup that accumulates, not to mention guano from birds, but of course it uses some of the energy we're trying to capture. So I thought, let's try the low-tech way, with human labor. Just as an experiment. They catch their own food through subsistence fishing, so it's actually quite efficient for us from an energy-expenditure standpoint."

Tara's brain flooded with questions. "So they live here? Permanently? How many? How will they get back to their island? How much do you pay them?"

"About a dozen or so. They've formed their own village down by what we call 'the beach.' They have access to the water, and they fish, even swim, on a daily basis. They practice their native rituals and religious rites. As long as they do the simple maintenance work we ask them to, we leave them alone. When we approach a shoreline, some of them get off, others come on. It's quite interesting, really."

"What if they want to get back home but they're too far away?"

Lightner shrugged. "The ocean is their home. For ages their people have voyaged by canoe from island to island, seeking a better life. This is really just a modern-day extension of that. If they want to get off, they leave at the next island stop or else wait until we get close enough to the island they came from."

Tara was still fuming from not being allowed to take pictures of the women. She let loose another question to keep her mind off it. "How do you handle medical emergencies here?"

Lightner tapped on the horn as he rounded a blind curve, then accelerated toward a building about fifty yards ahead. "All our staff undergo mandatory first aid and CPR training, and one of our technicians is also a trained medic. We carry first-rate medical supplies, including oxygen, antibiotics, painkillers, sutures, splints. For something more serious, we can radio for helicopter evacuation or even hold a videoconference with a physician."

Tara looked behind them, but the women were no longer in sight. Turning back around, she saw a man emerge from a squat, rectangular building and then immediately head back inside.

ELEVEN

Lightner pulled the cart to a stop in front of the building and got out. It looked to be a one-floor plywood building, its roof covered in what Tara recognized as the older-style photovoltaic solar panels. Simple stenciled letters over the door read "CONTROL CENTER."

"This building houses the computers and technicians that oversee the automated operations of our energy production," Lightner said. He opened the door, and Tara felt a cool draft emanate from within. "Come in," Lightner said as he entered.

Tara stepped into a fluorescent-lit tile-floored entryway. She followed Lightner to a plastic-strip door. "Antistatic, and keeps the heat and any airborne debris outside," Lightner said, holding a strip aside for Tara as they stepped into the larger room beyond.

Inside, the walls were lined with what Tara thought was an amazing amount of machinery. It looked like the inside of the starship *Enterprise*, she thought. Blinking LEDs everywhere, control panels, various boxes with metal conduits leading to and fro.

"I had no idea green energy required so many machines, so much technology," Tara said, and she meant it. She was pretty sure it was something a reporter would say to open up the conversation, too.

Lightner positively beamed. "So true! All people ever notice are the solar panels or collectors themselves; they have no idea what's behind the scenes. A lot of these boxes on the wall are power inverters, to convert the DC power generated by the collectors to AC power to run electrical equipment, like from your wall sockets.

"Of course, we sell energy on a large scale, so all this generation capacity isn't just for us on the island," he finished, sweeping an arm at the wall-to-wall technology.

Tara crossed her arms. "It certainly powers your air conditioner, all right!" She was dressed in shorts and a light blouse, suitable for the tropical conditions outside, but in here it was downright chilly.

"I'm sorry, I know it's cold in here, but it's necessary to maintain an optimal environment for the computers, which run 24-7. Personally, I find it refreshing after being in the tropics for so long, but you may want to put a jacket on if you have one," he said, indicating her backpack. Tara narrowed her eyes at him ever so slightly: Lightner had searched her pack earlier and knew that it contained a jacket. She removed a windbreaker and put it on in time to follow Lightner through a regular door set into the far end of the room.

It opened into a dimly lit space that belied the brightly lit world outside. It was staffed by two middle-aged men seated in wheeled desk chairs at computer workstations.

"Lady on deck, gentlemen," Lightner said. He turned to Tara and said, "Back in my Navy days when I did a stint as an electronics technician for four years to pay for my degree, the Captain would always say that when he brought a lady into a room filled with men. Of course, these days, they probably don't do that much anymore because there are more women; but here on Solar Island, unfortunately, we don't see a lot of females."

"And certainly none that look like you, if I may say so," one of the technicians said, rising from his chair and offering his hand to Tara. She shook it politely.

"Matt Dobson," the tech said. "I'm a statistician." Tara thought the man looked tired, possibly stressed. Did Lightner understaff Solar Island to save on salary costs?

"Dr. Dobson here analyzes the mountains of energy data we generate. His reports help to optimize our systems." Lightner proceeded to introduce Tara as reporter Amanda Greystone.

"And who is this?" Tara said, indicating the other technician who still sat at his station, facing a screen. He spun around slowly in his chair and stood up.

"Robert Benson, machinery-control specialist. I program the computers that automate everything around here."

If Dr. Dobson is tired, this guy is barely awake, Tara thought, eyeing the bottomless circles under Robert's eyes. He moved slowly.

"Robert's job is to make sure the machines don't take over the island. Right, Rob?" Lightner joked.

Robert managed a smile, but said nothing.

"And you gentlemen are Americans?" Tara asked, holding her notepad. They nodded while Lightner looked on.

"California," Dr. Dobson said.

"Nevada." This from the sleepy Benson.

"And how long have you been on Solar Island?"

"About a year," Dobson said, with Benson barely moving his head in agreement.

"Wow!" Tara exclaimed. She meant it. She hadn't yet even seen most of the island, but she'd been here less than an hour and couldn't imagine living here for a year. "That's a long time. Do you have families—wives, kids?" Both men shook their heads. Lightner spoke. "Some of our employees do. But I know what you're thinking: What kind of people would sign up for a job like that, where you were gone months or even years at a time?"

"The thought did cross my mind," Tara said.

"Lots of people," Lightner went on. "Same as those who work on oil rigs, or join the military, commercial fishermen, scientific expeditions, that sort of thing. No shortage of those kinds of people."

"I suppose not," Tara said, writing in her pad. At first she had caught herself merely doodling to make it look like she was taking notes, but then it occurred to her that if someone were to see her notepad filled with nonsense, it could compromise her cover, so she started taking real notes. They might even prove useful later, too. While writing, she caught Dobson and Benson exchange knowing glances.

"Well, gentlemen, I'll let you get back to work. Amanda will be here for three days, so you'll have a chance to catch up with her later." Lightner turned and strode for the exit.

The statistician, Dobson, shook her hand again, saying once more that it was nice to meet her, before turning back to his workstation.

Then Benson, moving with a surprising degree of alacrity, approached Tara while looking past her at Lightner, who was almost to the plastic strips.

"So glad you're covering Solar Island for your magazine," Benson said, overly loudly. "People really need to know about the work that goes on here."

He stared directly at Tara and raised his eyes as he said this last sentence. It gave her the chills. He shook her hand, pumping it vigorously while pressing something into her palm.

She opened her mouth to say something, but his eyes told her not to. She could feel a piece of paper in her hand. Benson broke his grip and sauntered back to his work area. Tara could see Lightner holding the plastic strips aside for her. She strode toward him and passed through the plastic into the entry room. She stood there until Lightner passed her and headed for the outside door. She then shoved the paper into the pocket of her shorts and hurried after Lightner, who had stopped at an electronic panel just inside the door. She heard a voice emanate from a speaker and realized he was using an intercom.

While she listened to Lightner speak to an employee somewhere else on the island, informing him that he and "the reporter" were heading over for a visit, Tara took a few steps away and pretended to study a schematic on the wall. Careful to face away from Lightner, she removed the crumpled piece of paper from her pocket and unfolded it.

At first she was confused, because she was looking at a Coca-Cola label—*Did that sleepy guy give me some trash to throw out?!*—but when she flipped it over, she saw writing on the reverse side. Not really writing, she told herself, but a message cobbled together from typed words and letters that looked as though they had been torn from various books or manuals and then glued in place on the label back. All of the message was in a small black typeface; this was not magazine cutouts with letters of wildly different styles and colors.

Tara's eyes widened in disbelief as she read the note:

I'M CHRIS TENNER! MEET ME TONIGHT, MIDNIGHT—THE MARINA.

TWELVE

She stuffed the note back into her pocket and turned around. Lightner was finishing up his intercom call. She walked to the door as he concluded it, and the two stepped outside. The full tropical daylight was blinding after the dimly lit computer room, and Tara scrambled to throw on her sunglasses, a high-end designer pair that she fantasized a world-traveling reporter might wear. She noticed that Lightner didn't wear any, yet it didn't seem to bother him. She asked him about it to distract from what had just gone on inside.

"I never wear them. Like to see things the way they really are, and being out here for extended periods of time—*living* out here—I find it best not to become dependent on anything."

Tara wondered why his face was so pale around his eyes if he never wore sunglasses. "Sunscreen?"

Lightner nodded solemnly. "Oh, yes, religiously. In fact, I had a little bout with skin cancer not too long ago. Doc advised me to stay out of the sun. Of course, that's not exactly possible in my line of work, now, is it?" he added with a laugh.

"I suppose not." Tara found it ironic that the man who had founded a personal empire based on the sun had also been damaged by it.

"Are you all out of questions for me?" Lightner asked after the silence that ensued.

"Do you have a marina on Solar Island?" The question carried some risk with it, but he had put her on the spot to ask something, and she did need to know where this marina was.

"As a matter of fact, we do! Did you see it from the air on your way in?"

"I saw something that looked a little out of place," Tara tried. During the helicopter descent to the island, she'd been so fascinated by the great field of solar collectors in the middle of the ocean, not to mention discussing logistics with Dillon and Rob, that she had not absorbed as many details as she might have. Dillon had managed to snap a wide-angle shot of most of the entire island, though, and he had given her that same camera. She made a mental note to review the shot later.

"Indeed, it is out of place!" Lightner said as he climbed back into the cart. "In fact, back when I was in the design phase of Solar Island, I had more than one marine engineer tell me that the concept simply wouldn't work at all, for a multitude of reasons."

He pressed a button to start the electric vehicle while Tara slid back into the passenger seat. It made her somewhat uncomfortable to be sitting so close to Lightner, the man behind an island where things weren't quite right. The man who had confiscated her little derringer. The man under investigation by the CIA....

She took out her notepad and forged on. "Why's that?"

She wanted to keep him talking, to continue divulging more about Solar Island and, on a different level, about his own personality. Tara was a trained observer of people: the more someone talked, the more she picked up on their overall demeanor through visual cues as well as directed questioning. She also needed to learn the location of the marina without having to blatantly ask where it was.

Lightner rolled the cart back out onto the track, which bisected two opposing rows of solar-collection apparatus. "For one thing, they thought it would be too fragile. But they were picturing a marina—this is a small-craft marina to house our fleet of about a half dozen boats—that would be appended to the edge of the island like a bump on a log."

He laughed aloud at the memory of it. "This one designer even showed me a drawing that had an artificial breakwater going around the marina to protect it from the waves."

"What's so funny about that?" Tara asked. It seemed reasonable enough to her, although she was certainly no marine engineer.

"From a hydrodynamic standpoint, it's just preposterous," Lightner spat. "The thing would break away after, at most, a few weeks of exposure to the ocean's forces."

"So, then, how did you handle it?"

Lightner stopped the cart at a fork in the path. The left route took them deeper into the maze of solar collectors, while the right led toward open daylight—the edge of the island.

"Would you like to take a look right now?"

"At the marina? Sure!" Tara thought back to Tenner's note. *Midnight... The marina...* It would be advantageous to get a look at the rendezvous point in the daytime before having to sneak there in the middle of the night.

He drove off toward the daylight. "It's on the other side of the island, but we're almost at the perimeter road, so it won't take long."

"How long does it take to drive around the entire island?"

"The circumference—do you recall your high school geometry?"

"The distance all the way around a circle," Tara said flatly. Lightner's lecturing was getting to be annoying.

"Yes. The circumference of Solar Island is about three and a half miles. So it can be walked in under an hour or driven in one of our carts like this in as little as fifteen minutes. Did you know that doubling the diameter of a circle increases its area four times?"

Tara confessed, on behalf of Amanda Greystone, that she did not. Lightner continued.

"Yes, well, that was one of the design issues inherent with choosing a circular shape for the island as opposed to something angular."

"Why did you want a circle?"

"It's hydrodynamically superior. With no straight edges to resist, water just slides off. From a fabrication standpoint, it was a little more difficult, but still doable, as you can see."

They reached the edge of the platform and turned left on the track, the ocean to their right. Also to their right was the perimeter jogging track. Tara was surprised to see a man in shorts and a T-shirt about to use a set of pull-up bars. He waved at them as Lightner passed in the cart without slowing.

"The perimeter track features an exercise trail. There are bars, rings, little stations like that at regular intervals around the track so that we can stay in shape out here."

"I might want to avail myself of their use at some point, if that's okay," Tara said. While it was true that she was a regular exerciser, she was also trying to establish a basis for having some free roaming around the island, *sans* escort.

"Certainly, please do. It's even lit at night."

Having gotten what she wanted, Tara quickly moved on, lest Lightner change his mind or alter the terms of the freedom she had just established for herself.

"Ah, that brings up one of the questions on my list," she said, flipping through her ever-present notepad. Overhead, the sun peeked through the solar-collector array that they were driving under like it was a long tunnel.

"How do you provide electricity at night, when there's no sun? Or—and I suppose this doesn't happen much in this part of the world—but when it's cloudy?"

Lightner pulled the cart to a stop beneath a solar collector.

"It's time I explained how our energy-collection and power-generation processes work," he said, climbing out of the cart and pointing at a solar array. It was a curved trough design, with a slick mirrored surface. A tube of some kind ran along the length of the glass trough.

"These look different than other solar panels I've seen," Tara said.

"That's because these are not the old clunky photovoltaic panels you learned about in grade school. In fact, they're technically not solar panels at all. While we do have a few photovoltaics around—especially the newer thin-film type, the principal design in use here is called concentrated solar power, or a solar thermal electric power plant. We actually employ two different variants of solar thermal: parabolic trough, and solar power tower." Lightner paused while Tara took notes.

"Both are types of high-temperature collectors. The parabolic trough system, an example of which you see to our right, uses curved mirrors to reflect sunlight onto fluid-filled pipes. The fluid—it's oil, like a cooking oil—is heated to produce steam, which is then sent via the pipes to turn a turbine."

"What's the second type?" Tara asked, unabashedly scribbling on her reporter's pad. Lightner pointed to the row of solar equipment on their left. Unlike the single continuous trough, these were large square mirrors placed in a row with perhaps six inches of space between them. A system of motors and gears occupied the metal support base of each one.

"The second type is known as a power tower design. It uses a field of individual square, flat mirrors called heliostats, which can collectively focus the sun's radiation on a receiver contained within our power tower—that's the tower in the center of the island."

"The same tower we climbed down the outside of from the helipad?"

"Yes. Inside that is a set of powerful turbines. Due to the unique constraints placed on us because we are an island, we use the same turbines for both the parabolic trough system and the heliostat system. From there, we have a set of cables that we can use to deliver the power to the land."

"So these parabolic troughs," Tara said, looking down at her notes, "focus the sun's rays on the thin pipes that run along the mirrors, and heat the oil inside them?"

"Correct, along with the computer-controlled tracking system that both rotates the deck platform and tilts the individual heliostats and troughs to keep them aligned with the sun for maximum radiation exposure."

"So the parabolic troughs are the long, continuous curved mirrors with the pipes in front of them, and the heliostats are the individual square mirrors. Correct?"

Lightner nodded. "That's right. We use alternating rows of each type throughout the island's solar farm. Right now, on our right is a parabolic trough, and to our left is a row of heliostats. I don't like to depend too much on any one system, and, since this is a pilot project, we're collecting data on the efficiency of the different systems to inform future efforts."

Tara looked down at her notepad as if reading a prepared inquiry. "Back to my original question. I've heard reports that Solar Island is capable of producing power twenty-four hours a day. How do you produce solar-derived energy at night?"

"The trick is that we don't actually *produce* energy at night, but that we *store* some of what we make during the day for use when the sun isn't shining."

"How is that storage accomplished?"

"For smaller-scale use, we have a battery bank of a type of sealed battery known as 'absorbed glass mat' or AGM, which stores more than enough power for our own use at night or in the rare event of days without sunshine. AGMs were originally developed for military aircraft and later saw use in marine deep-cycle applications, and we've further modified them here to suit our purposes. They're especially great because their charging systems never need to be recalibrated. Anyway, it's critical that we have power at night, not just for our own comfort or so we can work, but for the navigation and running lights that surround Solar Island, so that ships can see us at night."

"And what about for larger-scale use, like powering entire towns, which I heard Solar Island has done in the past?"

Lightner nodded. "We also have some new experimental technologies for storing power that we can get to later. But enough of the technical stuff for now. Let me show you something that's sort of fun!" Lightner got back behind the wheel of the electric cart and restarted the vehicle.

"Okay," Tara said, resuming her seat. She already felt like she was learning a lot about solar power. But she wondered how much Lightner was leaving out.

They emerged from the tunnel formed by the overhead heliostats and trough back out to the island's perimeter. Lightner made a left onto the utility track, which ran parallel to the exercise course. Ahead of them, their world followed the curve of the massive structure, while to the right the ocean once again reminded Tara that there was literally nowhere to go off of Solar Island. But in front of them, the terrain was changing.

An abutment forced the utility track to the left, inward toward the island's center. A highway road sign with an oversized left-turn arrow outlined in reflectors guided them. Tara craned her neck but couldn't see over the abutment.

"What's this?" she asked.

"You remember the design issue we had over the marina?"

"That it would stick out too far and get snapped off?"

"Yes. I solved it by having the marina become *part* of the island rather than appended to it. So the island remains a perfect circle, and the marina is contained inside a small part of the circle. This is a compromise, because it does take up precious space that could be used for the solar farm, but it's infinitely more efficient."

"If it's inside the circle, how do the boats get in and out?"

"Excellent question, Amanda. You're about to see for yourself, but the answer is a gate that can open and close to allow access for our vehicles."

They rounded the abutment, and Tara was surprised to see a view looking down on a small boat marina—"small" being the operative word, Tara decided. There were two tugboats, two Zodiac inflatable boats, and an odd yellow craft that Tara couldn't place, resting on its own dock. Lightner rounded the abutment and pulled the cart to a stop in front of a gate.

"The road doesn't go down to it, but this is the entrance," he announced. "We've got two tugboats of our own, in the event that we need to tow our island. They've proven useful in navigating through some uncharted atoll formations on occasion, or if one of our energy clients doesn't have towing capabilities."

"What's the shiny yellow contraption on the dock?" Tara asked. She could now see that it featured some kind of clear dome.

"Ah, that's my one true luxury aboard. It's a two-person submersible. Not a deep-water craft: it's just for use either for pleasure diving on the coral reefs, or as an inspection vehicle if we want to take a look underneath Solar Island."

Secretly, Tara hoped she'd never have to do that. Having been diagnosed with hydrophobia in childhood, her fear of water was now under control; but she knew it was still there, lurking somewhere beneath the surface. "Interesting," was all that came out.

Lightner positively beamed. "I quite think so! Perhaps if there's time during your stay, I could take you for a dive. Get you a real in-depth tour, so to speak," he chuckled.

"Maybe," Tara said, trying to sound noncommittal yet not afraid at the same time.

"So you can see that what we've done is to basically indent the marina inside the circle of Solar Island, and then gate off the outside with what's known in marine engineering circles as a 'containment boom,'" Lightner explained. "It's just a floating tube that we pull across like an artificial breakwater. The island itself creates a protected cove on three sides. It's a little like drilling a hole near the edge of a coin to make a necklace."

Tara nodded. She was about to say something when they heard a commotion from the other side of the marina: people shouting, a loud clanking noise.

"Hop in, please." Lightner said, his voice fraught with unexpected tension. Tara jumped back into the cart, and Lightner floored it down the path that ran along the marina to the other side, where once again the track resumed its course around the perimeter of the island, twenty feet above the sea.

A group of people was knotted in the path ahead, clearly focused on something beyond the chest-high steel railing that guarded the island's edge all the way around. Lightner pulled the cart to a stop and hopped out. Tara followed.

Four men were huddled at the island's edge. Tara had seen none of them before. Three were Americans, judging by their accents, while the fourth was a Pacific Islander.

"I could take one of the Zodiacs," Tara heard one of the men say.

"No, I got it, I got it!" one of the other men, wielding a fishing rod, said. He had stuck the rod through the cables of the railing and was now reeling something in. Tara saw that a long metal pole lay cast aside on the track. A failed attempt at whatever they were trying to do, she thought.

The three men not fishing saw Lightner approach and immediately snapped to attention.

"What's going on?" Lightner demanded.

"I was doing a jog and spotted something in the water. Clothing, maybe. Not sure. Alan's reeling it up right now," one of the American men said.

Lightner pushed his way up to the rail to see whatever was coming up. Tara could feel the eyes of the men on her as she also made her way to the rail. She peered over the side at the object. It was a piece of cloth of some kind, maroon in color. She couldn't see why these men were getting so worked up over it. Casting a sidelong glance at the man next to her, she could see his eyes bugged out as he focused intently on the object coming up. "Careful. Don't jerk the line," he said, touching the shoulder of the guy doing the fishing.

"I got it, I got it," came the response in an almost reverent tone.

"It's a baseball cap," someone said.

The man flicked the fishing rod, and the cap flew up over the rail onto the deck. It bore the letters "ATM," with the "T" dominating.

"That's Bernie's hat," the man with the fishing rod said. "He went to Texas A&M."

A hushed silence fell over the group. None of them touched the cap.

"Who's Bernie?" Tara asked.

A man wearing shorts and a T-shirt with the Solar Island logo answered her. "Bernie Riley. He's been missing for about a week."

THIRTEEN

Everyone in the group began talking at once. Tara heard the words "overboard," "Bernie," and "missing" spoken several times. Dr. Lightner stepped forward and raised a hand in the air to gain attention.

"Hold on!" he said. "First of all, proper introductions are in order. Gentlemen, this here is Amanda Greystone, the reporter from the *National Reader* I was telling you about."

Tara knew this was meant to remind the men not to say too much. Someone was missing, judging by what was being said and the dead-seriousness of the group.

So Chris Tenner was right, she thought, eyeing the soggy cap on deck. Something *was* going on out here.

"Amanda, this is Greg Rush. He's one of our power-generator specialists," Lightner said of the fisherman, who leaned his pole against the rail and offered Tara his hand. He was a gruff-looking man with a thick head of curly black hair and a beard to match. She shook his hand politely.

"And this is Luke Burke. He oversees the day-to-day operations and maintenance of the solar farm."

"Ma'am," Luke said simply, tipping his head. He had short blond hair, a ruddy complexion, and rough-looking hands that spoke to a life lived largely outdoors.

"And I'm Ray Baxter," the third American man said, offering a hand. His hands were rough, but well manicured, Tara noticed, and his eyes had a vague friendliness to them.

"Ray here's one of our mechanics, and our Chief Vehicle Mechanic," Lightner said.

"Pretty much everybody on this island's got to be a mechanic, no matter what their job title is, to keep all this stuff working," Luke joked.

The fourth man in the group, a South Pacific Islander, smiled at Tara. "And who is this?" Tara asked.

"I am Matiu," the man said, smiling brightly as he offered his hand. Tara shook it.

"Matiu is from Tonga," Lightner said. "He's also part of the power-generator team."

Tara wanted to ask if he lived on "the beach" with the other native South Pacific Islanders she'd seen, the ones who cleaned the mirrors, but decided now was not the best time to ask.

"So, what happened here?" Tara asked, pointing at the cap.

There was an uncomfortable silence. Lightner broke it.

"We think one of our employees, Bernie," he said, nodding toward the cap, "may have fallen overboard."

"He's been missing for a week," Luke the mechanic said, echoing what the man in the shorts had previously said.

"A Solar Island employee has been missing for a week?" Tara said directly to Lightner. She figured any reporter would ask.

"Unfortunately, that is correct," Lightner answered. "When he didn't report to his station a week ago, we looked in his quarters, and then searched the entire island, including a perimeter search by boat, and even underneath the platform with the sub. He was not found."

"This is the first trace of him at all," Luke said, nodding at the cap.

"So, was he reported missing to the authorities?" Tara asked, again looking right at Lightner.

"What authorities?"

The question caught Tara a bit off guard. Out here in the middle of the ocean in international waters, who did have authority? But she played it off like a reporter.

"I don't know; the Coast Guard? The nearest government's police, the man's family—anybody?"

"If you mean the U.S. Coast Guard, they have no authority out here. International waters."

"But they still might be able to help. You didn't call his family?"

"He has no family listed in his personnel file," Lightner said.

Tara could see Luke take on an expression of distaste at this comment, but he said nothing, and then Lightner turned and strode back toward the electric vehicle.

"Take out the Zodiacs and do another perimeter search," Lightner ordered. "Come on, Amanda, let's continue our tour."

Tara said goodbye to the four men, who nodded in return. Luke seemed to shake his head ever so subtly, or was she reading something into the gesture that wasn't there? As she walked to the cart, she turned around once and saw all four men still staring at her, just watching her go. Then they sprang into action, two of them heading for the ramp leading down to the marina.

Tara felt almost in a daze as she climbed into the cart beside Lightner. *No official search? No one notified of a person missing at sea?* She was horrified. And none of the men, with the possible exception of Luke, showed the slightest bit of resistance to the idea that allowing a man's disappearance at sea to go unreported was anything but business as usual.

Lightner said something about continuing the tour, and Tara responded on autopilot. She was thinking now. *If Lightner had anything to hide, or didn't want the missing person to become known, then why had he agreed to have a reporter visit at all?*

She didn't know. Maybe he needed the money the "magazine" was paying him? The exposure it would generate would be good for business? Or maybe, Tara thought as the cart glided down a path that took them toward the center of the island, Dr. Lightner just didn't care. *Seems like he's gone a little overboard with the private-island–nation thing,* Tara thought.

"It's time you saw the power tower!" Lightner enthused as they entered a tunnel of heliostats. As the relative darkness enveloped them, Tara turned to look at Lightner. He was looking straight up between the solar collectors to the sky, not even looking at the road.

"Mind your driving, Dr. Lightner!"

Lightner put his hands back on the wheel and brought his gaze back level with the road. "Not to worry. If the expression 'I know these roads like the back of my hand' ever applied, it's to me, here. Just checking the weather."

Tara glanced up at the sliver of brilliant blue sky visible through the trough. "Does it ever change much?"

"Oh, yes." Lightner stepped on the accelerator a little. "You'd be surprised how things can turn on a dime out here."

Tara was numb as they drove toward the island's center. Here she was, being toured around an island when a man was missing.

"Dr. Lightner, I've got to ask: Has everything possible been done to find Bernard Riley?"

FOURTEEN

Lightner slowed the cart to a stop under the shade of a parabolic trough. He looked at Tara. "Why, of course! You heard me back there—my men are looking for him right now."

"Yes, but the fact that no third parties were called...."

"Dear, we monitor all standard and emergency marine radio channels on Solar Island."

"Dr. Lightner, please refrain from calling me that. Have you heard anything on those channels?"

"My apologies, dear. Oh, really! I'm sorry, I just can't seem to help myself. No, we haven't heard anything. But if anyone found a person or a body for hundreds of miles around, we'd know about it. Let's face it, if someone does manage to fall overboard from our island—not an easy task: you've seen the rails, right?—they're not in the best of predicaments. It's a twenty-foot drop. And if they were to be sucked under the support pods...."

Lightner let the sentence trail off into oblivion. Tara shivered at the thought of being crushed beneath the massive structure. It could happen that way, she realized. At the same time, Lightner isn't going to let anything slip. But she now had the name of a victim.

"Has anyone ever fallen overboard or gone missing from Solar Island before?" Tara asked. The question put her on edge a little as she looked up at the narrow slice of blue sky available between the trough and the heliostats. She was crossing into special-agent questioning now, leaving reporter territory behind. Would Lightner notice?

"Nothing like this before, no. We have had an accidental fall into the ocean—one from quite high up on one of our windmills, which you'll see later—but fortunately the worker landed in the water and was immediately rescued in one of our boats. Solar Island, as I pointed out to you, is an industrial facility and as such does have inherent dangers."

"But no one's ever gone missing before?" Tara pressed.

Lightner hesitated. "Not missing as in gone overboard; but in the early days we did have issues with workers who went on shore leave to a port city. When we occasionally must make landfall for extensive repairs or resupplies, or to hold meetings for a new energy deal, we have port visits. Also reminiscent of my old Navy days. But sometimes not every worker was back on board when we were ready to leave again, that kind of thing. But we've since implemented procedures, including roll call and electronic sign-out protocols, to eliminate those sorts of problems."

"What was Bernard Riley's job here?" Tara persisted.

This time she could see in Lightner's face that she'd crossed a line. His cheeks reddened somewhat and his skin drew tighter. He looked at his watch and seemed to restrain himself.

"He was a battery technician. Worked with the power-storage mechanisms that allow us to provide energy at night, which I'm trying to show you if we could move along."

"I see. And did Bernard have any family members? Did you notify them of his disappearance?"

"Mrs. Greystone! If I am to give you the complete tour of our facilities that your magazine requested, we are going to have to move along. I myself have much to do in order to keep Solar Island running, in addition to continuing to search for my missing employee and shepherding you around. As you can see, there aren't a lot of personnel for an installation of this size," he finished, putting the cart into gear.

"I'm sorry, sir," Tara replied, stepping back into character. "I'm just trying to get a feel for what life is like here, besides just the technical stuff."

"You'll get a good idea of that over the next couple of days. I'd bet that by the end of that time, you'll be bored stiff and asking when the helicopter is going to return," Lightner said with a snicker.

They reached a fork in the path where their inward track joined a circular roadway. A sign indicated that it was called Core Circle Road. A simple wooden stake stuck into a potted palm, the sign had a tiny solar panel perched atop its post. No space was wasted here, Tara realized. Every inch of this place was a protest against the idea that humans could not harness the power of Earth's nearest star in order to survive.

As he drove, Lightner pointed at the island's core structures. "You saw the helipad and the customs station," Lightner said, perhaps with a bit of a smile, Tara thought, "but there's another building on top of customs, and it's very important."

"The jail for people who don't pass your little inspection?" Tara couldn't stop from throwing the jab. She was still angry about the unannounced search of her belongings and having her biometric data recorded.

Lightner laughed good-naturedly. "I see you have a sense of humor. That goes a long way out here," he said, pulling the cart to a stop in a designated spot that Tara now noticed featured a sign reading "RESERVED, JL." *Jacob Lightner's private parking space. Like there's so much traffic around here. Gosh, this guy has an ego!*

"So now that you've seen the solar farm and the lay of the land, so to speak," Lightner said, stepping out of the cart, "I think you're ready to see the power generator."

"Why didn't you just show it to me when we were already here?"

"To understand how Solar Island works, it's extremely important to see things in a specific order. All the solar infrastructure you've seen only *collects* radiation—it can't actually *do* anything with it. The generating station is what allows us to direct that energy to where it is most needed."

"You mean to a village or town that is willing to pay for it."

Lightner cocked his head to one side, as if slightly offended; but when he spoke, his voice was amicable enough. "Well, yes; Solar Island is a for-profit business, after all. I spent millions of dollars building it. If I can, I want to get a return on my investment."

"How do you decide which countries to sell energy to? Does politics play a role?" *That's for you, CIA,* Tara thought.

"Politics? Oh, heavens no," Lightner said. "Most of the time we just drift where Mother Ocean takes us. If that happens to be to some island or shore that wants the services we can provide, then so be it. If not, that's okay too. Here on Solar Island, we're in no hurry: we're on island time. Come, this way!"

Lightner beckoned Tara to follow him to a side door above the customs building. She trotted along after him. He scaled the ladder that they'd climbed down from the helipad earlier, to the door set into the side of the tower.

Tara continued her interview as she climbed. "So you wouldn't—just hypothetically—do something like deny a small island nation your energy unless they agreed to..." Tara looked up and could see that Lightner had reached the door and was just standing there, listening to her, a serious expression on his face.

"Agreed to what?" he prompted. He watched her climb. She reached him at the small platform set into the wall, but he just stood there, waiting for her response.

"Oh, I don't know...agree to stop trading with another country, say? Would you refuse energy to a country that wouldn't cease trade agreements with a neighbor?"

"Hypothetically?" Lightner asked, turning back to the door and using a metal key to unlock it.

Tara nodded. Lightner pushed the door open. She saw Lightner's lips moving as he answered her, but his words were lost to the roar coming from beyond the open door. He beckoned to her as he disappeared inside.

Tara was sure Lightner knew that his answer would be drowned out by the machinery. She followed him inside. Lightner flipped a switch, and wall-mounted fluorescent bulbs flickered to life around them.

"Welcome to the power tower," Lightner exclaimed with obvious relish. He had to raise his voice to be heard, but he didn't need to shout. "This is where the concentrated solar thermal energy collected on our island is converted into usable power," he said, waving an arm at the high-ceilinged cylindrical room filled with machinery.

Tara took it in with a sense of wonderment. She found it difficult to believe that all these moving parts were crammed into such a small space. Outside, Solar Island was so tranquil, so bright. They stood on a metal grate for a floor, a strong vibration rattling their feet. Looking down through the floor, Tara could see a collection of pipes and machinery below them; and then, under that, she could see the turnstile and part of the counter in the customs room. She noticed a narrow access ladder running down through the center of the power tower all the way down into customs.

"It looks like there's a lot going on, but in essence all we have is an inlet pipe, a turbine, and a generator," Dr. Lightner lectured.

"What are those?" Tara asked, pointing at two rapidly spinning objects that reminded her of fans.

"Those are the twin turbines. The noise comes from fans feeding air to them. The pressurized steam coming from the inlet pipe—which in turn comes from the solar field—is what's turning the turbines."

"When we flew over in the helicopter, that was steam coming out of the top of this building, right?"

"That's right," Lightner said, starting to walk in a circle around the big inlet pipe in the center of the space. "That's the spent vent steam coming out of the stack after it passes through the turbines."

"And what's that up there?" Tara asked. She pointed at a metal catwalk structure about ten feet over their heads that circled the turbines. On the catwalk was a small structure of some kind, with a door set into the catwalk in front of it. A prominent sign admonished "DANGER / HIGH VOLTAGE / KEEP OUT."

Lightner followed her gaze upward. "That's the Energy Transfer Station. It's a special signal-processing unit that handles the electrical flow before it gets to the cable set."

"So, how is the power actually transferred to someone who wants to use it on shore?" Tara asked, notepad at the ready.

"With the cables. They're heavy-duty, very long, and can be run under or above water for almost a mile. The energy buyer usually sends a boat out to us and we pay out the cable."

"What if it's not long enough to reach where they need it to go?"

"Usually in this part of the world that's not a problem. These islands are small. But on occasion we have had clients who also supply their own coupling cable to join ours—you can think of it as a giant extension cord—to get the power where it needs to go."

Tara took out the digital camera Dillon had given her and aimed it up at the Energy Transfer Station. Lightner immediately put his hand over the lens.

"I'm sorry, Mrs. Greystone. No photos of this area, please."

Tara feigned an expression of disappointment. "How about if I just climb up there, then, and have a look? No pictures," she said, offering Lightner her camera.

He waved it away. "One time I lost a worker due to a high-voltage accident—not on Solar Island, but with equipment similar to the ETS here. This is as close as I can allow you to get. I might add that even my employees who aren't directly responsible for working with the ETS aren't allowed on that platform," he said, gazing upward.

"So it's proprietary technology that you don't want anyone getting ahold of, is that it?" Tara asked.

"We have a lot of proprietary technology on Solar Island, but the ETS is not particularly sensitive in that regard, although it is a fairly elegant implementation of traditional technology. But mostly it's just dangerous to be around unless you've had training."

"Is it patented?"

"Patent pending." He looked at his watch, which Tara noticed contained a tiny solar panel in its face. *Even this guy's watch is solar-powered. Talk about obsess—*

"This will conclude the opening section of our tour," Lightner said, heading for the door. "It's time I got you to your guest quarters, and then I've got a technical meeting to attend. After that, it'll be dinner time. I'll send someone for you." He opened the door and flipped off the lights.

The sun was blinding after the relative darkness of the power tower. Tara stepped out onto the platform.

Lightner was already descending the ladder. "Just pull the door closed, please. It'll lock," he said, continuing on his way down. Tara grabbed the steel door by the handle and pulled it shut. It made a clanging noise as the edge contacted the frame, but she could feel that it hadn't clicked all the way shut. Looking down, she could see that an old rubber doorstop had become trapped under the door, preventing the lock from catching. She bent down to remove it, then hesitated.

From below, Lightner's voice came. "You coming?"

Tara left the door as it was and made her way down the ladder.

FIFTEEN

Dillon Marconi cast a worried glance over at the helicopter's fuel gauge. The island of Guam now grew larger in their windscreen, but he'd caught Rob eyeing the gauge too many times not to feel concern.

"Don't worry. We'll make it," Rob said, reading the rookie agent's mind. "Worse comes to worst, I could always whistle up a mid-air refuel."

"Maybe I should have just jumped out with Agent Shores onto Solar Island anyway," Dillon said, for the second or third time during the flight.

Behind his mirrored aviator glasses, Rob rolled his eyes. "You're playing Monday-morning quarterback now, buddy. What's done is done. And besides," he said, banking the aircraft into a turn, "it was pretty clear that you weren't wanted there. Would have just made things more difficult for both of you if you had disobeyed their request. Shores had the option of not going, too. Ask me, she's got a screw loose when it comes to this kind of stuff."

Dillon laughed. "True, not a lot of agents would have volunteered for that like she did. She could have waited while we did more investigating into the background of the island, but she wanted to go now."

Rob shrugged. "Loose talk around Guam is, that place is weirder than a UFO over the Bermuda Triangle, and about as reliable. I've lived on Guam about a year now, flown all over the South Pacific, and it's like it's become this urban myth or something; this floating island everyone's heard of but almost no one's even seen, let alone been to."

"Well, we've seen it, that's for sure. I probably don't need to tell you this, Rob, but it's best that it stay a myth for now, until we get Tara out of there. No details in the pub or wherever you flyboys hang out on Guam."

Rob looked over at Dillon. "Loose lips sink ships, is that it?" He spoke into his headset mic to engage in some chatter with the control tower for Guam International.

Dillon nodded. "Guam's a pretty small island. Never know who could be listening."

As soon as the wheels hit the tarmac, Dillon was on his cell phone to Tara's supervisor in Honolulu. Rob stayed with the helicopter for post-flight operations while Dillon got into a taxi. He gave the driver the name of their hotel and was wondering if Ozakawa was going to pick up, when he heard Ozakawa's assistant say, "FBI Honolulu, Special Agent in Charge Daniel Ozakawa's office. How may I direct your call?"

Dillon looked out the window at some passing palm trees and a group of Japanese tourists climbing onto a bus. He gave her an agent's field code that would authenticate him as a working agent. Then he said, "I need to speak with him right away."

"I'm sorry, but he's in a meeting. If you require immediate assistance—"

"Tell him it's about Special Agent Shores's current case."

A slight pause, followed by "Please hold."

A minute later, Daniel Ozakawa's voice greeted Dillon's ears. "What happened?"

Dillon relayed the events of Solar Island's welcoming committee. He cringed in the back seat of the cab as Ozakawa let loose a string of colorful language. "She's there by herself? You deviated from the field protocol that I signed off on?"

Dillon cleared his throat. "Sir, for what it's worth, I wanted to jump anyway—what could they do after our helicopter left?—but she told me not to. Said it would make them angry and—"

"That's enough, Agent. You don't need to tell me how Shores is. She must like my office, is all I can say, because that's where she's going to be the second she gets back, to explain this mess."

"Yes, sir."

"Remember this, kid: A special agent's job is to serve the public, and you can't serve the public if you're dead. You got that?"

"I do, sir."

"Good. Then do me a favor and remind Agent Shores of that. Meantime, I want you to investigate the hell out of the people behind that island. You get your butt over to the Guam station and start uncovering things we can use, you got that? Shores's life may depend on it."

SIXTEEN

Lightner drove Tara along one of the paths that radiated outward from the center of Solar Island. "We have a compound in a loose ring formation about two thirds of the way from the island's center that serves as our living quarters," Lightner said as he waved to a pair of Tongan women cleaning a section of parabolic trough on the side of the path. They returned his wave.

"How many people can it accommodate?"

"Probably about two dozen, although most of the time, as is the case now, we only have about half that number living there."

Tara winced as a shaft of sunlight piercing the gap between the heliostats reminded her to put her sunglasses back on. "Not counting the...natives?" she asked, watching the women clean the solar apparatus in their wake.

"All of us who live here are natives of Solar Island," Lightner declared happily. "But the South Pacific Islanders don't live in the staff or guest quarters. As I mentioned, they live down on the beach in their own village."

"And is this segregation of their choosing, or yours?" Tara asked.

"I don't think of it as segregation at all."

"Then how do you explain confining them to one small outdoor area of your island while the rest of you live within modern accommodations?"

He shrugged as he slowed the cart to negotiate a turn on the path ahead. "I think of it as what it is—allowing them to live as they wish. They're not *confined*, but rather they choose to live that way. You see, when we first took on a group of them—there were four, I believe, from Tonga—we put them in the guest quarters. But then in their free time they started going down to the island's edge to fish, and eventually down to the marina, where ocean access is easiest. Pretty soon, there was a small tent down there and they began staying less and less in the staff quarters. I asked them if there was something I could do to make life more comfortable for them in the quarters, but they said they prefer to live at the water's edge. Over time, as we took on new islander labor, they would all join the village. So I just let it be."

"Interesting," Tara commented as she made a notation on her pad.

"We're coming up on the first of the staff-quarters buildings here," Lightner said, as the row of heliostats they were following gave way to a long one-story plywood structure. The end of the building was decorated with a painting of an Aztec-style sun. He parked the cart there, and they got out. Lightner pointed to a sundial set into the deck.

"There's a reminder of one of man's earliest attempts at harnessing the power of the sun to do useful work. Still practical today."

"So, what time is it?" Tara asked, tilting her head to look at the ancient clock. Lightner looked at his wristwatch, and Tara made a clucking noise. "Aha! Yet you rely on modern technology for the answer!"

Lightner regarded Tara coolly. "Since our island is not stationary, the sun dial is not reliable," he said. He waved an arm at Tara to follow him around the end of the building. "Let me show you to your quarters."

He opened a screen door and led her into the barracks-style building. They walked down a wood-floored hallway that for now was lit only by skylights. Closed doors leading to private quarters were set on the right side, with an occasional screen door leading outside on the left.

Lightner stopped at a door about halfway down the barrack. The number 07 was stenciled onto the door. He opened it without knocking, and they entered the room.

"I think you'll find the accommodations Spartan but livable," Lightner said, gazing at the wooden walls, which were crudely painted with various symbols representing the sun—scenes depicting the solar rays drawing crops out of the ground. One of these showed what Tara guessed to be the mythical Icarus's wings melting as he flew too close to the ball of fire, while another portrayed the Egyptian sun god Ra, with an orange disc resting on his falcon head.

"Did you paint these yourself?"

Lightner smiled amiably. "I'm afraid my talents lie in other areas. These were done by various visitors, Pacific Islanders, employees, friends—anyone, really, who wanted to paint images that pay tribute to our purpose for being on this island—the sun. Each room is different. Would you care to contribute one of your own while you're here?"

"I confess that my talents lie in other areas as well," Tara said, taking in the rest of the room, which was unremarkable. A simple bunk bed was situated in one corner, while on the opposite wall was a small wooden desk. A kitchenette occupied one corner, and a window, curtains drawn, was set into the wall opposite the door. There was also a narrow closet. Tara watched as Lightner disappeared into the only other room besides the main one—a small bathroom.

"Every quarters features a toilet and shower," Lightner said, clearly proud of this accomplishment. Tara walked to the bathroom and peered inside. A mirrored medicine cabinet hung over a basic sink.

For a few days, it would be fine, Tara thought, but she couldn't imagine living in such small and simple confines for very long. She wondered if Dr. Lightner's personal accommodations were different.

"So, what do you think?" Lightner asked, stepping back into the main room. "Will it suffice?"

"Oh, it'll do. It's certainly...rustic. One question," she said, glancing back at the bathroom. "What happens to the, uh, waste?"

"That's a good question. We don't simply dump the wastewater—isn't that a lovely euphemism the industry has come up with?—overboard as the cruise-ship industry used to do and in some cases continue to do today when their ships are in international waters. We have our own advanced wastewater-treatment plant on board, and it's treated in that before being expelled, even out here in international waters, where such treatment is not required."

"So you do dump it overboard, but it's treated first," Tara said, making a note in her pad.

"Yes, we do have a treated-waste stream," Lightner said. "Of course, we don't have anywhere near the population density that the floating cities of the cruise ships have—Solar Island is more like a floating farm—lots of area but with low population. But we still possess advanced wastewater-treatment technology—solar-powered, naturally."

"Could I—"

"Yes, those facilities are scheduled as part of your tour here," Dr. Lightner preempted her.

"Thanks."

"And now I must go to my meeting. At dinner time I will send someone for you. We all try to have supper together nightly in the dining hall. As our guest, we'd be delighted to have you, and it will be a terrific opportunity for you to meet most of our staff, and to get some more questions answered as well."

"Sounds great," Tara said. "See you there."

She watched him leave the room and heard him walk down the hall until one of the screen doors squeaked open. She went to the door and noticed that it did have a simple lock, which she engaged. Then she dropped her backpack on the bed and walked to the window, drawing back its curtains. She wasn't sure what kind of view she expected, but the window was almost entirely blocked by the back of one of the solar troughs. She pulled the curtains shut again and went to the bed, opening her backpack.

Tara selected a dinner outfit of slacks and a T-shirt with the logo of the magazine she was supposed to be working for emblazoned on the front. Then she went into the bathroom to take a shower. A sign in the shower stall proclaimed "HOT WATER CONSUMES OUR PRECIOUS POWER—USE IT SPARINGLY!"

Tara stood outside the shower as she turned the water on. She'd experienced solar-powered showers before and recalled waiting several minutes for lukewarm water. She was surprised, therefore, when a forceful blast of steaming water jetted from the showerhead as soon as she turned it on. She thought of all the steam coming from the power tower and its powerful turbines as it scalded her arm, making her scramble for the cold-water knob.

She considered her upcoming meeting with Chris Tenner tonight. Lightner, who seemed to know everything under the sun about this place (literally), didn't know that Tenner had gone far out of his way to arrange a meeting with her.

Or did he? What if this was some kind of setup, and Lightner was waiting there to greet her when she showed up at the marina at midnight?

As she showered, Tara tried to imagine all the possible ways Lightner could have learned about Tenner's activities. She couldn't think of any.

And then there was the missing employee, Bernard. Could the man who knows every inch of this place, who had built it by his own hand, not know what had happened to him?

Stepping out of the shower, Tara was determined to find out.

SEVENTEEN

Tara had just changed into her new outfit when a knock came at the door. "Mrs. Greystone?" an accented male voice inquired. Tara unlocked it and pulled the door open with a smile.

A tall, thin Pacific Islander stood grinning at the doorway. "If you please, ma'am, my name is Waisea. I am here to show you to the dining hall for dinner. I have a cart waiting just outside." He waved a hand down the hallway behind him.

"Nice to meet you, Waisea," Tara said, extending a hand, which he shook cordially. "Shall we go?"

"Very well," he said, smiling as he turned and began walking down the hall.

"So, what island are you from, Waisea?" *Please don't say Solar Island.*

"I am from Fiji," he called back in a sing-song lilt. They reached the end of the hallway and Waisea flung the door open. He climbed into the cart's driver's seat, his head barely clearing the roof of the vehicle.

"What made you want to leave beautiful Fiji to live here?" Tara asked, taking a seat next to him in the cart.

"I try something new, make good money for my family," he said, putting the cart into gear.

"How long have you been on Solar Island?"

"Eight months."

"A long time."

He shrugged. "One of my sisters is here with me."

"Do you live on 'the beach'?"

He turned to smile at her. "Yes, the beach! We live down by the water."

"When will you go back to Fiji?"

"The next time we are near, I will probably go back. I am in no hurry. Fiji will always be there."

Tara took a deep breath. She felt a question coming on that she had to ask. She knew that if it got back to Lightner, it wouldn't bode well for her; but she had to know.

"Waisea, are you and your people treated fairly here? You can tell me the truth."

Waisea eased the cart to a halt. He looked her in the eye. "Mrs. Greystone, you are here to write about our power from the sun. It is best if you do not ask many questions outside of that. Everything is okay here. Please, do not concern yourself with such matters."

Tara rubbed her temples and let her head fall back against the seat. She said nothing more as Waisea put the cart into gear again.

Only a couple of minutes later, he announced "This is the dining hall. I will return for you when dinner is over to take you back to your quarters."

Oh, really? Tara couldn't help but think. *And what if I don't want to go back to my room?* She was starting to see Lightner's tight schedule for her as a way of controlling her during her stay. She doubted he had allowed for any free time. "Thank you very much, Waisea," she said, nodding and stepping from the cart.

"That way, Mrs. Greystone," he said, pointing behind her as he drove off.

Tara turned around to see another long, low building in the same style as the living quarters. With the exception of the power tower, there seemed to be no structure on Solar Island taller than one story, and they all seemed to have been constructed long and narrow in order to fit into one ring of a set of concentric circles. The vast majority of the island's space was devoted to the solar farm.

As she approached a screen door set in the end of the dining hall, Tara realized that she was not even sure where on the island she was. She looked around but could not see the power tower. It was either blocked by the parabolic troughs behind her or else by the building itself. Nor could she see the ocean.

The sound of clinking silverware and social chatter drifted through the screen as she stepped up to the door. Peering inside, she could see that fifteen people or so were seated at benches around wooden picnic tables that had been arranged into one long line. Opening the door and stepping inside, she spotted Lightner, who was seated at the far end of the long row of tables. He waved her over as she stepped inside.

Tara strode past the row of diners on her way to Lightner's end of the table. Other than the dining tables, the room itself was mostly ordinary. The floor was wood, and there were a couple of screened windows. Simple light fixtures hung from the ceiling, as well as a couple of fans. On one wall hung a sun sculpture in an American Southwest design, with a hand-painted disc and wavy rays.

Tara could see Lightner indicating an empty seat near his end of the table. She now noticed another table behind the dining table, farther down the room, with food-warming trays where a man was fixing a plate. Then she looked to her left and recognized Chris Tenner. He nodded to her as she passed, and she smiled in return.

Midnight, his eyes seemed to say.

And then she had reached the empty seat that Lightner had saved for her, and she was sitting down to dinner on Solar Island.

"I've taken the liberty of having a plate prepared for you," Lightner said. Tara looked down and saw a steaming plate of fish, rice, and vegetables, with a tall glass of ice water garnished with a lemon slice. The meal smelled delicious; she was a fan of seafood.

"Looks great! Tell me about your food production here on Solar Island. The fish," she said, poking at it with her fork, "the vegetables—even the water—where do you get it?"

Lightner, who appeared pleased with the question, introduced her to the group as a reporter. Tara glanced quickly around at the other diners to gauge their reactions. Some of them she recognized from her tour of the island. Many seemed to have a kind of forced courtesy with her, like they were straining to stay polite. Across from her she saw Darrien from customs, who refused to look her in the eye. "Almost all of our food is produced here on the island," Lightner began. "I say almost, because we do have a store of comfort items such as candy bars and ice cream; but all the food on your plate was harvested here on Solar Island."

Tara tasted the fish. "Delicious!" she said, truthfully.

"Tonight we have a kind of tropical fish that was line-caught off Solar Island, called a wahoo."

Living in Hawaii, Tara was familiar with the fish—it was one of her favorites—but Amanda Greystone was from back East.

"Mmmm. Never had it before, but it's absolutely delectable! Great fresh veggies, too," she said, sampling a ripe tomato.

Lightner indicated a tall, thin man seated next to him. "Dr. James Cobb here is our lead food-production scientist. Perhaps you recall the old Biosphere2 experiment in the desert where a group of people lived inside a giant greenhouse in a closed system, growing their own food?"

Tara nodded.

Lightner said, "James was one of them."

"There was some controversy about that experiment, wasn't there?" Tara asked.

James smiled at Tara from under a thick red beard. "The term 'closed system' can only be loosely applied in that particular case, I'm afraid," he said with a laugh. "I do recall some Snickers bars smuggled in, along with a bag of machine parts after a Biospherian had to be evacuated and then returned for a medical emergency. Solar Island here is actually much closer to the true spirit of what the Biosphere set out to accomplish. We really do grow most of our food. We are very isolated from civilization ninety percent of the time. Unfortunately, I can't claim credit for the wahoo. Matiu caught those this week," he said, nodding to the Tongan man Tara had met down at the marina when Bernie's hat had been fished from the water.

Matiu regarded Tara coolly, acknowledging her without saying anything. James continued.

"I run the aquaculture and farming operations for Solar Island. So anything that's not wild-caught from the sea...that's me!" he finished with a laugh.

"Well, by the taste of it," Tara said, between forkfuls of rice, "you're doing an excellent job!"

"Tomorrow, I believe, Dr. Cobb will give you a tour of his facilities," Dr. Lightner said.

Cobb nodded enthusiastically. "Absolutely!" Then he picked up a bottle of wine. "But for now, I suggest that you sample some of my more experimental product. This is a mango wine I produced here on Solar Island. We brought two mango trees on board from somewhere near Tahiti, and I made this over the course of several months from their fruit." He poured some into a glass and passed it to Tara. The bottle was passed around; more glasses were filled.

"A toast," Lightner said, raising his glass. Down the length of the table, another bottle was making the rounds. More glasses were raised. "To Solar Island!"

"To Solar Island!" came the cheers.

But Tara could tell that not everyone at the table was enthusiastic. Chris Tenner, she could see, merely grumbled the words, although she noticed he did drink the wine.

"I have a question," Tara said when the cheers had died down. Lightner and those seated around him eyed her expectantly.

"What do you say to your environmentalist detractors who claim that Solar Island is bad for marine life because it—and this is ironic—blocks out the sun for all the plants and animals it passes over?"

"Oftentimes that blockage is only temporary," Lightner said, jumping on the question ahead of those around him who also looked eager to respond. "We're constantly passing over, not usually remaining in one area for very long."

"Although the doldrums could be an exception to that," James said. Tara saw Lightner glare at him before the food scientist continued. "Truthfully, we haven't spent much time in the doldrums, though," he said, as if to placate Lightner, who resumed jabbing with his fork.

"What are the doldrums?" Tara asked.

Another diner, one Tara hadn't heard from before, spoke up. He had longish dirty blond hair and wore a scuba diving T-shirt that proclaimed "Divers Do It Deeper!"

"Before coming to Solar Island as a marine mechanic, I worked on transpac yachts—big sailboats that cross the Pacific, some of them for races. The doldrums are an area of the tropical Pacific around the equator that sailors dread because it's an area of little or no winds. So *if* Solar Island were to drift into the doldrums, it could stay there in one place for a relatively long time. Blocking out the light," he finished, looking at Lightner as if to see if he would protest.

"True, Fred," Lightner said. Then, for Tara's benefit, he added, "That's Fred Jackson, one of our marine mechanics. Of course, we could tow ourselves out with the fleet of boats that you yourself maintain," Lightner said. Fred nodded. Lightner went on. "But more importantly, what are we blocking the light for? The water is thousands of feet deep. There are no coral reefs, no seaweeds. Only plankton, which will drift past in the currents anyway. Or maybe large pelagic fish like swordfish and tuna, which can move out from under it with ease. So I consider it a baseless criticism."

Tara thought for a moment about her next question. Amanda Greystone wasn't here to do a fluff piece. She was doing an exposé on a controversial new energy facility. So it was time to start exposing. She looked directly at Lightner.

"Forget about the environment for a second. I think what you've done environmentally is a good thing overall." Lightner smiled and nodded in thanks. "But what about the criticism that you may be withholding the sale of energy to small island nations who have policies you disagree with?"

Tara judged the reactions of those at the table. Most eyes grew nearly as wide as the dinner plates before them, she observed. Lightner himself turned positively red. She had struck a nerve.

"What specifically are you referring to, Mrs. Greystone?" Lightner asked. "What nation?"

"It's time for dessert," Dr. Cobb said, getting up and heading for the food table, where a Micronesian man in a white chef's uniform had just deposited two new trays. "Fresh fruit with cream!"

Lightner and several others at the table also got up and headed for the serving table. Tara saw Fred Jackson making eye contact with her and returned his stare.

"I know you're a reporter just doing your job," he said in a low voice, "but if I were you I'd drop the political angle. Just forget about it."

"But—"

Fred tapped his knife on his plate, clanging her into silence. "I'm telling you, if information about this place is what you want, then pissing Lightner off is contrary to your goal. Personally, I think he should lay off the sovereignty crap and just stick to energy production—a bunch of us here do—but it is his island. I was there when he launched it from this little atoll in the Philippines, and it wasn't easy. The guy worked his ass off to make this place happen."

"I don't understand what he's got to hide," Tara said, deliberately vague. Lightner and those who went with him for dessert were streaming back to the table now with full plates. "You're right, it is his island. If he doesn't want to sell energy to someone, I suppose that's his right. But why won't he just admit it?"

Fred hunched forward over the table, holding a glass of wine up to hide his face from the approaching Lightner as he talked. "He's got some kind of plan, but none of the people I'm friends with here are sure what it is. Others are more susceptible to his sovereign-island-nation B.S. We were supposed to go ashore for energy talks with Japan a few weeks ago, but—"

"Amanda!" Dr. Lightner's voice boomed. "You simply must try the dessert!" Tara looked up at him. He wasn't smiling.

"Well, fruit's not really—"

"When you travel to a foreign country, you sample the local cuisine, right? Here on Solar Island, we grow our own fruits right here in the middle of the Pacific. It's divine. Star fruit, dragon fruit, kiwi, even coconuts! You must partake."

Tara stood up from the table. She was about to call Dr. Lightner a modern-day Captain Nemo, but realized the negative connotations associated with the fictional submariner and restrained the impulse. "When in Rome," she said, heading for the dessert table. She caught Fred nodding at her as she passed.

EIGHTEEN

A few minutes later, Tara stepped out of the dining hall. The sun was lower in the sky now, and Waisea was waiting for her in the electric cart. Lightner had bade her good night, warned her not to leave the safety of her quarters without an "escort," and promised that her tour would continue early the next morning. She assured him she'd be turning in early.

"Did you enjoy your dinner, Mrs. Greystone?" Waisea asked as he put the cart on a trackway.

"Oh, the food was excellent," she replied, deliberately not mentioning the company. "I'm quite tired, though, and I'm sure I'll sleep well tonight," she said, feigning a huge yawn. Waisea seemed gentlemanly enough, but she knew there was a good chance that his loyalties lay with Lightner.

"It is very peaceful here at night. Quiet."

"Except for the generator, right?"

He laughed. "That is true. But I don't even notice that anymore. None of us do. It is like something that helps you sleep... how do you call it...white noise."

Tara bristled with recognition. *White noise*...where had she heard that in relation to this case? *The recording!* She had talked with Dillon about how Chris Tenner's disguised call for help sounded like white noise. Odd that the same term could be used to describe the generator. Could Chris have recorded the sounds inside the power tower?

"White noise or not, after all the travel and activity I've had today, I'm going to sleep like a baby."

Waisea grinned. "Well, then, here we are at your quarters, Mrs. Greystone. If you should need to contact any one of our staff for any reason during the night, there is an intercom button in your room next to your front door. It will ring the operations manager. Sweet dreams to you."

Tara thanked him, exited the cart, and walked into the barracks building. She could see no one else, although now she could hear a shower running in one of the rooms. She made her way down the hall to her quarters and went inside, locking the door behind her.

She flopped down on the bed, thinking that she really could use a nap before her midnight rendezvous with Chris Tenner. But she forced herself to get up and go to her backpack, which she had stashed under the bed. There was work to do. A clock on the wall—she supposed it was powered by rechargeable batteries—showed her 7:00 p.m.

From her backpack she withdrew her satellite phone, the use of which on Solar Island she had cleared with Lightner by saying it was required as part of her reporter duties. Back on Guam she had almost not even mentioned the phone to Dillon when telling him to work out the terms of her stay with Dr. Lightner. She had taken for granted that it would be allowed. Now, as she switched the device on, comforted by its glowing screen and familiar logo, she wasn't so sure that it wouldn't have been confiscated along with her derringer had it not been for the pre-arrangement.

And she did feel isolated here, floating around in the middle of the largest body of water on Earth on a giant man-made disc. It was crazy, she thought, as she went to the bathroom and turned on the shower. It would provide cover noise while she talked. She didn't know who might be listening in, but she was taking no chances. She knew there was no way for Lightner to tap into the signals of the FBI-secured sat-phone; but was it possible that her room was bugged? Through the intercom, perhaps? She didn't have a bug-detection kit with her and she couldn't ignore the possibility.

Tara dialed Dillon's number at the Guam office. She was a little surprised to find herself relieved when he picked up on the third ring.

"Marconi here."

"Amanda Greystone reporting in, sir," Tara said. She froze as the sound of footsteps came clunking along on the wood hallway floor somewhere outside her quarters.

"Amanda, glad you called. How's the assignment going?" Dillon's voice came through the phone. Tara smiled. He was playing the cover to the hilt. The footsteps continued past her door, and Tara relaxed. She reached up and shut the small window that looked out on the back of a solar collector.

"It's going. Started the tour today. Just had dinner."

"Good. Learn anything?"

"I met Chris Tenner."

A pause ensued while Dillon processed the bombshell. "You met him? So he is alive. What did he say—did you ask him about the recorded message he sent us?"

"Didn't get a chance. Lightner introduced him to me on a tour of the..." she consulted her notepad, flipping through pages until she found that portion of her tour "...Control Center. Tenner introduced himself to me, in front of Lightner and another colleague, as Robert Benson."

"So they don't even know about his fake death. They didn't help him do it."

"It certainly seems that way. But as we were leaving the Control Center to continue the tour, Chris slipped me a note without anyone else seeing. It said to meet him at midnight at the marina."

"Are you going?"

"Well, yeah, I'm going. Why wouldn't I go?"

"Alone?"

Tara laughed. "Unless you're going to drop in on me later on."

"Listen, *Amanda*. You need to be careful. I did some more digging into Lightner's background like you asked, picked up where we left off in Honolulu. Guy's really smart, but also unbalanced."

"Criminal record?"

"Not in the U.S., but he's lived much of his adult life as an expat, so

I can't be sure yet. I'll email you the reports. Your Internet connection working out there?"

"Haven't tried it yet, but if the sat-phone works, it should be fine since it's also a satellite connection."

"Be careful out there tonight. At least you have your little friend."

Tara told him about the customs search and how Lightner had confiscated her derringer.

"A customs station on that floating solar panel? I'm not really liking this. It does sound in line with what I found on him, though. You know, Ozakawa about had a heart attack when he found out you deployed to Solar Island alone. I explained the last-minute change of plans, how they wouldn't let me board, but he was still pissed."

Tara sighed. Technically, she had ignored FBI protocol when she decided to enter Solar Island alone, even though she was under cover. The plan had called for her partner to be with her, also under cover. She knew Ozakawa would maintain that if Dillon was unable to go, then she should have scrubbed the mission.

"I made a go/no-go decision based on the information available to me at the time," Tara said.

"I know. I'm just saying, be prepared for a little meeting with him when you get back. You have anything else?"

"Yes. Apparently, a worker went man overboard here not too long ago, and his body was never recovered—or, get this—never even reported! But I saw some workers fish a baseball cap out of the water today, and they say it belongs to the missing man."

"Why wasn't it reported? Did you get his name?"

"They said his name is Bernie Riley. The cap that they say is his is a maroon baseball cap with the letters 'ATM.'" Tara waited for Dillon to jot the information down, then continued. "Dr. Lightner says he didn't report it because they are in international waters and there are no authorities to report to."

"That sounds like Lightner."

"What do you mean?"

"It fits his background that he would have that mentality. I tracked down some of his old associates. A few of them talked to me for quite some time. I'll say one thing about Lightner: people who meet him don't forget him. You'll see when you read the report."

"I should get going so I can check out your report before my little meeting tonight. I'll call you around the same time tomorrow."

"You got it. Oh, and *Amanda*?"

"Yeah?"

"Be careful."

NINETEEN

Tara turned off the noise screen of the shower and left the bathroom. In the bedroom, she powered up her laptop and connected it to the Internet via the sat-phone. She watched the screen, hoping Solar Island didn't employ some kind of signal-jamming technology.

Connected.

She found Dillon's email waiting in her inbox. An appreciative smile formed on her lips as she saw the characteristic thoroughness with which Dillon had prepared and written up his interviews. It was one of the reasons she had chosen him to assist her on this case out of dozens of agents who would have been eager to work with an agent of Tara's reputation.

She settled onto the bed and started reading:

CASE REPORT #002232A64

F.O.: Honolulu

Reporting Agent: Agent in Training Dillon Marconi

Case Agent: Assistant Special Agent in Charge Tara Shores

Case Name: Solar Island

Subject of Investigation: Dr. Jacob M. Lightner

Sex: Male

Race: Caucasian

DOB: April 17, 1960

Place of Birth: Blythe, CA

Education: Ph.D. electrical engineering, University of California, Berkeley, 1985

Occupation: Alternative-energy entrepreneur

Interview Subject #1: Childhood neighbor, Mrs. Jane Ellison, longtime Blythe resident

Audio transcription from telephone interview:

Dillon Marconi (DM): You lived on the same block as his family for many years. Tell me if you would, Mrs. Ellison, about your experiences with Dr. Jacob Lightner.

Jane Ellison (JE): Being a small desert town on the border between California and Arizona, Blythe was a place with a real sense of community. Everybody knew each other. I recall the Lightner family very well, especially Jacob. Doesn't surprise me if he's gotten into some trouble, although I hear he's done quite well for himself. That's no surprise either. It was clear from early on that he was a genius with machines and electronics and just knowing how to make things work.

DM: Can you give me an example?

JE: Well, you know how most ten-year-olds have jobs like paper routes, or lemonade stands, maybe cutting the grass? Little Jacob installed home solar panels for everyone on the block. Mind you, this was in the early seventies, when solar power was a new thing. One time, I think it was the summer after that—he built a solar system to power the town library. His father may have helped him to design it, but Jacob installed the thing completely by himself, and explained how it worked all by himself. To this day, that library still has solar power, although Jacob's original panels were replaced years ago by newer models. But there's a plaque with Jacob's name on it that says how our little library became the first solar-powered library in the country, back in 1971.

DM: I see, thank you.

JE: But I haven't really told you the whole story yet. You see...[pause] This is hard for me.

DM: Take your time. It's important to give me as clear and accurate a remembrance as you can, Mrs. Ellison.

JE: [taking deep breath] Okay. Well, shortly after the time he worked on the library, I was doing some gardening in the far corner of my yard. Our properties were next to each other, you see, and I didn't mean to snoop, but a row of cacti separated our yards, instead of a fence—that's Blythe for you—and I was doing some weeding there, when I heard young Jacob crying. He must have been about eleven years old at the time.

DM: Go on, please.

JE: I heard him say—and I still recall this distinctly after all these years, because it's so unusual to hear an eleven-year-old say it—"But Dad, there aren't enough flux capacitors to make it work!" And then I saw Jacob's father—he was an electrical technician who worked a night shift for the Cal Edison power plant in town—grab his boy by the hair. "You are not thinking straight! Always looking for the obvious, the easy way out. Think!" And he struck Jacob on the back with a piece of wood, knocking him over. He cried out, and...[sniffling, unintelligible]...kicked him in the side—hard! And then he said, "You figure out how to make this work with what you have, Jacob. No more parts! If this timer system isn't working by the time I get home from work, you're not gonna want to see me. The light turns on when the sun goes down and off when it comes up, you got it!"

DM: Thank you for that account, Mrs. Ellison.

JE: And that night, when the sun started down, I couldn't help but watch out my window into Jacob's yard, staring at that light pole, wondering if it would come on. I was so nervous for little Jacob! But sure enough, when it was almost dark, that light bulb on top of the pole flickered a couple times and then caught. I just about whooped and hollered!

Interview Subject #2: Co-worker, Dr. Warren Rothstein

Audio transcription from telephone interview:

DM: Dr. Rothstein, when and where did you work with Dr. Lightner?

Warren Rothstein (WR): I worked with him at Mojave Solar, out in the Mojave Desert in California, way back in the late eighties. It was the first full-time professional job for both of us after earning our doctorates. Mine was from Stanford, and he came out of Berkeley—Bezerkley, we used to joke. Anyway, our job was to help design components for a large-scale solar farm used to generate electricity that could be sold to the grid.

DM: And how would you characterize Dr. Lightner as an employee? What was it like to work with him?

WR: [deep breath] Definitely a brilliant guy. There's no doubt about that. Whenever we needed to brainstorm some technical solution, he was always a major contributor, a real go-to guy. He took "outside-the-box" thinking to a whole new level.

DM: Can you give me an example? Anything stand out in your mind?

WR: I remember it got around at Mojave Solar that Lightner was this crazy genius because he won this bet.

DM: What was the bet?

WR: [laughter] Okay, this might seem kind of strange, but keep in mind we were young engineers way out in the middle of the desert with not much to do, outside work.

DM: I understand.

WR: We used to have this break room with a television. Lightner said one day that with $50 and fifteen minutes in a Walmart, he could come out with all the supplies he needs to tinker with a TV set so that it can kill someone in five different ways—explosion, electrocution, mercury poisoning.... It seemed unbelievable, so the guys took him to task on it and he made a bet. When he diagrammed out all the modifications, it made perfect sense. There were some disagreements over the finer points, but in the end he won the bet and everybody paid him.

DM: You mentioned three ways to kill someone with a TV. What were Lightner's other two ways?

WR: Oh, [laughter]. One of them he said was just throwing it on somebody's head.

DM: That's some serious engineering.

WR: It could work, though, couldn't it? At least with the old CRT TVs we had back then—today's skinny little flat screens might not do the job [laughs]. And he saved money on that one. He does have a reputation for coming in under budget. Now, with Solar Island, we're seeing what he can do with millions and all the time he wants!

DM: Yes. I'm curious—so what's the fifth way?

WR: Oh, well, he said just tie you up in front of the set with it tuned to C-SPAN. The guys let him have that one.

DM: Ah, so he wasn't fond of U.S. politics, even back then.

WR: He wasn't. He didn't go around talking about anarchy or anything silly like that, but he used to ask, "Why do they (the U.S. government) think they know what's better for me than I do?"

DM: Thank you for your time, Dr. Rothstein. Is there anything else you'd like to add before we conclude?

WR: I've told you everything I know about him. There have been a lot of years between then and now. Today, I think because of the influx in funding for Solar Island and Jacob's overall success, you're seeing his personality magnified in ways that only wealth can do. He's like a kid burning an ant with a magnifying glass, only now his magnifier is Solar Island.

Interview Subject #3: Neighbor from last known permanent U.S. residence, Mrs. Dawn Grossman, long-time Los Angeles resident.

Audio transcription from telephone interview:

DM: Mrs. Grossman, you live in a suburb of Los Angeles where Dr. Jacob Lightner used to be your next-door neighbor up until about three years ago, correct?

Dawn Grossman (DG): Yes, that's right. He lived next door to my family for almost five years until he started taking a lot of trips abroad, and eventually sold his house, he said to help pay for that weird island of his. I must say, we were somewhat relieved when he decided to move.

DM: Why is that, Mrs. Grossman?

DG: [sigh] Well, being from the FBI, you've probably already heard how he got into that spat with the City about all the solar panels on his roof? It was a zoning issue?

DM: Yes. The courts ruled in Dr. Lightner's favor.

DG: Unfortunately, yes, they did. Let me tell you, that was the most disruptive thing to ever happen in this neighborhood, and I've lived here almost my whole life. All because that man had to have his own way. He plastered his entire house and roof and yard with solar panels, windmills, all kinds of strange energy generators, so that he could live off the grid. Imagine, living off the grid in the middle of Los Angeles! We told him, this is ridiculous! If you want to live off the grid, then move to the desert somewhere where people have the space to do that.

DM: And what was his response like?

DG: Condescending. He lectured us like we were children, telling us about "peak oil" and how sooner or later we were going to have to stop depending on the government's imported oil for our energy needs. He would make it sound like any day, all the roads would just shut down and no more gas would be available. It got to the point that one of our other neighbors told him he was scaring their kids. The kids were asking their parents, "Are all the cars going to stop working and the lights go out? Why don't we have sun power like Mr. Lightner?"

DM: And how did he react?

DG: He was unapologetic. At first, he just said that he was only trying to help. But as time went on he became harsher, and things came to a head one day at a neighbor's barbecue.

DM: What happened?

DG: It was football season, and some of the husbands had been drinking beers. Jacob never drank—that we saw, anyway. My husband tried to include him in their gatherings, but Jacob almost always refused. I asked my husband why he wanted such a weird guy around anyway, but my husband, Roger, he's such a nice man, he would say, "Rich people aren't weird, they're eccentric." Anyway, Jacob did come to this one gathering, and of course the guys started picking on him about his solar stuff and how he was driving down property values with his eyesore industrial house. But Jacob just started in again on the oil shortage and how gas prices would see ten dollars per gallon soon and then what would we all do? So one of the guys told him point-blank to stay away from his kids, and Jacob responded that someone had to educate them. And our friend threw his beer on Jacob—dumped it on his head. [Pause.]

DM: What did Dr. Lightner do?

DG: He said, "You can't fight Hubbert's peak," and left. Later we looked up what that meant. It has to do with peak oil and how oil production is declining. He sold his house about six months after that, and then when we saw Solar Island on the news, it didn't even really surprise any of us. It was just like, "Yep, that's Jacob Lightner, all right." So, what has he done? Why is the FBI investigating him?

DM: I can't comment on that, Mrs. Grossman.

DG: Well, it wouldn't surprise me if he's done something bad. He was always so arrogant, flaunting his education and his wealth that allowed him to do whatever he wanted. But he never had much compassion for anyone else. He had no empathy. That's my take on him.

TWENTY

After rereading them several times, Tara looked up from Dillon's interview transcripts. She knew from her own preliminary casework that Jacob Lightner's father had died of a heart attack when Jacob was seventeen, shortly before the future Solar Island inventor left Blythe to attend college. His mother had succumbed to cancer seven years after that, just prior to his earning a Ph.D.

Together with Dillon's interviews, it gave Tara a good picture of the man behind the energy empire. Like her, he had lost both parents at a relatively young age. Also like her, she suspected that he had filled that void by pouring himself into his work. Unlike her, somewhere along the way he had developed a mistrust or dislike of government. Enough that it seemed to be taking over his focus on Solar Island, Tara thought. At the very least, it was a distraction. Even some of his own employees saw it that way, she could see already. Sure, he was producing energy and selling it, but he also put a fair amount of his own energy into the independent-nation status of his personal floating island. Had that become his main focus?

With these thoughts, Tara dozed off next to her laptop on the bed and awoke a couple of hours later. She woke her computer and checked the time: 11:03 p.m.

Chris Tenner...Midnight!

She had to find her way down to the marina for her meeting with Chris. Quickly, she changed into an outfit of black leggings and a black shirt. She did not wish to be seen by anyone tonight, except for Mr. Tenner. She grabbed her camera, her notepad, and her precious pen. She wished she still had the confiscated derringer. She considered taking the sat-phone just in case of an emergency, but decided it was too bulky. She didn't want to risk losing or damaging it. The idea of being here without any connection whatsoever to the outside world was less than comforting.

She switched off her room lights. She didn't want to advertise that she was up late to anyone glancing at her window or under the door. Looking out her small window, view blocked as it was by the solar trough, she could see the moon, big and full, high in the sky. She cursed her bad luck. Tonight would *have* to be a full moon, she thought. On the one hand, it would make it easier for her to see where she was going in unfamiliar surroundings. On the other, she would be bathed in light. She would have preferred darkness.

She opened the door to the hallway. She looked, listened. She saw no light coming from beneath the door frames of the neighboring quarters and heard no sounds. Life at sea in general was early to bed, early to rise, Tara knew, and Solar Island was no exception.

She walked down the hall, cursing the creaking floorboards. Reaching the outside door at the end of the hall, she paused with her hand on the knob. What would she say if someone saw her outside? *Just going for a stroll? Needed some air? Love the full moon?*

Tara remembered how Lightner had offered her the use of the exercise track, and she decided that her outfit was just suitable enough to support a claim that she was going for a late-night workout in the cool air.

How to get to the marina? She wasn't even sure where it was in relation to her quarters. Lightner had provided her with no maps or references of any kind to Solar Island. She could walk until she reached the edge of the giant circular platform; but if she came out on the wrong side and then had to walk along the edge, it would increase her chance of being seen, as well as likely make her late for her meeting. She doubted Tenner would wait long for her, were she to be overdue. He would assume she'd chickened out or wasn't taking him seriously for some reason.

Tara skirted a row of heliostats, walking along the side of the building. *Does Tenner know for sure that I'm FBI? Or is he desperate enough that he would reach out to anyone who came to the Island, even a reporter who knew nothing about him?*

She doubted it. He'd sent the message, and the FBI had responded. He knew that much. But that meant that someone on this island knew she was undercover, and that in itself was troubling. Had Tenner told anyone else about her undercover role?

Ahead, she saw one of the electric carts parked on the other end of the quarters building. Beyond, she could now see the power tower rising above the center of the island. A red light blinked atop the helipad, a warning to ships and aircraft alike that they were not alone in this dark ocean.

Tara climbed into the driver's seat of the cart and pressed the start button. She cringed when the headlights blazed a path through the darkness to reflect off the solar mirrors ahead. Scrambling to turn the beams off, she held her breath until relative darkness enveloped the island once again. Only the big moon overhead, full and bright.

She waited a minute for her night vision to return and then put the cart into gear. Grateful for the nearly silent engine, Tara eased her ride onto the nearest marked path. She could see none of the occasional road signs that dotted the island, so she continued along the path away from the living quarters. She was relieved when the route was swallowed up by rows of solar collectors. Still not daring to turn the headlights on, Tara rolled the cart onward at a pace that was faster than walking but less than a jog. Crashing into anything because she couldn't see was not an option.

Ahead, she saw moonlight on Solar Island's deck. Then the mirrored troughs and heliostats came to an end and her cart emerged into an open space at a junction of three pathways. She brought the cart to a stop as she considered her options: left, right, or straight. Looking up, she saw that the tower with its red warning light was closer to her now, so she must be heading toward the island's center. Deciding that if she continued straight she'd pass through the center and be on a path to the edge, she gave the cart a burst of speed, shooting across the intersection and back into the cover between two rows of solar collectors.

After several minutes of plodding along, Tara felt a stab of adrenaline when she saw light up ahead. A small, jiggling light. *Flashlight, carried by a man! Must be a night watchman of some sort.*

She wasn't sure why they needed them here, since they all knew each other, but she supposed there could be legitimate reasons. Report problems, possibly make small repairs, that sort of thing. She fleetingly wondered if pirates would consider Solar Island a target.

Tara pulled the cart over as far as she dared underneath the heliostats on the right-hand side. She watched as the patroller shone his beam down the corridor in which she was hiding. Were he to see the cart parked here, he would check it out. Tara cursed the vehicle's white color.

She watched as the flashlight's beam sparkled and refracted off the solar mirrors, dazzlingly bright at this hour. Then the beam changed directions, and Tara saw distant pinpoints of light scattering off the mirrors in the opposite direction, across the intersection. Then those, too, faded and she heard footsteps receding off to her left. The night patroller was taking the track perpendicular to her own.

Tara waited five minutes. When there was no sign of him for that long, she decided she'd better move on in case he walked up her row from the other direction—behind her. She kept to the right side of the track, creeping her cart forward. Reaching the intersection, where she would have to shoot forward across an exposed path before reaching the cover of the solar collectors again, she exited the cart. On foot, she crept to the end of the row and then low-crawled to its edge.

Still seeing no one, Tara went back to the cart, got back into it, and raced across the intersection. She drove faster now, and, after passing under a sign pointing to the marina, she accelerated. She had to make a left onto another path but soon saw another marina sign and knew she was getting close. She had managed to drive to the correct side of the island. Had she gone in the opposite direction, she would now be driving around the edge. She was grateful for that bit of luck.

Tara left the cart and started walking the rest of the way toward the marina. With the cart, it would be obvious to anyone who saw it that she was up to something. Without it, she was just a late-night exerciser. She was almost there.

She walked through the field of mirrors, moonbeams bouncing off of them all around her. Emerging from another row of troughs and heliostats, she saw the entrance to the marina across the same perimeter track she'd earlier ridden on with Lightner. In the distance, she thought she heard noise, but she couldn't be sure. She saw no one, though, and walked to the marina entrance itself—a white archway set back from the path leading down a ramp to the docks.

Tara had just walked under the arch when she heard a forceful whisper behind her.

"Amanda!"

TWENTY-ONE

Guam, The Mermaid Pub

"Nice place, Rob," Dillon said, taking a seat in the tattered booth that Rob already occupied. Wooden barrels and bags of yeast were piled along the walls, seemingly in any available space. Even at this late hour, the place bustled with activity. A group of twenty-something Japanese tourists giggled in the booth next to them. A cluster of local fishermen occupied the booth on the other side, and a row of American enlisted men, many of them Guam National Guard, were bellying up to the bar across the room. The walls were haphazardly decorated with framed photographs of old planes, ships, and nautical memorabilia. A figurehead of a mermaid from the prow of an old wooden vessel looked down on the activity from its mount on the wall high above.

"See that?" Rob asked, pointing to a black-and-white picture of an old airplane. Dillon's gaze followed his finger. "That's the *Enola Gay*, the bomber that dropped Little Boy on Hiroshima, when it was here on Guam. It actually took off from the island of Tinian, though, near Saipan, for the mission itself."

"Lot of history on this island," Dillon said, looking around. "So, where do all these people come from? Been working non-stop ever since we landed, haven't had a chance to poke my head out anywhere yet."

"Well, on Guam, for the most part you have your American military, your local islanders—called Chamorros—and your Japanese tourists. The Japanese who come here are pretty much the ones who can't afford to go to Hawaii," Rob finished, taking a swig from a mug of beer and sliding one over to Dillon, who jerked his thumb subtly toward the next booth.

"They don't speak English," Rob said, unapologetic about his statement. "Some of the Japanese corporations, when they give year-end bonuses, also give away vacations. The lowest tier is to go to Okinawa, because that's still part of Japan, but the southern tropical part. Next tier up is Guam, and then the top-tier performers get to go to Hawaii."

"Doesn't seem like there's a whole lot here unless you're into fishing or scuba diving," Dillon said. Rob nodded his agreement.

"Or flying," Rob added with a grin.

Dillon took a sip of brew and said, "Thanks for meeting me, Rob. I really appreciate it."

"No worries. So, what's up?"

"Talked to Shores tonight. She made contact with our target—the guy working out there who contacted us. Meeting tonight at midnight."

"So...right now," Rob said, glancing at his aviator's watch.

Dillon's eyes widened a bit as he nodded. He tapped his cell phone that lay before him on the table. "I'm standing by in case she needs anything. Anyway, I had time to ask around town a little bit about this Doctor Lightner. Turns out he's been here, on Guam, about a year, right around when Solar Island launched. Bought some supplies from that hardware store across from the beach—it's owned by an elderly... Chamorro?...gentleman."

Rob nodded. "I know that store."

"He told me Lightner came in once to buy bulk amounts of screws, nails, bolts—ordinary stuff—but he wanted to basically clear out the guy's inventory at a steep discount."

"Yeah?"

"He said Lightner was an extremely tough bargainer, even rude at times, accusing him of being some backwater local yokel and knowing nothing about modern business practices. Said he wasn't expecting a guy with his own private island to be such a penny-pincher, but that he was really persistent in getting the best possible deal. In the end, he said that he did manage to get Lightner what he wanted and still make a little profit off him, but that the bargaining process basically wore him down and he would have preferred to have sold the inventory off slowly rather than deal with Lightner."

Rob shrugged. "You were wondering earlier how he built Solar Island so cheaply. The guy gets what he wants, gets the best deal for himself that he can. No law against that," he finished.

"If he was that tough for everything he acquired to build it..."

"Doesn't look like he penny-pinches on his bullets, judging by our reception today."

Dillon laughed heartily. "I'm glad you're our pilot on this, Rob. You got me out there and back in one piece today. Not to mention that Shores says you're the best, and that's more than enough for me."

"You need anything, you just let me know. I have the same bird on standby until the scheduled pickup, but I'll do whatever it takes to pick her up. If I had to buy a copter on my own dime to fly out there and get her, I'd do it."

"Thanks, Rob." Dillon wondered if Rob and Tara had ever had more than a working relationship. They were both single, after all, as was he. Sort of had to be in this line of work, but it made it that much more lonely being out here in the middle of nowhere on Guam, an island most people didn't even know was a U.S. territory.

Then he thought about Tara, way out there on Solar Island alone, deep undercover. If he was feeling lonely here—a touch claustrophobic, even—with a field office to work out of, and at least Rob's company in the pub at night, then how must Tara feel on Solar Island?

TWENTY-TWO

Startled, Tara turned around to see Chris Tenner standing behind one side of the archway. He waved her over. "Don't stand in the main path. Patrol comes by once an hour."

Tara walked back to Chris. "You scared me," she said.

"Sorry, but to be seen meeting with you would not be good. You're FBI, right?"

She hesitated, not expecting to be so bluntly confronted about her true identity. He continued. "Look, I sure as hell hope you're not just a reporter. You listened to my audio tape, right? You called the number?"

Tara nodded. "I'd show you my badge, but I didn't bring it for fear of blowing my cover. And with Lightner's little customs charade, it's a good thing I didn't."

Chris looked concerned. "It's not a charade. You made the right choice not bringing it. But you have backup, right? You can call for backup?"

Tara stared hard at the man in front of her. If possible, he looked even more fatigued than when she had seen him in the Control Center. She doubted he had gotten any rest after dinner. His eyes oozed fear, constantly darting back and forth, pupils wide, dark circles beneath. Even by moonlight, she could see the red in them.

"Backup is pretty far away, but yes, if necessary I could. I guess I don't inspire much confidence," she finished with a laugh.

Chris did not appear amused. "So you have a sat-phone?"

Tara nodded. "Yes. But so far, although I've seen some strange things, what I haven't seen is evidence of any crime. Only circumstantial things. Tell me about what's going on here."

Chris nodded. "You saw they found Bernie's hat today?"

"Yes. Tell me about Bernie."

"I'll have to admit some wrongdoing here. Maybe I'll be arrested for it at some point, I don't know; but what Bernie and I did is minor compared to what Lightner did."

"Go on."

"A few weeks ago, right before I sent the FBI the message, Bernie—Bernard Riley—and I had a plan to smuggle an engineering schematic and chemical formula out of Solar Island."

"Schematic and formula for what?"

Tenner pointed to the succession of light poles that ringed the island's perimeter, bathing the island in light. "For the battery technology that lets this place use solar power all night long, not just for the island, but to power villages as well."

"I've seen CIA pictures of Solar Island lit up at night. They're very interested in the technology. Apparently you and Bernie were aware of its worth too."

Chris kicked at the deck, looking down. "It was wrong of us, I know. Somehow Lightner was onto us, I think, because the night before we were supposed to land in Japan for energy talks, he changed course and canceled the talks. The next morning, Bernie was missing, thought to have fallen overboard."

"Maybe he did just fall overboard."

Chris gave her a doubting look. "This isn't a cruise ship where people drink too much and do stupid things."

"You tried to steal something from your employer. Most people would say that's a stupid thing."

He paused, looking down at the deck. "You got me there. But seriously, you've seen the railings around this thing, right?"

Tara nodded. They were a chest-high series of heavy-gauge wire, and extended around the entire perimeter, not something one could accidentally fall over. "So, what do you think happened?"

"I think Dr. Lightner—either personally, or through his goons—had Bernie thrown overboard."

Tara leveled her gaze into his eyes. All of her investigative experience told her that he was being sincere.

"But if he wanted Bernie thrown overboard for trying to steal from him, how come *you're* still here?"

Chris took a deep breath. He looked around, head on a swivel, before answering her. He stammered a bit, as if unsure how to respond. "I—I don't know. I'm not sure. But I think Lightner knows I was somehow involved. Bernie was the point man, though—he was the one who actually had the schematic on his person—literally." Chris explained to Tara the sunburn-transfer method they had used.

"I guess that's why Lightner limits access to these," Tara said, holding up her BIC.

"Absolutely. You're lucky to have that one. You could get a lot for it if you want to sell it when you leave."

"Maybe I'll pretend to drop it overboard and then give it to you," she said, hoping to signal him that she appreciated his help. "So you think he saw Chris getting the sunburn during the day and then threw him overboard that night?"

"That's what I think."

"But he doesn't know of *your* involvement?"

Chris shook his head. He looked depressed. "I think Lightner knows I was involved. I don't know what Bernie may have told him before he went overboard. I—this might sound weird, but—I think he's toying with me, like a cat with a cornered mouse. Maybe he thinks two people overboard at once would be too suspicious. So he only got Bernie. But me...he's got me trapped on this island... He's been having his people follow me around. He's put monitoring programs on my computer. I think he may have bugged my quarters. He's been deliberately keeping the island far away from any land."

Tara sighed. "Again, what I'm hearing is a lot of 'I think...he may have...' I need something concrete."

"I know you wouldn't have come all the way out here if it weren't for the CIA involvement, but there's more. Lightner knows the CIA is watching him. He loves it. He says it's a sign he's on the right track with what he calls his 'foreign energy policy.'"

Tara thought for a moment and recovered a bit. *This guy knows a lot.* "He may suspect CIA involvement, but there's no way he can know for sure. I hope he doesn't think *I'm* CIA," she said.

Chris shook his head vigorously. "He wouldn't have let you on if he did. But whatever you do, don't let him find out you're FBI, either."

"He took biometric information from me."

A look of concern crossed Tenner's face. He had just started to respond when, in the distance, they heard sounds, something different than the wind.

"You said there was more," Tara said.

Chris nodded. "Yes. This isn't the first time something like this has happened. Someone 'falling overboard,' that is."

"Tell me."

"A number of undocumented workers have disappeared since I've been working here."

"'Undocumented'—you mean the Pacific Island people?"

"Yes. One time, I actually saw him do it. On a night like tonight."

"How was it like tonight?"

"Full moon."

"You realize that if you are lying to me, it's a federal offense punishable by imprisonment?"

"Yes, I know it. I wish I *were* lying, but I'm not. I once saw him, with the help of two other men who are both still working on this island as we speak—pitch an older man from Samoa over the side in the middle of the night during some kind of bizarre ceremony. No rescue attempt was made. And then there was the battery explosion," Tenner added before Tara could interrupt.

"Battery explosion?"

"About six months ago, a Filipino worker was killed in a battery explosion—we have gigantic batteries containing molten nitrate salts, along with some other exotic chemical processes, for storing solar energy so it can be used at night—they're pretty dangerous—and Lightner just tossed his body overboard without reporting it."

"That's a very serious accusation, Mr. Tenner."

"The FBI doesn't send its agents halfway around the world for something that's not very serious, does it?"

Tara ignored the point. "Can you prove it? Were there any other witnesses besides yourself?"

"About a dozen. They're all too afraid to come forward."

"Afraid for their lives?"

"Maybe, but it's not just that. You may have noticed that a lot of the guys who work here weren't the most upstanding citizens before taking a job on Solar Island. What Dr. Lightner offers is decent pay for technical and engineering work to people who for one reason or another would be hard-pressed to find a job in the States or elsewhere. People with criminal records, people—"

"—who faked their own deaths," Tara interjected.

Chris swallowed hard, then hung his head a little, as if in shame. "Yes, I'm guilty of that too. I wanted to start over. A lot of us here did; that's what brought us to Solar Island. But Lightner knows this and began to use it against us, basically holding us prisoner here. But..." He trailed off.

"But what?"

"But he does have real followers. Since I've been here, Solar Island has sort of split into two camps: those who support independent-nation status and, by extension, Lightner's incendiary political actions; and those of us who don't—who just came here for the work, nothing more."

"I did get a sense of that at the dinner table."

Chris nodded. "I've sort of become the unofficial leader of the so-called Anti-Sovereignty Movement—those of us who want protections afforded by developed nations—while Lightner himself heads the Sovereignty Movement."

Tara shook her head. "It all seems so silly, though—this fighting over a floating plastic dish in the middle of the ocean. It's not even real land!"

Chris shrugged. "It's a dish that serves energy to a hungry world, though, and there isn't any more real unclaimed land left. Artificial islands are a future trend."

"What about the Pacific Islanders—are they split on this issue? They must feel loyalty to their own islands."

Tenner's eyes widened. "I thought that, too. But they're split, just as we expats are. Some of them come from tiny countries ruled by kings or even tribal lords with absolute ruling power, and they see Solar Island as a chance to have a greater say in how they live. Some of the others really don't care, I think, as long as they are fishing and eating well, and Lightner counts their votes as his."

"Votes?" Tara stepped back under the gate, out of the moon's spotlight.

Chris chuckled softly. "Yes, *votes*. A while ago, Lightner started having polls to vote on certain things. At first they were trivial things, like what to have for dinner, what kind of recreation activities to have, that sort of thing, and it was fun. But then gradually the votes took on a more serious nature, like which direction the island should sail in, and should we sell our energy to this island first or that one?"

"And the island's residents became split along the lines of those votes."

"Exactly. It became divisive. And it allowed Lightner to identify who was like-minded. He's been weeding out the dissenters ever since. Literally."

The wind changed direction, and momentarily the sound of primitive drums could be heard.

"What's that?"

Chris glanced up at the sky. "That would be the full-moon party down on the beach. Once a month, Lightner communes with the Pacific Islanders. More weeding. You wanted some kind of proof. Let's go."

TWENTY-THREE

Tara and Chris ran down the marina ramp to the docks below. Chris, in the lead, held a hand in back of him, warning Tara to freeze. The sound of the drums was louder now, and mingling voices could be heard on the breeze. They saw no one among the boats tied up in the marina. Chris ran forward in a loping crouch to the cover provided by the hull of the largest vessel, one of Solar Island's two tugboats.

Tara could tell by Chris's careful evasive maneuvering that he absolutely did not want to be seen by anyone. As the sound of the drums grew louder, his fear became hers as she prepared herself to spy on the alleged killer who had inspired so much fear on this strange island. Tara joined Chris at the tugboat.

"Where are they?" she asked.

"The beach. It's just around that corner at the end of the marina, there." He pointed past a strange-looking yellow craft, to a wooden dock that ran around the lip of the marina.

"What kind of boat is that one?" Tara asked, pointing to the unusual vessel. She already knew from Lightner's tour earlier that it was the submersible, but she sought corroboration. Would they both give the same answer? It would also concern her if Tenner honestly didn't know what it was. She was depending on him to guide her around this island in secret. *He better know his stuff,* she thought.

"Minisub. Doesn't go real deep. It's used to perform inspections and maintenance on the island's underside, but it's also Lightner's favorite toy whenever we're over shallow reefs...which isn't all that often," he added.

That's what Lightner said. It is *possible to get a straight answer around here*, she thought. Then she heard tribal chanting coming from around the corner.

"What's around that dock?" Tara asked.

"It leads to the beach, which is set low against the side of the island. It even has a few trees, and those block the view of it from the edge of the island above."

"They won't see us when we come around the corner?"

"Stay low. There's some shrubbery at the entrance; we'll have to hunker down in that."

Tara nodded, and then Chris led the way across the marina docks toward the other side. The acrylic dome bubble of the minisub gleamed in the moonlight as they passed by. The drumming became more intense, crescendoing to a loud level. They reached the far end of the marina, where small waves lapped against the dock. Tara felt water wash over one sandaled foot, and she took a step back. Looking out over the water, she saw only moonbeams lighting the empty sea.

And then Chris was waving her around the corner, and she ran onto the flimsy wooden docks that led outside the marina. As they rounded the corner, Tara was surprised to see an upward grade. The beach occupied a shelf that sloped up to the island's outer wall. Sugary white sand gleamed in the moonlight, and a row of coconut palms lined Solar Island's outer wall at the beach's upper reaches. The promised cluster of shrubs lay at the entrance, and Tara was glad when Chris pulled her into them, because she had frozen in the face of the spectacle unfolding before them on the beach.

A towering bonfire occupied the center of the sandy shelf—a beach in the middle of the ocean where none should be. A crowd of about twenty people danced around the fire in elaborate tribal garb. Many of them played simple drums or percussion instruments. All of them chanted words that meant nothing to Tara, but their fervor was unmistakable. Most of the people were Pacific Islanders, Tara noticed—but not all.

There were Americans, too. Peering through the bushes, she recognized a couple of them from dinner—Fred Jackson, the marine mechanic, and another guy whose name she hadn't caught, who had been quiet. They were now dancing around the fire, wearing only shorts, skin smeared with some kind of body paint. Tara watched as another two figures scaled a wooden platform, similar to a lifeguard tower, near the back of the beach. A white man accompanied by one native Fijian. The Caucasian raised his arms, and the drumming and chanting died down. A few of the men knelt on the beach around a large bowl of *kava*, a South Pacific drink made from a plant root that Tara knew was rumored to be mildly hallucinogenic. She wondered how many people on Solar Island drank it, and how often.

She didn't have time to speculate, though, because, as she brushed some leaves from her face, she was stunned to recognize Dr. Jacob Lightner standing atop the platform, decked out in tribal garb. The esteemed electrical engineer and alternative energy pioneer shouted something in a foreign tongue, to which the small crowd responded with rowdy cheers. Lightner waited for near-silence and then spoke in English.

"Tonight we give thanks to our solar sister, the guardian of the nighttime sky—the moon." He raised his arms toward the stars and the glowing moon, while the Fijian man next to him on the platform translated his words into an island dialogue.

To Tara, Lightner's words were strange enough, but it was his appearance and demeanor that impacted her the most. He had completely transformed himself, and yet he was instantly recognizable. Wearing only a pair of dark shorts, the sun medallion still graced his neck. It flashed in the moon's rays as he gyrated through a fiery oration, the people on the sand below thrusting their fists in agreement. Streaks of dark paint—*blood?*—adorned his body in the form of crude line drawings. Tara recognized the Egyptian figure of Ra, the sun god on Lightner's chest. His hair appeared bright silver.

"Great moon goddess, protector of night, we thank you for your nocturnal rays, for your bountiful radiance which has guided our people across these very waters through the millennia! On these, your fullest hours, we commune before you with humility, with spirit, and with singular purpose!"

More cheers erupted as Tara cast a sidelong glance at Chris Tenner, ensconced next to her in the bushes that shielded them from the moon's illumination. He was staring at Lightner, eyes narrowed into what Tara took for a look of intense dislike, even hatred. Oblivious to the non-believers in his midst, Dr. Lightner went on.

"Tonight we gather beneath your silvery orb to deliver justice to one who has fallen, to one who has betrayed your brotherly sun." Hushed tones of reverence rippled through the crowd until Lightner shouted, "Bring him!"

A commotion ensued at the far end of the beach, and then Tara could make out a four-man procession in which one man was being dragged by three others. The prisoner was yelling something in his native language that Tara could not understand. She looked to Chris next to her in the bushes, but he only stared at the spectacle with severe interest.

The man was brought in front of the makeshift tower where Lightner stood with his assistant. The crowd hushed. Lightner addressed them.

"Faipa, you have angered the sun by neglecting your duties. As punishment, our great sun's sister, the moon, shall bear witness to your expungement from our circle." Faipa tried to run, but his hands were tied to a rope held by his captors, and he was easily corralled.

"There is no escape, Faipa. The sun sees all. The moon will now see all."

The drum circle began anew, the rhythmic pounding and chanting building while Faipa's captors tied one end of the rope binding his hands to a large stone. Faipa was screaming now, tossing his head back and forth, frothing at the mouth, but his cries were overwhelmed by the ritualistic music.

"We are but a tiny island nation amidst the great sea of countries who would have us bend to their will," Lightner orated as one of Faipa's captors hefted the stone now tied to his arms. Tara glanced at the Americans on the beach to read their expressions, but they appeared to be willing participants, chanting and drumming when appropriate and then listening to their leader's words with rapt attention. Lightner waited for his translator and then continued.

"Our machine of freedom has no tolerance for faulty gears. Every cog must be in place, each broken part must be replaced. Faipa, you represent a broken part. You would have our island of the sun given over to your own countrymen, were it so possible. You would have our precious energy sapped to feed the greedy instead of the needy. You have failed to see us as *us*, and instead look for ways we can be assimilated into the fraternal system of legacy nations."

The captive stopped struggling for the first time and paused to look up into Lightner's eyes as his sentence was handed down.

"Faipa, this Court of the Full Moon finds you guilty of high treason. The penalty for high treason against the sovereign nation of Solar Island is death. Let any citizen who opposes this verdict now speak."

From the foliage, Tara watched the gathering for signs of someone coming forward. No one did. She started to rise, but Chris jammed her back onto the ground with a forceful shove. "You crazy?" he whispered. "Don't. He'll have this mob kill us."

Lightner spoke before she could respond to Chris. "Then, in the name and honor of Solar Island, the sentence shall now be imposed." The man standing next to Lightner raised a conch shell and blew into it, producing a mid-range trumpet sound. After a series of short blasts followed by one sustained note, Faipa's captors began to drag him down the beach toward the water's edge.

The ritual music began again. Faipa crumpled to his knees, but he was dragged in spite of that, leaving behind a frenzied trail in the sand. Someone threw another log onto the bonfire, sending up a shower of sparks to vocal approval.

They reached the edge. Faipa tried to work his ropes around his captors' ankles, but they sidestepped him easily, one holding the heavy stone—the stone that was attached to Faipa by a rope—off to the side. This one glanced back at Lightner, whose nod cut through the chaos, and the executioner dropped the stone into the sea.

TWENTY-FOUR

"We are on the verge of something great here on Solar Island," Lightner intoned forcefully as Faipa's body was dragged beneath the waves. "Threats to our rise must not be tolerated. No longer will the same corrupt nations of the world—be they run by iron-fisted dictators or by self-acting corporations—tell us what to do. We are running our own country here—wherever Solar Island floats—and our people have spoken. Actions that compromise our ascent as a unified nation will not be tolerated. At this moment, our Lord Sun journeys across the night sky to light our way in the morning. By the time he arrives, we will have our house in order, our resolve steeled."

A rousing chorus arose from the beach in response to Lightner's discourse. In the foliage, Chris seemed to be almost shocked into a state of paralysis. Tara could scarcely believe what she had just witnessed. If she had not seen the killing for herself, she had to admit, she never would have believed that Dr. Jacob Lightner had had an employee drowned in full view of about twenty people for some perceived threat against his nascent "nation," which Tara saw as nothing more than a giant raft.

But as the full-moon "party" kicked into full swing again with drumming, dancing, and *kava*, Tara knew that not only what she had observed was real, but that the man hiding next to her in the bushes was right: that Lightner had to be stopped. The longer she remained on this island, the greater the danger she would be in. She had to get back to her room and call Dillon on the sat-phone.

Tara watched as another log was thrown on the bonfire, sending a shower of sparks out over the ocean to mark Faipa's unfathomable death. She tapped Chris on the shoulder and indicated for him to lean closer. "How late will they go?" she asked.

He shrugged. "I came down here once at 2:00 a.m., and they were still going. But after that execution, they're pretty fired up. Could go until sunrise."

"I've seen all I need to see," she whispered back, and Chris nodded.

He pointed back the way they had come, but then leaned close. "Do not let them see the bushes move on our way out. If they see us, they will have no choice but to kill us."

Tara nodded and indicated that she would go first. Chris held branches out of her way while she picked her path out of the shrubbery. With Chris close on her heels, she then retraced the path they had followed on the way in, the sounds of the gathering fading behind them as they rounded the point that divided the beach from the marina.

As they sneaked across the docks, a chilling thought came over Tara as she looked up at the main-deck railing high above. "Are there surveillance cameras on Solar Island?" she asked Chris.

"There are a couple up in the solar field, still in the experimental stage. But not down here or anywhere else, as far as I know. Believe me, I checked that out thoroughly before I started sneaking around at night, keeping tabs on Lightner. It wouldn't surprise me if he puts them in island-wide sometime soon, but initially I don't think he saw internal security as much of a problem."

"I sure hope you're right. Because he could have used them now," Tara said as they passed the sub to the other side of the marina.

"I agree that he slipped up on that. But this floating solar panel is a huge operation, and he's preoccupied with turning it into his own country. People make mistakes, even Lightner."

They reached the ramp and took it up to Solar Island's main deck, crouching when they neared the top to check for patrols. Tara also looked back down toward the beach, half-expecting to see a throng of torch-wielding natives chasing after them; but she saw only the boats bobbing in their slips under the moonlight.

Tara grabbed Chris's arm. "My cart is right across that path. I want to take it back to my quarters and call in to my field support."

"Let's go."

The two dashed across the wide path into the narrow corridor between opposing rows of solar collectors where Tara had left her cart. The fact that it was still there bolstered their confidence. Tara started to get behind the wheel.

"Let me drive," Chris said.

She acquiesced. He knew the roads. A few seconds later, they were wheeling between solar troughs and heliostats, lights off, toward the center of the island. Chris was zigging down a path here, zagging around a corner there; before Tara knew it, they were pulling up to the crew-quarters building. They hadn't seen a soul on the drive over.

"Go to your room and stay there the rest of the night," Chris said.

"Gee, no one's told me that since I was ten years old," Tara joked. She supposed it was her way of coping with the horror that they had just witnessed.

"Very funny. I'm serious. Don't turn the room lights on. Keep your voice down on the call. Make sure you're up bright and early for the tour as scheduled. You've got to act like nothing happened. I'll find you tomorrow."

Before Tara could nod in response, Chris had vanished on foot into the shadows. Silently, she entered the still barracks. In her room, she opened the curtain to let in the moonlight, leaving the lights off. She stalked around the room, inspecting it, checking in the bathroom, looking up at the ceiling. Satisfied that there was nothing out of the ordinary, she went to the bed and pulled her backpack out from under the covers.

She unzipped the pack and reached inside. She pulled out the satellite phone and hit the key for Dillon's stored mobile number.

"Marconi here," he answered before the end of the first ring.

"I'm back from the rendezvous."

"How'd it go? I'm still researching Lightner's background. I just sent out a few inquiries to some of his old college professors who I managed to locate. I'll let you know if anything comes of it. There's—"

"Dillon, listen, this is serious. Listen to what I just saw."

She heard some shuffling on the other end of the line as Dillon moved to turn off a TV. "Go ahead," he said.

Tara relayed an account of her meeting with Chris Tenner and Lightner's full-moon event.

"Jesus, and the guy was still alive when they threw him in?"

"Definitely."

"We've got to get you out of there."

"Tomorrow's the last scheduled full day of the tour, anyway. Pick me up early in the morning on the day after tomorrow. I think we should stick to the plan, avoid tipping our hand at this point. Later, we can send an arrest team out to Solar Island for Lightner."

"You sure you don't want us to be there at end of day tomorrow?"

"No. If I tell him I'm leaving early, he might suspect that I know something and throw me overboard before you get here. It's just one more night."

"One more night with a guy who doesn't have all his cups in the cupboard. Why do you think he had the worker killed?"

"He's obsessed with turning Solar Island into his own country where he can do whatever the hell he wants. He saw this guy as in his way for some reason—Chris Tenner said sloppy work habits—and he set an example."

"Remind me not to apply for a job on Solar Island," Dillon said. There was a pause while Tara heard him shuffling papers, then he continued. "CIA intel is coming to us out of Southeast Asia, too, that some kind of insurrection started between two islands, over energy! They say one of them used 'a floating energy carrier' to temporarily power their military to ensure a takeover. I checked, and Solar Island was there six weeks ago."

"Lightner's building alliances. Practicing that 'half-assed statecraft' that the CIA warned us about."

"They're worried that he might try to influence—or even disrupt—the Pan-Asian Energy Summit next month, in Singapore. They say he's been fortifying—"

"Dillon, listen. I can catch up on the intel later. Right now I've got to get some shut-eye so I'm bright-eyed and bushy-tailed for a one-on-one tour by the Sun God himself first thing in the morning. I'll report in tomorrow night."

"Right, sorry. Listen, though, there is one more thing." She heard the sound of paper ripping. "Rob just sent me a weather fax. There's a hell of a storm building east of your position, heading your way."

TWENTY-FIVE

6:00 a.m.

Tara rubbed the sleep from her eyes, looking about her Spartan room. This was certainly no Hilton with a stocked minibar and an assortment of breakfast options laid out on a table. "Why did I not bring a coffee maker?" Tara said aloud to herself. She had thirty minutes until she met with Lightner to continue her tour. She vaguely remembered something about the dining hall being open early for breakfast, so she looped her fake press credential around her neck and made her way outside. She walked over to the dining hall, noticing that the sun was already up in the sky. She couldn't help but recall bits of Lightner's speech from his demented festival. Then she remembered Dillon's weather warning. Gazing skyward, she saw only a ball of orange low in the clear blue sky. The air was still, too, but with a weighty humidity to it.

Stepping inside the dining hall, Tara was surprised to find it mostly empty: only four people were seated at the table, grungy-looking American expats. *Everyone else must either be working already or still sleeping off last night's festivities.* She supposed the legitimate night crew, those few who had actually been working to keep Solar Island running smoothly during the night, would now also be asleep.

Tara did not recognize any of the diners, but she studied the reactions on their faces as she walked in. Did any of them know of her midnight sojourn?

"Morning, ma'am," one of them said. "Coffee and toast are over there." He pointed to a table against the wall with a warming tray and a coffee maker.

How did he know I wanted coffee so bad? She recalled with a start that she had wondered aloud why she hadn't brought a coffee maker. *Had someone been eavesdropping?*

Tara shook it off and headed for the brew. *It's morning, stupid; coffee is a normal thing to offer someone.* She poured herself a cup, grabbed some toast, and headed back to the table. As she did, all four of the men stood up to leave.

"Apologies, ma'am, but we're the morning-shift crew and we need to get to our stations."

"Maybe some other time, then, gentlemen." The men filed out and Tara sipped her black coffee alone. The brew wasn't that good, she decided, but it would have to do.

"I trust you had a good night's sleep?" The voice startled her and some of the hot liquid splashed onto her hand. She sucked in her breath from the pain, quickly wiped away the coffee, and turned around.

Dr. Jacob Lightner stood in the doorway with the sun at his back, shadowing him while he gripped each side of the doorframe with one hand. How long had he been standing there, observing her?

"Oh, hi there, Dr. Lightner!" she managed, standing to greet him. "Yes, I slept well, thank you. I was just having some coffee and toast. Have you had anything this morning yet?"

"I'm quite all right," he said. "It's time to continue our tour."

"Great! So, what's on the agenda for today?" It made her sick to think that she was speaking to a man who had deliberately ordered a man drowned only last night; and she knew that if she were to dwell on this, she would lose her composure.

"Well, so far you've seen a great deal about how the energy-production side of our island works, but there still remain two cornerstones of our human existence here: food production, and desalination. This way, please."

Tara rose from the table, stuffing the last of her toast into her mouth and taking her coffee mug—printed with the Solar Island logo—with her.

She followed Lightner through the long cafeteria hall, past the dining tables, the warming trays, and to a door set in the far end. He held it open for her. She felt his gaze upon her as she passed through it into a large-scale kitchen and food-preparation area.

Lightner explained that all of Solar Island's meals were prepared here. He stopped just long enough to introduce Tara to a man in a white uniform and hat as Solar Island's head chef—Tara was relieved not to recall seeing the chef at the full-moon party—and then continued through to a heavy door at the far end, preceded by another of the plastic-strip curtains she had seen in other areas. Lightner parted the strips for Tara, and she passed into another world.

An intense humidity draped itself around Tara's body as the temperature jumped ten degrees from what it was in the kitchen. The enclosed space they now stood in (it seemed far too large to call a room: it was more like a small stadium in size) had walls of glass panels and a ceiling of the same. Stands of various plants in wooden trays and pots stretched out in rows before them, tended by a half-dozen native island workers, one of whom Tara thought she recognized from the previous night's ceremony as one of the few women in attendance. This woman looked up from trimming leaves to glare at Tara as she snapped her clippers.

"Welcome to the greenhouse," Dr. Lightner said.

"Hot in here," Tara said, wiping her forehead with her sleeve.

"They don't call them hothouses for nothing," Lightner said with a cryptic smile. "Other than what comes from the sea, this is Solar Island's main food-production facility. I'm going to give you an overview, then in a minute I'll be handing you off to Dr. Cobb, our food-production scientist, whom you met last night at dinner."

Tara nodded her acknowledgement as she gazed in wonder at the floating greenhouse. A double row of taller fruit-bearing trees lined the middle of the rectangular space, with the wooden trays of smaller plants occupying the sides. A few butterflies fluttered about, and she even spotted a hummingbird hovering over a flower.

Lightner watched Tara's eyes tracking the bird. "We keep a few pollinators around. Also, it helps to make it more like a natural ecosystem."

Tara pointed out the vines creeping from the support struts above. "Those look like regular jungle plants. Do they produce some kind of food?"

Lightner nodded as he looked across his greenhouse. "The indigenous jungle plants are of course not necessary, but they do have a certain aesthetic appeal. It's nice to be able to go for a walk in the park, so to speak, when spending so much time at sea."

"I can see how that would be desirable."

"Also, for me," Lightner said, a faraway look taking hold in his eyes, "this space affords a feeling of total connection with my environment like no other area of the island. It's difficult for me to explain, but when I stand here, it's almost like I can visualize the sun's rays catalyzing the photosynthetic process in the plants' leaves. I can picture the dynamics of the marine food web occurring in the water below our feet. I can even comprehend the psychology behind my workers singing as they clean the solar panels and farm the tilapia ponds, tending to Solar Island much as our pollinators tend to our plants...." Lightner trailed off for a moment. "I feel as though I understand exactly how I fit into the biosphere and how everything interacts."

Tara didn't know how to respond. To her, Solar Island was still only a floating platform with solar panels and some buildings on it. But it was obvious that, to Jacob Lightner, it was much more than that. He saw himself as some kind of god over this place, Tara realized. He had created it. He was its lord, its master. And, Tara thought with some discomfort after flashing on last night's beach killing, he would control its fate as well as the fate of all those who lived here.

He probably thinks he's performing some kind of needed ecological function, Tara thought. She watched as Lightner held a hand up to a cloud of water descending from a mister system. *Like a predator catching prey, maintaining a balanced ecosystem.*

Lightner pulled his hand down out of the mist as he caught Tara staring at him a moment too long. He reassumed a businesslike demeanor, once again becoming the tour guide.

"So, this food-production facility is divided into two main sections. We're standing in the crop area, where all of our plants are grown. Then, around the corner down there—the greenhouse is actually L-shaped—the shorter wing contains our aquaculture facility. Dr. Cobb will be able to provide you with as much detail as you desire. Come, he should be over this way."

Lightner walked down the length of the greenhouse, threading his way between trays of plants. Tara recognized tomatoes and bell peppers, but many of the plants were unidentifiable to her.

They came to an area of leafy trees, where they began winding through a maze-like path around the big pots. Before long, they came upon James Cobb, dressed in shorts and a T-shirt that proclaimed "Fresh is best. Support your local farmer."

The scientist was standing in front of a tree, talking with two workers while he consulted a handheld electronic device.

"Last harvest on this specimen was three months ago, so our yield should be considerably higher than this," he was saying. He interrupted himself as Lightner and Tara arrived. "Check the sensors, the watering lines, the phosphate drip," he admonished the workers before turning away from them to face his boss.

"Good heavens, we're not going to run out of coffee, are we, James?" Lightner asked. To Tara, he added, "This place practically runs on caffeine!"

And kava, she thought, but hefted her mug and said, "Don't I know it! Good stuff! So the beans are grown right here?"

Cobb threw his hands up in a gesture of surrender. "Well, some of it is, but these few trees here are really more of a token effort to provide a few gourmet cups now and then. I confess that the bulk of our supply is purchased and delivered during our quarterly helicopter supply drops."

"So what I had this morning was—"

"Bulk buy," James said, nodding.

That explains why it tasted like bad truck-stop swill, Tara thought.

"It wasn't that good, was it?" James asked.

"It didn't have what I would call a robust flavor," Tara said. Living in Hawaii, she was used to the rich Kona blends, although she couldn't let that slip for fear of blowing her cover.

"Well, you certainly are polite, saying you enjoyed it anyway," Cobb said.

Tara blushed.

"So we've caught her in a lie!" Lightner said with exaggerated dramatic flair. "A dishonest reporter; imagine that!"

Tara fumed, part of it genuine, part of it coming from how she imagined a reporter would react to such an insult, even a pretend one. But, to her, Lightner's accusation was veiled, which gave it an uncomfortable, unspoken edge: *What else is she lying about?*

"It's actually not any worse than the battery acid they force-feed us at the magazine. Believe me, I don't take any coffee out here for granted, especially at six in the morning!"

Dr. Cobb gave a natural laugh; but, as Tara watched, Lightner's eyes came together in an annoyed squint, which concerned her. Her comment had had the intended effect with Cobb. Why had Lightner not taken it that way?

Could he be onto me? She flashed back to the biometric security check, the metal orb swinging up to her retina, and coughed in order to disguise her involuntary shudder. Knowing she needed to focus undistracted, Tara shrugged off the doubt.

"Anyway, Mrs. Greystone, this is Dr. James Cobb. He's an agriculture expert with a PhD in agricultural economics, and in the past has consulted for NASA on food-production techniques for the International Space Station. I'll leave you in his capable hands for this part of the tour," Lightner said, turning and walking deeper into the maze of trees.

"Well, then, are you ready?" Cobb asked.

"I am."

"So you happened to find me here in the coffee trees, but, as I said, that's really not one of our staples. Let me show you our 'daily eats' section, the vegetables and fruits that truly help to sustain us here in the middle of the Pacific."

Cobb waved an arm for Tara to follow, and they began walking back toward the kitchen. Along the way, he gave her some dry facts and figures on the average human's minimum daily caloric intake versus what could be produced in the greenhouse. Tara pretended to be interested, even jotting down some notes as she walked. When they reached an open area of small plants in trays, Cobb stopped and pointed to the neatly tended rows.

"Recognize them?"

"Tomatoes."

"Cherry tomatoes, yes. We can produce these year-around here. I started with seeds that have genetic traits favorable to this environment and this situation: rapid growth, high yield. Oddly, pest resistance is not a huge factor out here in the middle of the ocean, so it was not necessary to trade that for slow growth, as is sometimes the case. Drought tolerance, too, is not really an issue since we produce our own water here through a desalination plant." Cobb pointed through the glass walls to the ocean beyond. "Endless supply!"

"Where is the de-sal plant?"

"It's housed in another building, next to the greenhouse."

"Doesn't it need to be on the edge, to suck up the water?" Tara asked.

Cobb shook his head. "The seawater intake is accomplished by piping it straight up from below. It would have been more expensive, in terms of energy usage, to have it on the edge and then have to pump it across a half mile to the greenhouse. So instead, we have it adjacent to the greenhouse and pump it twenty vertical feet."

Tara nodded. "Interesting. And do you also run the desalination process?"

"I was involved in the design, as it relates to food production, but the actual operation of it, chemically—the reverse osmosis and all that—is the domain of Dr. Henderson—Spencer Henderson, our chemical engineer. He is also in charge of the wastewater treatment processes, so that we're not dumping raw sewage into the ocean everywhere we go."

"Sounds like he has an important position here. Was he at dinner last night?"

"No, he's something of a hermit. Doesn't socialize too much. But I suppose that's fitting for one who lives in the middle of the ocean. All of us are hermits out here, if you think about it."

"Do you miss home? Do you have family in America?"

"My dear wife passed away ten years ago. We had no children. I was in a deep depression for about five years after that, not even working. Just living off savings as...well, as a hermit, really, in my house near Rockville, Maryland. And then one day Dr. Lightner emailed me out of the blue, asking me if I'd like to join his 'experimental energy project,' as he put it."

"What was the negotiation process like with Lightner? Did he offer a competitive salary, or did you haggle over pay?"

Dr. Cobb coughed slightly, covering his mouth. His eyes widened just a bit. Tara had surprised even herself with the directness of the question. It was highly personal; but then again, as a reporter charged with rooting out the essence of what Solar Island was all about, it also had the potential to shed light.

"I'm sorry, Dr. Cobb. If the question upsets you, you don't have to answer it."

Cobb shrugged. "No, I suppose it's a logical question to ask. The pay he offered wasn't comparable to what I had been making, and in fact I did negotiate up from there. But what Lightner really offered was the chance to be a part of something new, something experimental, something deliciously cutting-edge. That, combined with the fact that although the salary was lower than what I could make just taking a faculty post at a major research university, this job covers all my living expenses; so with nowhere to go to spend money, everything I make is just banked."

Tara raised her eyebrows. "That is quite a perk. Thank you for being so forthright, Dr. Cobb. Please, let's continue with the greenhouse tour."

Cobb nodded. "So, I mentioned how we start with genetically engineered cherry tomato seeds that need not favor drought tolerance or pest resistance. This same principle holds for all our subsistence crops." Cobb pointed to different trays as he named them. "Bell peppers, corn, squash, cucumbers, cabbage, lettuce, broccoli, brussels sprouts, alfalfa sprouts, watercress, potatoes, radish—we have a Chinese white variety here called *daikon*. And for the fruits: watermelon, cantaloupe, honeydew, oranges, limes, dragon fruit, breadfruit, plus a few more we can't quite see from here. A lot of fruits tend to grow on trees, which makes them more impractical, so I try to focus on the vine-producing species, especially the melons."

Tara pointed to the metal piping, hanging over the trays, that periodically emitted a fine mist. "So I see the misters are automated, correct? And the watering?"

"Yes, the basic life-sustaining functions for the plants are automated through what's called SCADA—Supervisory Control and Data Acquisition, the same technology that controls much of the island's machinery. There are also sensors that report the soil conditions, and alarms are triggered if those conditions exceed designated thresholds."

"So, with all the automation, what do all the workers do?"

Cobb smiled. "Automation can't replace everything. We're not a giant agribusiness here. We don't have mechanical pruners and sorters and graders and the like." He pointed to a nearby Pacific Island worker, busily trimming leaves from a mango tree. "Some things are just better done by hand. Especially the harvesting," he said, pointing to another worker, pulling radishes from the soil and placing them into a basket woven from palm fronds.

"I see," Tara said, writing in her notepad.

"In addition to fruits and vegetables, we also have a modest protein-production facility, which occupies the other wing of the greenhouse. Let me show you that."

Cobb led the way down the greenhouse toward the end farthest from the kitchen. Tara walked side by side with him through the center of the greenhouse. Her shirt was sticking to her back, rivulets of sweat streaming down her neck. A mister discharged over them as they walked, and Tara was grateful for its cooling effect.

They passed a section of medium-height green leafy plants being carefully tended to by a worker, and Tara asked what they were.

"Those are kava plants," Dr. Cobb said. "Their roots are used to make a popular South Pacific drink that has a mild trance-like effect. Have you ever had it?"

In fact, in Hawaii, Tara had taken the opportunity to sample it once. To her, it tasted like liquid dirt, and she hadn't enjoyed it. "No," she said.

"Well, most Westerners don't like the taste. Look at these plants over here," Cobb said, changing the subject. Tara followed his pointing finger to a low plastic tub filled with water. It was covered with a green aquatic plant.

"These are taro," Cobb explained. "They grow in flooded soil, and the roots are used to make a starchy chip or, especially in Hawaii, a pasty dish called *poi*."

Tara bristled at the mention of her state of residence. Was Cobb somehow trying to tip her off to the fact that he knew where she was from—and therefore who she really was? Or was it merely a coincidence? *Should I see if I can get the helo to pick me up at the end of the day today instead of spending another night?*

She wrestled with these thoughts as they wound their way through the facility, but placated herself by rationalizing that Hawaii was part of Polynesia and therefore had enough in common with the South Pacific for it to come up in conversation naturally.

When they reached the opposite end of the greenhouse's agricultural wing, they made a right turn through a wide plastic-strip door. A sign overhead read "PROTEIN PRODUCTION." The temperature dropped slightly but not much, and, if anything, Tara noted, the humidity increased.

Her eyes scanned the room before her. A row of round water-filled tanks, each about twenty feet in diameter and four feet high, occupied most of the available space. Overhead ran a complex array of PVC piping, wiring, and various electronic fixtures, giving the place an industrial-factory feel. As in the crop wing, a few workers were carrying out manual-labor tasks. To her left, she heard a splash and looked just in time to see a fin slap the water.

"Tilapia," Dr. Cobb said, answering the obvious question before it could be spoken. "A freshwater fish farmed in many tropical parts of the world, due to its suitability for aquaculture: quick-breeding, hardy, disease-resistant."

Dr. Cobb led Tara through the protein wing, which was smaller by half than the main greenhouse. He showed her various tanks of fish, shrimp, and chickens in a coop being fed by a worker. There were even small stables housing goats and a few pigs.

"These farm animals, with the exception of the chickens, are not actually bred here," Cobb said, "but we buy them from time to time when we make a port stop."

"So meat is a special occasion around here?"

Cobb nodded. "Yes, it's strictly rationed, but it's funny how you don't really miss it. I've become a vegetarian myself, by choice, since moving here."

Since moving here... Tara thought that sounded so final, like he wasn't just working here, but had *moved* here, permanently. She found that even living in Hawaii was somewhat inducive of "island fever" and could not imagine what it must be like to call Solar Island home. Only her second day here, and she was already looking forward to leaving, though of course she had other reasons for feeling that way.

"Well, you certainly look healthy," she said. She wondered if he missed the company of women. She supposed it must be like serving in the Navy and that the men found their women in various ports of call when they could. Cobb blushed slightly.

"Well, thank you, ma'am." Tara wondered if he had misconstrued her comment as a flirtatious line. "Healthful eating—that's my job here, and I live by it! That concludes the look at our food-production facilities. I'm happy to answer any questions before you continue with your tour."

Tara made sure to ask a couple of detail-oriented questions that might be used for an in-depth article. When they had been answered, Cobb opened a barn-style door on the far end of the protein wing, and Tara scrambled for her sunglasses as she stepped outside. Cobb looked at his watch.

"Jacob will be by to pick you up any minute now. Good day, Amanda."

Tara watched as the double doors were pulled shut and she heard the click of the latch echo inside the protein wing. Cobb certainly seemed nice enough; and, if she had to guess, she'd put him with Tenner's Anti-Sovereignty Movement as opposed to Lightner's fanatics. But was she sure?

She could not afford to be wrong.

TWENTY-SIX

Tara stood outside the aquaculture facility, alone on Solar Island for the first time since waking. Her feet hurt after so much walking over the last two days. She wasn't sure it would help, but she slipped off her shoes.

Alone in a lonely place, Tara thought as she scanned the roadways for some sign of an approaching electric cart. She saw only empty expanses of track. A worker was visible maybe fifty yards away, oblivious to her presence as he cleaned a solar trough.

Tara glanced at her watch. Lightner would be by to pick her up at any minute. That didn't give her enough time to head back to her quarters for an update from the field office, so she decided to have a look around, as any good investigative reporter with idle time while on assignment would.

The only notable feature in her immediate vicinity was a corrugated metal shed adjacent to the aquaculture wing of the greenhouse. A painted sign over its partially open door indicated "MAINTENANCE." After a last glance around, Tara stepped into the shed.

She allowed her eyes to adjust to the dim light while taking in the room's dimensions. It was small, maybe eight feet on a side. She was able to distinguish dim outlines that momentarily took shape as recognizable objects: a heap of potting-soil bags, a shovel, various other long-handled tools, a pile of garden hoses, an old outboard motor.

Tara took a step farther into the structure. She thought about returning for her shoes, which she had left on the ground outside, but decided she would only be in here for a few seconds. As a shed, it differed from those on land in two respects: it was free of dust, and it contained no bugs or spiderwebs that she could see. Judging from the haphazard storage organization, Tara guessed that these "lackings" weren't attributable to meticulous upkeep, but rather to being far out at sea most of the time, beyond the reach of spiders or copious dust.

She was about to turn and head back outside when a faint noise registered her attention. She froze. The sound had emanated from within the shed. *Below me?*

Tara's eyes scanned the floor and lit upon a metal grate set near the shed's back wall. She padded softly toward it; when she stood almost directly over it, she peered inside. It was dark, but she thought she detected some depth, a kind of shadowy three-dimensional form suggesting at least some space below.

And then she heard the sound again. She recognized it this time: the sound of a page turning. In the whisper-quiet environment of the shed, far from the power-generating machinery at the island's center, the rasp of paper on paper was unmistakable.

Someone is down there.

She was leaning down toward the grate for a closer look—*was that a blue glow?*—when she heard voices outside. Pulling back from the grate, she recognized the radio chatter coming from a cart; and then, with a start, she heard Lightner's voice in response giving some command. *Damn those silent golf carts.*

Tara slipped noiselessly out of the shed just before Lightner drove his cart around the corner of the greenhouse. She stepped into her shoes while he parked the cart and got out, waving to her.

"Amanda, sorry I'm late," Lightner said as he strode toward her outside the shed. Tara had her notepad out, writing busily.

"Hello, Dr. Lightner!" Tara said, mustering a false enthusiasm. She was surprised at how much energy it sapped from her to keep up the cheery reporter-on-assignment façade. "Just jotting down the reams worth of information I got from Dr. Cobb!" she continued, looking up from her pad with a final scribble, which actually read check grate.

"I only hope James didn't throw too many dry factoids at you—kilocalories and biomass per hectare and such. He's a brilliant agronomist, but I'm not sure he has much experience with the press."

"Oh! No, he was great, explaining how it all works in general terms. It's amazing, the diversity of foods he's able to produce out here."

"Such is the bounty of our ultimate sustainer, the sun," Lightner said, reaching a hand to the sky. His sentence and posturing reminded Tara of the rhetoric he had used during the full-moon ceremony, and she shivered involuntarily in the tropical heat.

"Are you ready to continue your tour?"

Tara said that she was.

"Excellent. Only one major section remains; but without it, Solar Island could not function."

Tara held up a finger while making a show of flipping through the pages of her notepad. "The battery bank?" she asked, snapping her pad shut with a flourish.

Lightner was expressionless as he looked at her notebook. He slowly lifted his gaze to meet hers. "Forgive me; the approaching weather has me distracted. There are actually two major sections remaining—the battery bank, and the desalination plant, which is next up. James probably mentioned it since it is inexorably linked to food production."

Tara sensed that Lightner was deliberately de-emphasizing the battery bank portion of the tour, but she didn't want to appear overly interested in it, so she moved on for the time being.

"He did mention it, said that..." she riffled back through the pages of her notepad, grateful to have an excuse for looking away from his eyes "...Dr. Spencer Henderson is in charge of that. And the wastewater treatment as well."

"That's correct. You'll be meeting Spencer momentarily. Climb aboard," Lightner said, indicating his electric cart.

When they were under way in the vehicle, Tara said, "So, I don't believe I've yet seen Dr. Henderson. He doesn't eat with the group at dinner?" Tara thought it better not to tip her hand that Dr. Cobb had dished to her that Spencer was a hermit. She liked Cobb, felt a little sorry for him and his self-imposed exile out here following the death of his wife, and did not want Lightner to devise any negative consequences for him based on anything she said.

"You'll see him in about..." Lightner negotiated a curve with the cart before looking at his solar-powered watch. "...five minutes. Again, I'm afraid I'll just be dropping you off for the tour of his domain and will pick you up afterward."

"No problem. I understand that you have lots to do in terms of keeping things running here..." *and killing and terrorizing your would-be citizens* "...besides chaperoning me around, and so I really do appreciate your hospitality."

"Ah, well, the work we do here—providing energy for this often-forgotten, isolated part of the world—is something the general public should hear about, and so I thank you, Amanda, for playing your part."

And no doubt for my ten-thousand-dollar "journalist touring fee" that goes to fund your quasi-political terrorism, Tara thought but did not say.

"You're quite welcome. If what I've learned so far is any indication, I have no doubt that the public will be paying close attention to what's happening on Solar Island."

Lightner smiled as he entered into a final series of tight turns through corridors lined by white-painted metal tanks and pipes before pulling into a parking space next to another cart. A placard over the other cart read "RESERVED FOR DR. SPENCER HENDERSON."

After two days on the island, Tara was amazed at how many nooks and crannies contained things that she hadn't seen before. Here was some kind of industrial complex, no doubt a little world unto its own—the world of Spencer Henderson—Tara thought, but before now she hadn't even known of its existence. *What other secrets does this place hold?*

As she stepped out of the cart, Tara was no longer sure that she wanted to know. It was her job to find out, but she had to admit that this place represented a new level of potential crimes against humanity. An area of special sovereignty, drifting around the largest ocean on Earth through the seas of developing nations and impoverished communities, violating human rights and wreaking havoc wherever it goes.

And this was just the beginning, Tara thought. If Lightner was successful with Solar Island, could other would-be fanatics and seasteading despots be far behind?

She was glad the CIA was involved, though exactly what they would be doing remained to be seen. Were they watching her right now through a keyhole reconnaissance satellite? If so, would they intervene should she find herself in immediate danger? She liked to think so but knew from experience that the CIA was unpredictable. Ozakawa had suggested that they were most concerned about the special-battery technology—which allowed Solar Island to provide power at night—falling into dangerous hands, particularly those of North Korea.

She was on her own. She worried that perhaps she had underestimated the seriousness of the situation she had willingly placed herself in.

Tara waved goodbye to Lightner, who pointed her up a metal utility staircase to a closed metal door reading "DESALINATION PLANT." She felt a strong breeze ruffle her dyed blond hair. Remembering Dillon's weather warning, she paused on the top step and looked out toward the sea, which was not visible from her perch of only three feet up near the center of the island—almost a half mile from the edge.

Looking up, she saw white, heavy clouds pass over the sun and felt the loss of heat immediately. Then the first raindrops fell.

She banged with her fist on the metal door. When no one answered, and as the rain intensified, she pulled the door open herself and stepped inside.

TWENTY-SEVEN

Tara stood for a moment in the doorway to the desalination plant, absorbing the scene. The roof of this building was low. She had maybe a foot of clearance beneath the rows of fluorescent lights. She stared down the length of the rectangular building, marveling at the floor-to-ceiling racks of white pipes that lined both sides, several racks on each side, leaving only a narrow walkway running down the middle between the center racks.

And the noise! Compared to the near-silence outside, it was deafening in here. She almost didn't hear the voice yelling at her, "Close the door!" Tara looked around for the source of the voice.

"Door, please!" the male voice repeated, close now but still out of sight. Tara reached back and followed the command. When she turned back around, a forty-ish Asian man stood in front of her, wearing the customary Solar Island shorts and T-shirt, but with a yellow hard hat, safety goggles, and heavy work boots.

"I'm sorry to yell at you," the man shouted. "The high-pressure pumps are running. Come with me," he beckoned, before ducking between two racks of pipes on the left side of the room.

Tara followed, passing, along the way, an assortment of industrial heavy equipment including three-foot-diameter metal pipes with red-painted valve wheels, silver consoles with arrays of pressure gauges, and other small colored pipes with labels. Tara read a few of the labels: sodium chlorite, hydrochloric acid, sodium bisulfate, sulfuric acid, and sodium hypochlorite.

Then the man opened a regular door and stepped into a smallish, windowless office. Tara trotted inside after him and shut the door, blocking most of the noise. With a sigh, the man removed his hard hat and goggles and extended a hand.

"Amanda Greystone, I'm pleased to meet you. My name is Spencer Henderson. I apologize for the rude greeting, but Jacob was vague about when you would be here, and it's impossible to hear out there."

Tara shook his hand. "Thank you, sir. That's quite all right. So, those high-pressure pipes are part of the desalinization system?"

Spencer pointed to a tiny table with two chairs and indicated for Tara to sit, which she did. The rest of the room was occupied by a desk and computer, a wall rack with more hard hats and goggles, and a whiteboard covered with complex schematics and chemical equations.

"Correct. I have the capacity to produce 100,000 gallons of fresh water from seawater per day. It is pumped from directly beneath us."

"That sounds like an awful lot of water. Does Solar Island actually use that much?"

"No, you're right. While we have the capacity to produce 100,000, we only need about 20,000, including for the greenhouse and the solar thermal pipes that don't use oil."

Tara made a notation in her pad, then looked up as Spencer continued. "That max capacity is only a theoretical, though. We haven't been able to actually hit that in a long while. Dr. Lightner's on my case about it because he wants to be able to sell water, along with energy, to his clients wherever we go."

"What is it that keeps you from attaining maximum production?"

"Mostly it's marine life growth captured by and stuck to reverse-osmosis filters, but there is also a smattering of obscure technical issues I won't bore you with. Right now we have about fifty percent blockage due to marine life."

Tara gave Spencer a puzzled look.

"In the same way that ships have the problem of fouling—algae, and then barnacles, sponges, and other life forms will grow on just about any object immersed in seawater for any length of time—Solar Island itself, and in particular my osmosis filters, get clogged with growth as we float through this tropical ocean."

"But ships use antifouling paints, right?"

Spencer smiled. "Yes, they do. And in fact the bottom of Solar Island does too. But my filters are a special application where it can't be applied. The stuff is toxic, of course, and we're producing drinking water." Tara took down another note and looked up at Spencer again. He stared at the floor, lips turned into a frown.

"Those things are really the least of my problems, though," he muttered.

"How so?" Tara prompted. She could tell something was bothering him.

Spencer looked around the room before he answered her. He stared at the computer screen on his desk, at a walkie-talkie hanging from the rack, at the diagrams on the whiteboard, and finally back to Tara herself. "What I am about to tell you is off the record, okay? I don't want to lose my job over this. Or worse."

"Agreed." Tara set aside her notepad and pen. *So he knows what goes on here.* It struck Tara how eager some residents of Solar Island were to talk about their situation with an outsider. She was one of the only outside people they had seen and would see for a long time, as far as they knew.

"I'm not sure, during your relatively brief stay so far, how much you've been able to find out about some of the politics that go on here. Would you be interested in hearing about it?"

Tara decided to keep tight-lipped about what she did know and let Spencer talk if he wanted to. "Yes, very."

Spencer took a deep breath and began. "Two opposing factions have developed here. The stronger one, championed by Dr. Lightner himself, is known as the Sovereignty Movement. They are motivated by the prospect of Solar Island being its own nation, and by extension being able to construct their own societal laws and customs as they see fit."

"And you are not a part of that movement?"

"No. I came here to work on an engineering project because I lost my university post after I was banned from ever again receiving federal research funds."

"Mind if I ask why?"

Spencer cocked his head to one side and held his hands palms up. "For inadvertent administrative missteps for which I take full responsibility but don't want to discuss." Tara nodded her agreement, aware that his statement sounded rehearsed, as though he had carefully prepared and memorized it for whenever the question arose.

Spencer continued. "Suffice it to say that I was not attracted to Solar Island by the romantic elements of a life at sea. I had no choice. Lightner offered me interesting technical work in my field at reasonable pay, considering that I have no expenses while here, doing something I'm good at and can take pride in."

"The production of drinking water from seawater, that is," Tara clarified.

"Precisely. Providing potable water for a live-aboard green-energy installation, and maybe—if I could get it to work right—maybe even providing water for remote, impoverished nations who really need it. But Lightner put a damper on that by demanding high fees for my water, well above what it costs to produce, even though his clients are also paying him for the energy. He is not given to charity, I suppose, which is his right; but I found it disappointing."

"And the second faction?"

"So, the Sovereignty Movement is Lightner's manifestation of some warped belief system, what he thinks of as a utopia, but which has actually become more of a dystopia. I and a small band of residents—Chris Tenner among them—started what came to be called the Resistance. This name was not chosen by us, but was bestowed upon us by the Sovereignty people as a way of calling attention to what we are doing. I would have just called us the Normal People," Spencer laughed, "as we are not politically motivated in any way—I'm just a normal person who made a mistake and as a result had to take an unusual job—but they gave us that name, and it stuck."

Tara's thoughts turned to tactical matters. She needed hard information that she could convey back to the field office and to the CIA. "How many people make up the Resistance?"

“There are about six of us who are hard-core members. Used to be seven, if you count Bernie....” Spencer said, trailing off to see if Tara would ask who he was.

“I’m familiar with Bernie’s man-overboard incident,” Tara said, realizing that she was slipping a little too much into her FBI persona.

“Chris Tenner is our leader, I guess you would say. And besides the six of us, there are others who have somehow managed to remain neutral, especially among the Pacific Islanders, but Lightner has been steadily working to convert them over.”

“So how often do you and Chris work together on the Resistance?”

Spencer’s gaze bored into her blue contacts. “Enough to know that you’re not a reporter,” he said.

Tara shifted uncomfortably in her seat.

“Don’t worry. No one from the Sovereignty knows that there is a law enforcement agent here. Yet. We above all want to keep your role safe. I know that you responded to Chris’s plea for help—his sound file.”

Tara was shocked speechless. The situation was worse than she thought. Two people—that she was aware of—knew that she was FBI; how many others, she wondered. She needed to get to the point.

“I saw a man killed here last night, drowned on Lightner’s orders at the full-moon party.”

“Some ‘party,’ right? That’s what I’m talking about. At this rate, it won’t be long before he’s killing people not for any strategic purpose, but for some stupid sun-god sacrifice, like the Aztecs or something. He thinks he’s forging new ground, but in actuality he’s only repeating the distant past.”

Tara had to agree. “Spencer, how would you assess my chances of leaving Solar Island when my helicopter comes to pick me up tomorrow?”

Dr. Henderson appeared to consider the matter, looking down at the white tile floor, then up at Tara, then at his computer. He stood up. “So far as I know, Lightner doesn’t know you’re an agent, but he has been snooping around, grilling those you’ve talked to after they meet with you. I’m sure he’ll be coming for me later.”

"I'm sorry."

"Don't be. I gave you a tour of the desalination facilities, which is true." Spencer went to his desk and sat down in front of the PC.

"There is something that concerns me, though." He tapped a few keys.

"What?"

"You're scheduled to be picked up in the morning, you say?"

It made Tara uncomfortable to disclose her field timetable, but she needed information. "Yes. Early."

Spencer clacked away at a few more keys and then frowned.

"What is it?" Tara asked.

"Weather doesn't look good, but it's still a little bit too far away to be sure yet. I can tell you that a chopper landing is not a hundred percent possible at this time." He turned away from the monitor and looked her in the eye.

"Do you know where we are?" she asked. "Are we farther from Guam than when I was dropped off?"

"I believe so," Spencer said gravely. "I have heard the thrusters on lately, which also concerns me. Usually we just drift with no motor usage whatsoever. Let me check the chart...." He clicked the mouse and focused on the screen. He raised his eyebrows.

"My goodness, that is odd."

Tara stood up and walked behind the desk. She wanted to be sure he wasn't fabricating things. She didn't think so; but she was alone in this outlandish place, and so she had to be sure. He showed no signs of discomfort as she approached.

"What's odd?" she asked.

He pointed to a red dot on the screen in the middle of a nautical chart. "That's our position, which is *well* south and west of where we were when you were dropped off. Also," he added as Tara stared numbly at the display, "we appear to be heading straight *into* the storm, which NOAA is now tracking as a..." Spencer clicked the map, and a National Oceanic and Atmospheric Administration Pacific region weather page came up.

Peering at the monitor over Spencer's shoulder, Tara finished his sentence for him. "Cyclone."

Spencer nodded. "In the Atlantic, this would be called a Category 1 hurricane."

An awkward silence followed, which Spencer attempted to end by saying, "Cat 1 is the lowest severity, 5 is the worst."

"I know that. So it's just a little, itsy-bitsy cyclone. No need to worry."

"I'm sorry, I don't mean to make light of it. It's serious. We've been in tropical storms before, which we weathered without serious problems, but never a cyclone. But maybe it'll either change course or die off. We shouldn't panic yet. And the island was designed to withstand a Category 5, though of course it wouldn't be fun."

"But my helicopter..."

Spencer clicked a button, and a printer whirred in the corner. He walked to it and plucked out a piece of paper, then handed it to Tara. "Here. This has our current position. You can call your people, right?"

Tara nodded. "Tonight they're actually expecting me to call in."

"Good. So give them our coordinates. We'll have moved since now, especially with the winds picking up, but it's a hell of a lot more accurate than estimating our position based on your drop-off zone two days ago."

Tara folded the paper into a pocket. Spencer looked at his watch. "We should really be getting on with our tour. It would look suspicious if Lightner finds out I was in here with you for so long."

"Is there much else to see in the de-sal plant?"

"No. I'll show you the seawater-intake pipe, the finished product, oh, and the wastewater treatment, and then off you go to hopefully coordinate your pickup. I'll also send word through our little Resistance grapevine to help you however possible. Godspeed."

Tara nodded her thanks and opened the door to a rush of industrial noise. She scanned the facility but saw no other people. Spencer pointed to the left, and they walked down the corridor lined on both sides by pipes.

The rest of the tour was a blur to Tara while she thought about her situation. The weather. What if she couldn't be picked up tomorrow?

Spencer said Lightner had been snooping around on her already...and what of her biometric data? She passed by labeled gauges as she considered her options. "Drain flow meter"..."Sediment filter pressure"...*I'll have to call Dillon as soon as I get out of here, not wait for tonight.* "Booster pump pressure..."

Spencer showed her the intake pipe, a white PVC pipe housed within a circular barrier. "In boats, this is what they call a through-hull fitting," Spencer said of the pipe piercing Solar Island's bottom to feed water from the sea. Tara nodded absent-mindedly, no longer pretending to take notes. But Spencer kept up the tour anyway. "So, on the other end of that pipe down in the water, there are filters that are always clogging with marine growth...."

They started moving again, passing stacks of 55-gallon drums and steel frameworks housing machinery. Tara saw a small alcove off to one side, created by the deliberate stacking of large polyethylene tanks. Spencer was walking a few steps ahead, rambling on about the purification process. Tara sidestepped into the alcove.

An old mattress lay in the corner, a pile of paperback novels lying nearby. A hot plate sat atop a 55-gallon drum, while a small desk lamp was clipped over the mattress. The tiny space was cluttered with evidence of daily living, and Tara was filled with dread at the thought of someone existing like that in this place, hundreds or even thousands of miles from real civilization at any given time. A cockroach skittered across the floor. Tara took a couple of snapshots of the dingy space with her digital camera.

Spencer's voice made Tara jump. "Oh, uh, sometimes I need to work late..." Spencer stammered, but they both knew he was lying. Spencer the hermit...never at dinner, not in the living quarters. He *lived* in here.

Tara turned to him, trying to keep her lower lip from trembling. "Why don't you just bunk in the crew's quarters?"

"Well, I do; I..."

"Spencer..." she said in a soft voice, trailing off as her gaze roved around the cluttered, grimy space. He appeared ashamed, eyes downcast, face flushed.

"When I became associated with the Resistance, Lightner made my life...difficult," he said. "He told me he needed my room in the quarters for a group of four Pacific Islanders coming aboard to share, and that I would have to live in my de-sal plant until further notice."

"Spencer, this is inhumane. Why didn't you quit?" Tara was mortified.

"I can't quit. What would I do? I'm no longer employable as a researcher. I have debts to pay down that a non-professional job wouldn't pay. I really have nowhere else to go."

"It seems Dr. Lightner has made an entire operation out of exploiting a vulnerable worker population."

Spencer nodded. "Yes, he takes advantage of different people in different ways, depending on what they can do for him, what their weaknesses are...."

"I'm going to put a stop to it."

"First we've got to get you out of here. Let's finish up the tour."

She followed him through the rest of the de-sal plant, passing by various controls, a color video screen with flow diagrams here, panels of knobs and switches there, barely seeing them. They passed through another plastic-strip curtain into the wastewater-treatment area. Spencer gave her some dry facts, but Tara was no longer listening. Overall, the wastewater section didn't look much different from the de-sal area. Pipes, machines, tanks, filters.

And then they stood before a metal door underneath an exit sign. Tara turned to Spencer and gripped his hand. "Thank you, Spencer. I'll take care of this."

Spencer looked down at the floor.

"What's the matter?" she asked.

"Be careful. There's—" He looked back up at her but said no more.

"There's what?"

"I think we may have a mole in the Resistance. We should be able to keep you safe until tomorrow. But it's hard to keep anything a secret here for very long. Do you have enough to bring charges against Lightner?"

She lowered her voice. "My personal observation of the murder alone is enough. My case report will be thorough and convincing—do not worry about that."

Spencer looked at his watch. "Almost lunchtime. I take it Lightner will be expecting you there."

Tara nodded. "He keeps me on a pretty tight leash."

"I'll bet he does."

"I might try to call in to my field office, check the helicopter situation with the weather."

"Make sure no one hears you doing that. I'll be looking out for you tonight. If you need a safe haven, you can always come back here. I'll leave this and the other door you came through unlocked."

Spencer shied away from the light as he pulled the door open for Tara, and she stepped out into the day.

TWENTY-EIGHT

Guam, FBI Field Office

Dillon Marconi's desk phone rang as he looked up from the interview transcript he was reading. Scooting his desk chair closer, he picked up the phone and identified himself as an FBI agent.

"Hello, Agent Marconi. This is Dr. Lewis Putnam. I received a message from you yesterday regarding a former student of mine, Dr. Jacob Lightner."

"Thank you for returning my call, Dr. Putnam," Dillon began as he shuffled through various papers in his work area, looking for his notes on the potential witnesses he'd contacted yesterday. "I reached out to you because according to my information, you taught a Jacob Lightner at Berkeley. Is that correct, Professor?"

A smooth and easy laugh emanated from the other end of the call. "My, you realize that was *decades* ago, son? And let's make no bones about it—I didn't teach *a* Jacob Lightner, I taught *the* Jacob Lightner, the one about whom you're calling. That would be the one with his own floating island. And there's no need to call me Professor any longer, although I am emeritus at Berkeley—retired for quite some time now. You can just call me Lewis."

"Very well, Lewis; I appreciate your willingness to help. Tell me, which subject did you teach to Dr. Lightner—was it electrical or chemical engineering?" It was just a guess. Could have been mechanical, or a math class, Dillon thought. He scrambled through some more paper piles, looking for his notes. He disliked the lack of organization when using a temporary workspace.

A few seconds passed without a reply. "Lewis?" Dillon prompted.

"Yes, yes, I'm here. Oh dear, I'm afraid I may not be of much help to you, Agent. You see, I was Jacob's professor of English."

"English?"

"Yes, as in English Contemporary Literature I and II. Even back in those days, the science and engineering majors were forced to take liberal arts courses in order to afford them with a modicum of well-roundedness, you see. It's been so long, though, I dare say the word 'contemporary' in the title no longer applies! I'm sorry, but if you're hoping to pick my brain in order to trace back how young Jacob amassed the technical prowess he's putting to use nowadays, you'll find me quite inadequate."

Dillon found a notepad and folded over a new sheet. "Does anything stand out in your mind from your experiences teaching Dr. Lightner?"

"As a matter of fact, yes. I must confess, I would not recall the names of most of my students any longer, especially those who were not graduate students, or at least undergraduates majoring in English. But Jacob, he was quite interesting. Most of the engineering types who filtered through my classes were just going through the motions to satisfy the general education requirements. It's no secret to me that behind my back they'd dismiss literature as 'silly storybooks' or some other such derogatory term. If it wasn't going to help them advance their budding careers, they weren't interested in it."

"And Dr. Lightner was somehow different in this respect?"

"Well, yes, I do suppose he was. You see, he wrote one of the finest papers I have ever received from a student, including those in the major."

"Can you recall what it was about?"

"Clear as day. I'm old, son, and my body's starting to go, but my mind is still all there. Cruel joke that is, let me tell you. But it was a detailed analysis of the character of John Galt, from the novel *Atlas Shrugged* by Ayn Rand. Are you familiar with the book? I'm not sure what type of education one needs to become a federal agent."

Dillon hadn't been out of college all that long, and he recalled seeing lots of wide-eyed kids toting the book about, although he had never read it himself.

"I'm vaguely familiar."

"In fact, Jacob's paper was so arresting that I've kept it all these years. If you want, I'd be happy to brave whatever technological demons await me to get it from the paper into the computer so that you can read it."

Dillon knew that Rand was popular with libertarians and that her "objectivism" philosophy had spawned a fringe political movement. *Exactly the sort of thing Lightner had grown into. I've got to read that paper!*

"Dr. Putnam, I can assist you with any technical issues if necessary. Please, send me the paper as soon as you possibly can."

TWENTY-NINE

The wind hit Tara hard as she descended the few steps from the wastewater treatment plant, but not as hard as the sight of Jacob Lightner at the driver's seat of a parked golf cart, looking at her expectantly.

"Amanda, glad you're out of Spencer's tour. We've got a weather situation brewing," he said, gesturing at the sky, where Tara was surprised not to see any storm clouds.

Not wanting to give any indication that she'd been tracking the developing cyclone through her own means, she said "Really? Looks okay to me," as she put on her sunglasses. "A little windy, I guess. What's up?"

"I'm afraid that we're in the path of a small cyclone. They can develop quickly in this part of the Pacific. Unfortunately, this means we'll have to cut your afternoon tour short."

"The only thing left for me to see now is the energy bank, right? I mean, that was the only other thing that was left this morning besides Spencer's plant."

"Correct. You'll probably be able to see them yourself, but we won't be able to give you a guided tour as we batten down the hatches."

Tara wondered whether, if the cyclone hadn't existed, Lightner would have found some other excuse as to why she couldn't see the battery bank. "That's quite all right, Dr. Lightner. Please, don't let me get in the way of preparing for the storm!"

"Get in, then, and let's head to lunch." Tara got into the cart, and Lightner accelerated down a track that wove throughout the desalination machinery before emerging onto a straight path between solar collectors.

"Is there any way we can avoid the cyclone's path by motoring the island out of its way?" Tara asked.

Lightner was expressionless as he drove the cart, his wide-brimmed hat defying the breeze by remaining perched atop his head.

"Our tugs could tow us, but really it's anybody's guess which direction this thing will end up going. Best to just ride it out. We're big."

"So we're just going to float through it?"

"Hopefully not through it, but yes, we'll just drift."

"What precautions do you take?" She flipped a page in her notepad, ever playing the reporter hungry for a good story. And a cyclone would surely qualify, Tara thought as she scribbled away for show.

Lightner slowed his cart when they came upon an employee on the side of the track who was motioning to a valve wheel on a large pipe. "Yes, shut it off," Lightner said just before he sped up again. Then he focused his attention on Tara.

"Basically, like that gentleman there was doing, we shut off the energy production and water circulation systems. Close the seawater intake pipes and actually raise the pipe out of the water. We seal off the marina entrance and make sure the vessels are extra-secure in their slips. We cover the beach with a tarp to try to avoid losing all our sand. Board up all windows. We shut down the power tower."

"So you can't generate power during the storm?"

"We run off stored energy during storms. Batteries, and of course our special chemical salt technology.

"Chemical salt technology?"

"It's part of the battery bank. So don't worry, we'll have light tonight."

"That's good," Tara said, meaning it.

Ahead, the dining hall came into view, and Lightner pulled the cart to a stop in front of the building.

"Hopefully this storm will miss us completely, like most of them do," Lightner said. Exiting the cart, Tara silently hoped so. Mostly, she wanted off this floating asylum, but she had to play along for a few more hours.

"If not, though," Lightner said as he waited for Tara to get out, "you may have even more time for your tour than we planned. I say this because a helicopter cannot land here—indeed wouldn't even fly—if the cyclone is in our vicinity."

"Where can I get weather updates?" Tara wanted to see if Lightner would try to withhold this information from her, so as to exert further control over her.

"We have a central weather data station from which we broadcast alerts over Solar Island's bulletin alert system. Don't worry, you'll know what you need to do. We'll keep you informed."

I bet you will, Tara thought. Lightner started to drive off. She called after him, "You're not coming to lunch?" He stopped the cart and looked back.

"As much as I'd like to, I'm afraid I've got too much to do at the moment. But you go on. There are plenty of people there to keep you company."

"What should I do after lunch, since no tours are scheduled? Is there somewhere I should go?"

"Hopefully, even after we batten down the hatches, the storm turns out not to be a threat and we can resume normal activities. Until then, please remain either in your quarters or else in common areas. Avoid operational areas, please, and follow all instructions." He drove off without waiting for a response.

"Yes, sir," Tara muttered to herself as his cart disappeared around a curve.

Inside the dining hall, the table was full, the chatter lively. Tara recognized several faces, including Chris Tenner's and the group of men who'd fished out Bernie's cap, as well as Dr. Cobb. If they were concerned about the approaching storm, they didn't show it. As she passed the table on the way to the serving area, she overheard a lot of typical small talk. After making a plate of grilled fish, potatoes, and vegetables, she returned to the table.

Chris Tenner had made room for her, and so she sat next to him. Dr. Cobb was across from her, along with a couple of American engineer types she recognized but hadn't formally met. She wondered if she was sitting with the Resistance, if the lunch room organized itself that way, like in a prison with different gangs.

After Tara had a bite of fish, which she had to admit was delicious, she posed the question to no one in particular: "What's happening with the cyclone?"

"Category 2 now, but it's also shifted direction and is moving away from us," Dr. Cobb reported. "How's the meal?"

"Truly excellent," Tara said. "And I have a newfound appreciation for it after your tour."

They continued eating.

Tara wasn't sure what she was hoping for—talk of the storm, the Resistance, maybe another secret note slipped to her—but there was none of that, and a half hour later many of the men were standing up and depositing their dishes in the wash bin.

She was about to ask the remaining men, including Chris Tenner, what would be going on later in the afternoon when a voice over a loudspeaker interrupted. She recognized it as Lightner's.

"ATTENTION Solar Island residents: all personnel please report to their stations for cyclone preparedness, Stage 4. Repeat..."

With that, the table emptied immediately, the men scurrying to leave the dining hall, a few by way of the kitchen entrance to the greenhouse. Chris Tenner gave Tara a hard stare as he left, before cheerily saying, "See you at dinner."

Tara glanced at her watch. Dinner was a long way off. She had enough evidence already to bring a search warrant down on Lightner and Solar Island—but until she could get off of the panel, she thought, there wasn't much for her to do.

She walked outside through the main exit in time to see the last of the golf carts wheeling out. She could call in to Dillon, get a status update on the weather, on the helicopter, but she decided it was best to stick to the established protocol and call him that evening, after she had a better sense of what the cyclone was doing. She began walking along the dining hall, gazing nervously up at the sky as she mulled things over.

She took a couple more snapshots of Solar Island as she walked, continuing around the dining hall until it joined the greenhouse. She reached the end of the building and the entrance to the aquaculture area, its metal roller door locked down.

Then, as a fat raindrop hit her on the forehead, she saw the shed—the same shed she'd investigated earlier. The grate! *Something was down there.* Tara looked around to see if she was being observed. She didn't think so.

As more drops fell from the sky, Tara ducked inside the storage shed for the second time that day.

THIRTY

No sooner had Tara entered the shed than rain began to come down in earnest. She pulled the door most of the way closed to shield her from outside view. She looked around the simple structure, seeing nothing different from her last visit, and then she cast her gaze on the grate.

It was a square metal covering, about two feet on a side. Beneath it there was only darkness, but Tara remembered the dim light she had thought she'd seen and the sounds she had heard. She walked to the grate. She took her tiny keychain light from her pocket and aimed it down the grate, peering in along its narrow beam.

She could barely make out the contours of some kind of passage, one that appeared to drop a few feet and then level out, leading away, toward the back of the shed. She froze as a cart approached outside, its tires splattering water. She heard a worker chattering on the radio, voice fading as the cart continued, passing by along the path leading away from the food-production facility.

Tara knelt and pulled on the grate, testing it. She felt it begin to pull up out of its frame, and let it drop back. What would she say if someone came in while she was climbing through the grate opening? *Just doing some in-depth research for my report! Nothing to see here....* She doubted that would fly very well, especially with Lightner and his Sovereignty fanatics.

But what was down there?

Tara once again gripped the metal covering, this time lifting it from its frame and setting it aside. Next, she took the time to stack a few bags of potting soil in front of the open grate, to block the view of anyone peering in through the shed door.

Then it was time. Her keychain light in one hand, Tara gripped the edge of the opening and dangled her legs into the space below. Encountering no contact with her feet, she lowered her body some more. She was relieved when she felt the sole of her shoe touch a solid surface. She released her hold on the edge and dropped into the cavity.

Her light flicked off as her hand involuntarily squeezed it while she dropped, and she was thrust into darkness. Switching the feeble beam on again, Tara could see the walls of a narrow passage that stretched maybe six feet in front of her before coming to an end. She crept forward, the light clenched in her teeth, and saw that the passageway opened up to the left. That was when she heard the voice:

"Don't move. I have a weapon. Who are you, and what do you want?"

A male voice. One she didn't recognize.

"Okay. I mean no harm. Amanda Greystone, reporter. I saw a light down here and was curious."

A flashlight blinded Tara as the man assessed her from behind its illumination. She covered her eyes. "I'm sorry if I startled you," she pleaded. Who had she stumbled upon?

"Crawl forward, real slow. Keep your hands where I can see them."

Tara followed the instructions, keychain light still clamped between her teeth, until she emerged into a cramped room.

"Stop!"

She froze. The flashlight shifted and Tara could hear footsteps as the man walked around her in a slow circle, shining the light down from above.

"So it's true," the man said at length.

"What's true?" Tara said, still unmoving on hands and knees on the floor.

"There is a reporter on board. I've been out of the loop for a while. How did you find me here? Who told you to look in the shed?"

"No one. I found it on my own by accident. Dr. Cobb finished touring me through the food-production facilities, and I was waiting for Dr. Lightner to pick me up to continue my tour when I saw the shed. I stepped inside for a quick look, and I heard a noise coming from down here."

"Guess that'll teach me to be a little more careful. You got any weapons on you?"

"No."

"I'd say I need to pat you down, but you'd think I was a pervert, I imagine. Just turn your pockets inside out, would you? I have to admit, you don't look threatening, but you never know. I found that out the hard way. So just do it, please."

She did as requested. She heard a click as a small desk lamp was switched on, dim light emanating from its blue bulb. The flashlight beam clicked off, and she blinked a few times to adjust to the new light.

"Go on, get up."

Tara slowly rose to her feet, now looking around at her surroundings. The two of them were in a very small space—a crawl space, really—that had been converted into a living area. A mattress lie on the floor in one corner, a few books and magazines strewn about nearby. It reminded her of Spencer's place in the de-sal facility—a crude, improvised crash pad for a person in a desperate situation. There were PowerBar wrappers and plastic jugs of water, and, lying on a wooden spool being used as a table, she identified a handheld VHF marine radio amid a scattering of laid-out electrical components, including circuit boards, wires, and 9-volt batteries. There were also a few candles around the room, and taped to the wall was a detailed schematic of Solar Island, annotated with handwritten red Xs and various other notations. It was difficult for her to reconcile this space with her stored mental image of grand Solar Island as it appeared from the air when she'd first approached in the helicopter—gleaming brilliantly in the sun, its four windmills churning the air.

Tara could barely stand at full height, the ceiling a mere inch over her head, made even lower in some places where PVC pipes and electrical conduits ran through the space and back out again. The man whose room this appeared to be, she saw, had to stoop due to his height. He sat in an old swivel desk chair and held a length of metal pipe while he appraised her.

Standing stock-still while trying to appear as harmless as possible, Tara returned the scrutiny. She judged him to be a middle-aged

American man. He was barefoot in cargo shorts and a grimy T-shirt with a logo that read "Drifter's Reef Bar & Grill, Wake Island." He had a full black beard and thick, wavy black hair that looked like it hadn't been washed in some time.

"It's hot in here," Tara said, trying to break the uncomfortable silence. It was hot enough up on the island's main deck. Down here it was almost stifling. Even the greenhouse was cooler. The man got up, walked a few steps to a portable fan that sat on the floor, and switched it on. Then he went back to the desk chair and sat again.

"This is real awkward," he said, slouching in his chair. Tara gauged his demeanor closely. He did not seem menacing, like someone who had deliberately set a trap for her and now intended to exert control over her. Instead, he appeared genuinely caught off guard—as startled as she was—at having been confronted in the secret space.

"I apologize," Tara said. "Who are you? Have you been living down here? Did Dr. Lightner say you had to work down here?" Tara refrained from wrinkling her nose in disgust. Whoever he was, this person smelled bad, no doubt the result of many days of living in the confined space.

"Not exactly, no, although you're right that he has been known to do that sort of thing."

"Who are you?" she repeated. "What's your name?"

He didn't answer immediately, instead looking into her eyes while he made a decision.

"My name is Bernard Riley."

THIRTY-ONE

"Bernard Riley?"

Even though she was a seasoned investigator, Tara Shores was unable to contain her surprise upon learning the identity of this peculiar castaway.

"Yeah. Why? Heard of me?" He averted his gaze, staring at the floor.

"I thought you were dead."

"Everybody does. That's the way I want it."

Tara's head spun. Riley had been in on the attempted technology-design theft with Chris Tenner, who believed that Riley had been killed by Lightner—believed it strongly enough that he had sent off the message to the FBI.

"Why do you want everyone to think you're dead? They're all looking for you. They found your cap in the water the other day."

"I tossed that overboard on purpose. Knew it would be convincing." He grinned at her ever so briefly before staring down at the floor.

"But why?" Tara could see in Riley's face that he had reached his limit. His brow furrowed as he looked up from the floor.

"Look, lady, I know you're a reporter and it's in your nature to ask questions, but you're out of your league here. Trust me on that, okay? This is not something anybody wants in some article about alternative energy. You should get out of here. I would appreciate it if you say nothing."

Tara felt for the man. He was scared, lonely, and still he was not willing to threaten or coerce her into silence, as she feared he might try. Not that it would matter. She had a little trump card of her own that it was now time to play.

"I'm not a reporter. I'm Special Agent Tara Shores, FBI."

Riley's eyes widened. Then he broke into peals of laughter that he self-regulated for volume. He stood and walked to a battered old two-drawer filing cabinet, looking back to smile good-naturedly at Tara as he went. She stiffened as he bent to open a drawer. Riley laughed again, slapping his knee.

"I could be reaching for my .45, is that it?" he said, pulling an object out of the drawer. It was a fifth of cheap rum, three quarters empty. When she said nothing, he went on. "Wish it was a gun, have to admit that. But this here will have to do. Sip?"

He held out the open bottle to her, an offering that she refused with a curt wave of the hand. Now was not the time to let her guard down.

"Have it your way," Riley said, stooping down so that he could tilt his shaggy head back to chug the liquor.

"What I don't understand is why you wanted Chris Tenner to think you're dead."

Riley pulled the bottle from his lips. His mouth closed, his eyes narrowed. She could see him flexing the hand not holding the bottle. Some kind of nervous reflex, she supposed.

Her question was so loaded with implicit meaning that he didn't speak for almost a full minute—just stood there, stooped in the crawl space, one hand dangling the rum. Finally, he said, "You met Chris Tenner?"

Tara responded immediately, wanting him to know that the games were over. "Chris Tenner is the reason I'm here. He sent the FBI a call for help. Said you and he—together—were involved in a plan to steal one of Lightner's engineering designs—the battery technology, to be precise—by sunburning the schematic and chemical formula onto your back. Chris thinks that somehow Lightner got wind of your plan and threw you overboard the night before you were supposed to go to Japan on shore leave."

Riley was agape now, speechless. The bottle slipped in his fingers, but he gripped it before it could be fully claimed by gravity. That effort apparently was all he could muster, for he remained silent.

"F. B. I." Tara intoned slowly, over-enunciating each letter.

Slowly, Riley lifted the rum to his lips. After taking a long, slow pull, he looked Tara in the eye.

"Why do you think I'm down here? For the deluxe accommodations?"

"Why didn't you tell Chris you were going into hiding?"

Riley took another pull off the rum and then sat on the wooden spool, cradling his head in his hands as he spoke. "I couldn't go through with the plan Chris and I came up with to take the battery design to Japan. I did the sunburn part; but that night after I met with Chris, I got cold feet. I was scared Lightner would catch me in his inspection line to board the shore-leave ferry the next day."

"But you already knew about the inspection. Chris said you had both planned meticulously for this."

Riley looked up at Tara, fingers lazily dragging the rum bottle across the floor.

"We did, but planning it and actually going through with it are two different things. In the middle of the night I chickened out and decided I didn't want Chris to know. He'd just try to talk me out of it. I was also worried that somehow Lightner might find out how close we had come to stealing the battery design, and that he really *would* have me thrown overboard one night. I was the one with the design burned onto my back, not Chris. Rather than deal with him and Chris, I figured it would be easier to go into hiding and try to sneak off at the next energy-transfer stop. Just get out of here altogether and never look back.

"Look," he continued, pulling his T-shirt over his head and shifting so that his bare back was displayed to her.

Tara sucked in her breath as she looked at Riley's exposed back. The intricate etchings were easily visible, no longer red, but more like a decent suntan in contrast to the rest of his pale skin. Quickly she pulled out her digital camera and snapped a picture.

The camera's flash was blinding in the dim space.

"This will help to document the case against Dr. Lightner and what's been going on here," she said.

He sat up and put his shirt back on. "But what I did was wrong, too.

What about me? I was so worried about Lightner that I never stopped to realize that I was breaking the law too."

What about me? There it was. *It always comes down to that,* Tara thought.

By this point in her career, she had cracked many cases, most ordinary, some unusual, a few spectacularly so; but what they all had in common was that by the end, those she investigated had always asked, *What about me?* It was an eventuality she was well prepared for.

"Cooperate with me, help me bring Lightner down, and I'll help you. Besides, I'm not here about some industrial espionage or engineering-design theft. I'm here because the CIA is concerned about Lightner's volatile effect on South Pacific and Southeast Asian politics, and because people have been dying. I had thought you were one of those people." She gave him a hard stare as she said the last sentence.

"I did what I thought I had to do to survive. I had no way of knowing you were coming."

"Well, just so you know, Chris Tenner contacted the FBI after you disappeared. He was looking out for you."

Riley took a sip of rum and scratched his stubble. "How many FBI agents are with you? Where's the rest of your team?"

"You're looking at her."

Riley choked a little on his rum as he digested the news. "You came alone?"

"My partner was supposed to come along with me, posing as my photographer; but when we got here, Lightner said it had to be just me."

Riley grunted. "Guards this floating asylum like a junkyard dog, he does. So, when's the cavalry coming?"

It irritated Tara that no one seemed to think she was capable of handling things on her own. It was not her choice to have come alone, though. "Weather permitting, a helicopter will be here tomorrow morning to take me back to Guam."

Bernard shook his head. "Weather's not going to permit," he said, eyeing the handheld radio on the spool.

"So you know about the cyclone?"

"Sure as shootin'. Been getting updates every few hours. Honey, I'm not going to lie to you. It doesn't look good. The thing is heading right for us. At night I do some sneaking around, you know, to see what's happening. Last night I checked on our position from a GPS panel. Seems to me Lightner's heading us *into* the cyclone."

Tara nodded. "You're not the first one to notice that. Why would he do that?"

"Lightner's a cocky son of a bitch. To the public, he'll probably say it's to 'demonstrate Solar Island's resilience to extreme weather' or some crap like that, but I've seen him change course before, and he's always had his own reason for it, like I'm afraid he does this time."

"What reason?"

"He knows who you are, honey. He's figured you out, and wants you gone. What better way to do it than to say you were lost in the chaos of the cyclone?"

"I don't see how he could have made my cover. My satellite phone is encrypted; I only use it at night when I'm sure no one's listening. He did take my biometric data, but since I'm an FBI agent it's not easily cross-referenced."

Riley appeared to have trouble formulating his next words. He weighed them carefully, Tara could see. He swept an arm at the assemblage of electronic parts strewn on top of the wooden spool he used as a work table.

"See those?"

Tara eyeballed a soldering iron lying next to the pile of circuit boards, wires, and batteries.

"Yeah?"

"I use the parts to keep my radio going and a few other little tricks to avoid detection; but let me tell you, Lightner's got some tricks of his own. Take this, for example."

He went to the spool and brought back a small black box attached to a fuzzy rod about the thickness of a pencil. "This here's a sound-gathering microphone. I found it glued underneath one of the heliostats, over by the marina."

"I searched my room for bugs, manually, but with great care. Didn't find any."

Riley shook his head, pointing the fuzzy rod at her as he spoke. "This is not a bug, as in a teeny little mic people can look for if it's in their room. This thing can pick up and transmit whispered voices a hundred yards away. My guess is he has one or two of 'em somewhere nearby your living quarters. If it's only a few yards away, it'll pick up soft conversation right through walls and closed windows."

Tara felt a chill overcome her despite the heat of the cramped space. "You think he's been monitoring my phone calls from my quarters?"

"There's a decent possibility of it. Same goes for any private conversations you may have had with Chris. Where did you meet with him to talk about Lightner's activities?"

Tara gave Riley a brief account of her trip to the beach with Tenner. Riley again shook his head after hearing it.

"Like I said, I found this one near the marina. Who knows how many more there are?"

Tara suddenly felt claustrophobic in Riley's impromptu living quarters. More than ever, she wanted to get off Solar Island. She looked at her watch. "I think I should make a call to my partner and check in on the helicopter status now."

"Here, take this," Riley said, reaching back over to the spool and plucking a small device from the pile. He handed it to Tara, who gave the microphone back to him.

Tara examined the new device. Obviously something Riley had cobbled together on his own, it consisted only of a small piece of circuit board with a single black knob on it, a tiny switch, an LED, and a small silver disc that she recognized as a battery of the sort used in wristwatches or hearing aids.

"What is it?"

"Something I've been working on down here to pass the time. It's a radio frequency jammer. It stops the sound-gathering mics from transmitting what they hear. Tested it on this one I found," Riley added, wiggling the foam-covered antenna in the air before setting it back down on the table. "Just flip the little switch on and turn the knob until you see the LED light up. That means it's jamming something."

"Thanks." She pocketed the device.

"Would you come back tonight, give me an update?"

Tara thought about it. There was some risk to her snooping around at night, but then again she could use an ally. "I don't see why not. You want me to bring you anything? You have enough water down here?"

"Plenty of that," Riley said, reaching up to a white PVC pipe. He peeled back a piece of duct tape and opened his mouth, catching the trickle of water that fell from the pipe. "Tapped right into the de-sal outflow!" he said, wiping his mouth.

He was proud of himself, Tara could see; and yet, once again, it saddened her to see an intelligent man reduced to such extreme measures in order to survive.

"Maybe some food, if you can," Riley added meekly.

"I'll bring some," she said. Then she turned back to the exit.

THIRTY-TWO

Outside the shed, Tara strolled casually toward the living quarters, a calculated performance for the benefit of whoever might be watching.

Just out for a stroll before the cyclone hits, thank you very much. Getting some fresh air while I can.

And by the looks of things, Tara thought, looking up at the heavy clouds that now loomed and the blustery winds that caused her to rub her shoulders after the warmth of Riley's foul-smelling abode, she wouldn't have long to wait.

She picked up her pace, needing to get an update from Guam and to let them know about Bernard Riley. And maybe there was more to it than just that, she thought, waving to the driver of a passing electric cart loaded with plywood sheets in the back.

She missed Dillon, wanted to hear his voice. She was known for eschewing the advances of her male colleagues, but most of them saw her only as a potential conquest, a challenge.

She pressed on, fighting the urge to run. She heard the sound of hammering before she reached her quarters building. When she turned the corner around the dining hall, she saw people boarding up the windows.

"Just in case!" one of the men holding up a hammer yelled at her as she passed.

She gave him a thumbs-up and continued on to the door of the quarters building. She let herself inside and walked down the hall to her room. Around her, in the other rooms, she could hear conversations and rummaging as people prepared for the cyclone's onslaught.

She opened the door to her own room and stepped inside, closing it behind her. Her window was still unboarded, curtains closed. She removed the jammer Bernie had given her and squinted as she turned on the tiny switch. She turned the knob slowly from left to right. After about a quarter of a turn, the LED lit up green.

It's jamming!

But that excitement soon gave way to grave concern followed by mild nausea as Tara realized the implications of her discovery.

Lightner's been listening in on my conversations with Dillon! She wasn't sure which scared her more—that Lightner probably knew she was an FBI agent, or that he hadn't yet let on that he knew this. What was he waiting for?

She set the jammer on the windowsill and went to retrieve her backpack, which contained the satellite phone and laptop. But something was wrong: The pack was much too light.

She set the pack onto the bed and opened it. The laptop and sat-phone were gone. Tara dropped to the floor and searched under the bed in case the items had somehow fallen out of the pack.

Nothing.

She looked around the room, saw nothing out of the ordinary. Searched the desk and nightstand drawers. Nothing. She moved to the bathroom and checked there, again finding nothing unusual. All of her other belongings were untouched.

Someone came in here and stole my laptop and sat-phone!

She forced herself to sit on the edge of the bed and think this through. A little voice inside kept accusing: *I was stupid to leave it in here. Should have just worn the backpack during my tours.*

She could no longer directly contact Dillon on her own, but she had spoken with him last night and the plans to pick her up tomorrow morning, weather permitting, were already in place. She hoped that the helicopter would be able to be here in the morning, but as the sounds of hammering echoed outside, she was less than confident. If her air support wasn't here in the morning, she would have to reestablish contact to coordinate new plans.

She would also have to...what? She couldn't *confront* Lightner, but she would have to report the theft of her property. Not to do so would be odd. She would not accuse him, but would simply tell him that her items were missing and gauge his reaction.

After one more sweep of her quarters to make certain she wasn't overlooking anything, Tara went outside to search for Lightner. She couldn't find any golf carts that weren't already in use, so she started walking toward the center of the island. She wondered how many of Lightner's sound-gathering microphones she might be passing. After a few minutes, she came across a worker driving in the opposite direction. The man slowed as she waved.

"Do you know where I can find Dr. Lightner?"

"I heard he's in one of the windmills. I'm sorry, I don't know which one."

"How many are there?"

"Four, equally spaced around the island's edge."

Tara flashed on the white structures as she had seen them from the helicopter on the way in.

"I'm sorry," the worker was saying, "I would take you, but I have orders to get to the greenhouse right away to help with the cyclone-proofing."

"You better do that. Greenhouse and cyclone doesn't sound like a good mix." The man laughed as he drove off.

Tara took a path on foot that radiated toward the edge of the island. She emerged from a solar tunnel and looked at the sky. It was getting dark, and the storm was coming. The sounds of hammers on plywood rebounded around her as she made her way to the island's perimeter.

She saw the first windmill before she reached the guard railing. Tara had no experience with windmills, but she was surprised at how substantial this one was. A white tower ten stories high with the thickness of a lighthouse, it was not simply a fan on a stick. The vanes were gargantuan structures sweeping the air in a blur at close to a hundred miles per hour. Tara approached the building, wishing she could find out which of the four windmills Lightner was in without going inside each one. She saw no people around, though, and so approached the windmill.

Up close, the structure was impressive enough that Tara wondered why it hadn't been part of the tour. Probably because the energy from wind they provided was only a side project for the mighty Solar Island, but still. She craned her neck, looking up along the tower's sleek lines that reached for the gray sky.

In front of her, a door was set into the tower's smooth base. Beyond the tower, the sea was no longer calm. The wind had whipped its surface up into a white-capped mosaic. Tara could feel no difference in the stability of the island, but the angry water made her wonder how long that could last. She turned the door handle and pulled.

Locked.

She hoped that meant Lightner wasn't inside this one. She couldn't see the next windmill, so she started walking along the island's perimeter. It took her about fifteen minutes to get to windmill number two, and she was disappointed to find that it, too, was locked, its vanes churning the blustery air. Tara examined the area around the door closely, but there was no door buzzer, intercom, or any kind of signaling device. She even tried knocking, but when there was no response she hit the road again for the next windmill.

Naturally, if there are four of them, the one I want would have to be the fourth one I try, she thought. But when she reached the third windmill, she strode up to it and heaved the door open. The inside of the structure revealed a spiral staircase leading up. She stepped inside.

She yanked the door shut after her, leaving it unlocked. She looked, but there was no intercom or controls of any kind here either. Taking a deep breath, she started up the ten-story spiral staircase, making no effort at stealth. She didn't want to surprise anyone, especially not Lightner. She was here to get her things back; that was all. She would play the role of an angry reporter wanting her laptop and phone back so she could do her job of writing a green-energy piece for a popular magazine.

Tara could hear a machine-like noise that grew louder as she ascended. When she reached the top of the staircase, she was greeted with another vestibule area featuring a closed door. She could tell that the source of the noise would be much louder behind the door.

She knocked forcefully. After a few seconds, the door swung slowly open, and Dr. Jacob Lightner's white-tufted head peeked out from behind it.

"Did you know, Amanda, that wind power kills more people each year than does nuclear power? Not many people realize that, but fires, ice on the blades—not a problem here, of course—and falling blades kill hundreds of people every year. Nuclear deaths only occur every few decades in a major catastrophe."

Tara was still breathing heavily from the climb, but she kept her composure. Was he deliberately trying to catch her off guard? To annoy her? *If he actually knows that my stuff is missing, then he's really toying with me.*

"Dr. Lightner." She paused for breath. "That's all very fascinating. But I'm here because my laptop and satellite phone have been taken from my room. I left them in my backpack under the bed. Do you know what might have happened to them?"

"They're missing? No one has been instructed to enter your room at all, not even a cleaning service. This isn't the Hilton, after all." Tara tried to maintain eye contact with him while he spoke, but his shifty gaze made it impossible. He spoke rapidly, too, as if wanting to rush past the topic.

"That doesn't answer my question."

"Do come in; let's talk about this. I'm sorry you had to come all this way; it couldn't have been easy tracking me down up here."

"Third time's the charm."

"Dearest me, I'm ever so sorry. I've been on the communications team about installing an intercom system at the base of the windmills, but, well, you know...it's action item number forty-seven or whatever on the to-do list, right?"

Tara stepped into the room at the top of the windmill.

"There you are, do come in." Lightner pulled the door shut. He raised his voice to be heard above the machinery. "Now, then, you say you can't find your personal things?"

Despite how angry she was at Lightner's suggestion that she might have simply misplaced her things, the view from their lofty perch nearly took away what remained of Tara's breath after the stair climb. Acrylic windows like the kind used in large-scale fish tanks were set into the windmill's wall for a 270-degree view. They were one hundred and twenty feet above the Pacific, whose surface now churned with wind. The broad, curving expanse of Solar Island itself was visible to the right and left.

She could pick out electric carts driving along the paths like little white ants busily laboring for their queen. It was all very interesting, but it didn't change the fact that her gear had been stolen.

"It's not that I can't find them. They've been taken from my room. Either they've been stolen, or...I thought maybe it was part of one of your security programs."

Lightner turned away from her and put his hands on a control panel. "I've got to turn the blades off, you see, before the wind speeds get too high. I didn't take your things. But fear not, intrepid reporter. I can provide you with a computer and satellite phone to use until you leave."

"Dr. Lightner! I demand to know what happened to my things!"

At that moment, a gust of wind hit the tower and Tara could feel the structure sway. Lightner registered the concern in her eyes.

"Don't worry, these windmills are designed to have some play in them. I've shut this one down. Listen!"

Lightner cupped his hand to an ear and pointed out the window toward the blades, which gradually creaked to a stop. Tara sensed the change in the "play" of the structure that Lightner had just mentioned as the blades locked into place.

"Quickly, I need to move on to the others."

Tara stepped aside as he charged down the stairs. Skipping down after him, she could see him talking on a radio. Outside, he went around behind the windmill—to the ocean-facing side—and there was his cart waiting for him. He took the driver's place at the wheel and told Tara to take the passenger seat.

She got in, and Lightner started the cart as a fresh gust of wind blew across the island.

THIRTY-THREE

Guam, Big Eye Heliport

Rob Tanner completed a second check of the Sikorsky S-61R's hydraulic systems. He had flight mechanics at his disposal, but for this job he wanted to triple-check everything personally. The bird was fueled and ready—he'd gone through the post-flight checklist yesterday after returning from Solar Island and an early pre-flight this morning—but he wanted to be able to leave on a moment's notice. The scheduled pickup wasn't until the following morning, but from the sound of the regular updates he'd been receiving from Dillon, he might get the call for an urgent extraction mission at any time.

"Excuse me—excuse me, sir?" Rob closed an access panel on the Sikorsky and turned to look beyond the chain-link fence that surrounded the heliport maintenance area. A Japanese family of three stood there, a young boy clutching the fence, looking eagerly at the aircraft. "This where we go for aerial tour?" the father asked in accented English.

The question reminded Rob that he was wearing the civilian uniform of a private air charter company. These people thought he was a tourist helicopter pilot, which was his cover. With all of the politeness he could muster, Rob explained to them that they needed to check in with the front office first, and pointed the way. He felt strange playing at being some customer service–oriented touring pilot; but at the same time, the encounter gave him a newfound respect for what Tara Shores must be going through, so completely pretending to be someone else.

He picked up his tool kit and threaded his way down a flagstone path lined with ferns and small palms to a screen door set into the side of an old wooden building. He paused before opening it to look skyward. He saw the typical clear-blue tropical sky, but also noticed that the tops of the coconut palms were waving in a forceful wind.

Rob stepped inside the one-story structure that served as a combination maintenance garage and back office. A mechanic was working on a tail-rotor assembly on the far side of the garage. A narrow work desk supported an Internet-connected computer and a weather fax. Rob went to the computer and checked the National Weather Service page for an update on the area affected by his likely flight path out to Solar Island.

The red type on the page warned:

> Current conditions: Category 3 cyclone. All sea and air traffic urged to avoid area for next 48–72 hours.

"What's this?" Rob muttered under his breath as he zoomed in on the satellite image for closer inspection. In addition to increasing in intensity, the cyclone's path had shifted markedly since the last time he'd checked it.

"Hey, Rob," the mechanic on the other side of the room called. Rob jumped a little as he was ripped from his thoughts about how to deal with this new hurdle.

"Yeah, Fred, what's up?"

"I saw that storm you're looking at about an hour ago. Said Category 2, pretty far from here, but still, we're gonna get some pounding winds and rain. Looks like we got the day off tomorrow. You up for a pub crawl?"

Just then, the weather fax began spitting out an alert bulletin.

Rob almost told him he had to fly tomorrow, but checked himself. "Thanks for the invite, but I'll probably just catch up on my sleep," he replied as he ripped the paper from the machine. His "coworker" had been told that Rob was just a new regular employee and had no idea he was FBI. Only the owner of the air charter company was aware of this fact.

Sixty seconds later, Rob had stepped back outside and was on his cell to Dillon.

THIRTY-FOUR

Tara asked Lightner again about her stolen belongings.

"As soon as I shut down the windmills, I'll put an announcement out over the alert system."

This angered Tara. He was putting her off. But as she was about to protest once again, it registered in the still-reasoning part of her brain that Lightner was racing the cart fast—definitely faster than she'd seen him take it before. Was he really that worried about the windmills? He spat brief bursts of command into his radio with regularity.

"Why didn't you just have your people turn off the windmills earlier if it's such a problem?" she asked. "You knew about the cyclone hours ago." She knew it was a rude remark, but she was fed up with Lightner.

He turned to look at her as he sped around a curve. "Nobody's perfect! I built my own floating island that generates enough power to sell to other countries. Forgive me if I haven't shut my windmills down early enough for your liking. I'm doing the best I can."

He made a spitting sound as he turned away from her in time to pull the cart to a rough stop in front of the next windmill.

Tara was taken aback by his seemingly genuine outrage. He really had waited too long to shut off the windmills, she thought. Why else would he be so offended? Goose bumps cropped up on her legs as she exited the cart after Lightner, who was already running toward the tower while he fished out a key ring.

She heard a vibrating, thrumming noise. Looking up, she could see the blades of the windmill turning faster than before in the approaching tempest.

Tara ran for the windmill's door, reaching it just as Lightner got it unlocked. *Look at me, running for shelter with a madman. I've got to get control of this situation.*

Once up in the windmill's platform, Lightner turned some knobs and threw some switches on the control panel, identical to the one in the other windmill. They heard the whining noise decline in pitch. "Turbine's slowing," Lightner confirmed. He pointed to a trapdoor in the floor, indicating the access point for the windmill's energy-generation apparatus, including the turbine.

Tara didn't really care. She'd barely had time to pepper Lightner with more questions about her belongings before they were running down stairs again.

The rain started as soon as they emerged from shutting off another windmill. It blew sideways onto their faces, propelled by persistent winds. Tara noticed that the previous gust speeds were now the constant wind speed, with new gusts faster still.

"One more!" Lightner shouted, getting into his cart. Tara ran to join him, fearful that he might drive off and leave her behind. A streak of lightning cracked nearby. She couldn't believe how much the weather had turned in just the last few minutes.

"Is this it—the cyclone?" Tara shouted.

Lightner shook his head as he sped the cart around a curve.

"Not yet. We're caught up in a localized storm that looks like it's on track to be absorbed by the cyclone later!"

"Great. The perfect storm." Tara sank lower in her seat.

When they arrived at the last windmill, even Tara could see that something was wrong. A stream of black smoke was pouring from the turbine assembly at the top of the tower. As she stared up at the tower, a tongue of flame licked at the gray sky.

Lightner already had his radio out. "Fire, windmill two, all emergency personnel respond immediately!"

But as they stepped out of the cart, they heard a muffled explosion. Tara watched in horror as the entire top of the windmill canted over onto one side, flames shooting out of the created opening.

"Get clear!" Lightner shouted, but he didn't have to tell Tara, who was already hunkering down behind the cart, peeking around it to watch the ill-fated structure.

"Must have taken a lightning strike to the blade assembly and it traveled into the turbine," Lightner shouted into his radio. To Tara, he said, "There's hydraulic oil in them, feeding the f—look out! It's falling!"

Tara looked on as the hundred-foot tower began to topple—thankfully away from them. At first it canted like the Leaning Tower of Pisa, but then gravity took hold and it started to fall. The windmill sailed through the air, bits of flaming debris fluttering off of it, until it crashed onto three rows of parabolic reflectors and heliostats.

Tara and Lightner ducked behind the cart as an explosion of shattered glass ripped into the air above Solar Island. Tara covered her head with an arm, hearing the tinkle of glass shards landing nearby. When she looked around the cart again, Lightner was already surveying the situation. It wasn't good.

One of the absorber tubes in the center of a solar trough had broken, releasing oil onto the deck. The oil was already ablaze. A siren was heard approaching from behind them. "Fire cart number one is on scene," Lightner reported into his radio. "We'll need number two also. Step on it!"

The fire was now slowly spreading away from them on the deck, fed by oil from the ruptured solar-trough pipes. A fire cart rolled up to them and stopped. The electric vehicle was painted red. It contained a fire hose, oxygen tanks, and even a small ladder. Lightner headed over to consult with the driver. He cast a glance back at Tara and said, "Take my cart back to your quarters and remain there, please. Follow any instructions you hear over the PA system. Go!"

Tara was all too glad to put distance between herself, the disaster, and Lightner himself. She hopped into the cart and reversed it slowly onto a path leading away from the crashed windmill, then floored it toward the island's center.

Her mind raced along with the cart's wheels. By the looks of it, the fire was serious and would keep Lightner busy for hours. A smile formed on her lips as she hurtled through a solar-collector tunnel. But it wasn't going to be catastrophic.

It was just the distraction she needed. Even before the fire, it was clear that Lightner had no intention of assisting her with her missing items. If she was going to take matters into her own hands to retrieve her communications equipment, now was her chance.

THIRTY-FIVE

Tara drove toward the center of the island. To those passing her in the opposite direction in carts toward the fire, it looked like she was sensibly putting distance between herself and the blaze. But there was more than just that. Lightner and his staff were preoccupied, a situation she intended to take advantage of.

But how?

The rain ceased, which Tara was grateful for. In addition to staying drier, it would make the fire tougher to extinguish, giving her more time to think of something. She knew that what she needed was a radio, satellite phone, or computer from which to communicate with her field office in Guam. But where would she find something like that?

Tara crossed onto a new path between solar troughs and headed for the tower at the center of the island.

She could look for Chris Tenner, see if he had any ideas....

Her eyes remained fixed on the tower as she drove toward it.

The tower...the power tower, the helipad... Those things would be of no help to her right now. But there was something else, Tara thought as she emerged onto a junction of paths that gave her a clear view of the island's center structure.

The customs room—beneath the tower. She knew there would be short-range radios in there—walkie-talkies—but doubted she would find a VLF or ship-to-shore.

Was there a computer? She wasn't sure...she recalled Lightner's employee stamping her passport, checking through her things....

My things...I got all of them returned to me, except for...my extra pens and my derringer!

She recalled Darrien locking the little pistol in a drawer behind the counter. The thought stopped her in her tracks. She pulled the cart over and thought about it. In the distance she could hear the commotion of the firefighting effort playing out. Could she slip into the little customs building, grab her weapon, and get back out without being detected?

Tara left the cart where it was and set off on foot, now drawn to the center structure as if guided by some invisible force. If she did decide to enter the customs building, she didn't want the vehicle parked nearby to pique anyone's interest. By the time she reached her goal, she had made up her mind. She tried the door by which she had last exited. Locked. She knocked, loudly. If no one answered, she would attempt an entry. If they did, she would ask about making a phone call.

After standing at the door for nearly a minute, she decided that no one was inside. Looking about for passersby and seeing none, Tara removed a wallet from her purse. From that she extracted something Lightner had failed to detect in her customs search. A thin metal pin—a lockpick. Tara expertly slid the tool into the slot and, after a few moments of manipulation, felt a satisfying click.

Pushing the door open, she could see that the lights—in fact, all of the power—seemed to be off in the building. She slipped inside, pulling the door shut after her. She looked around, now able to relive her customs episode in much more detail. There was the high ceiling with the ladder leading up to the helipad entrance. There was the sign warning visitors to declare all goods. There was the conveyor belt, now motionless, on which her baggage had ridden through the X-ray machine, and the biometric station, its cabinet now closed.

Her pupils grew larger in the dim light. And there was the counter behind which Darrien had hidden her pistol. Deciding she needed to make this quick, Tara strode to the counter and jumped it, landing on the other side where Darrien had stood.

She began quietly rifling through cabinets and drawers. Most contained routine items and those necessary for customs work—stamps and ink pads, routine office supplies, hanging files. She smiled when she found a flask of rum in one drawer. It made Tara wonder if Bernard

Riley had ever been assigned to customs duty, or if Darrien was also fond of the traditional drink of seafarers.

The smile vanished when she encountered a locked drawer. Figuring this must be where Darrien had put her gun, Tara again went to work with her trusty lockpick. The locked drawer was even easier to pick than the door. She opened the drawer and saw her derringer lying there, along with her box of extra rounds.

Tara loaded the little pistol and then put it and the ammo into her purse. She felt much more secure—much more like a federal agent—now that she had a weapon, even though she would have preferred her Bureau-issued 9-millimeter Glock to this diminutive handgun. Nevertheless, it would have to do, and it was much better than nothing. She didn't know exactly what kinds of weapons people had on board Solar Island, but she had already seen the high-caliber rifle Lightner had greeted her helicopter with. She locked the drawer again and crept toward the exit.

The only windows in this room were placed up high, where the spiral-staircase entrance was. There was no way to tell without opening the door whether anyone was nearby. If somebody saw her leaving this off-limits area, she would definitely be questioned, and Lightner would definitely be notified. She put her ear to the doorjamb and listened. Nothing.

She pulled the door open a crack and peeked out.

A golf cart sat parked on the roadway in front of the customs building, not twenty feet away. It was a longer pickup-style model with a cargo bed, now empty. A Pacific Island worker she didn't recognize was kneeling by the front left wheel, inspecting the tire. She watched as he stood and got back into the cart, driving it out of sight on one of the tracks that radiated out from the center.

Tara slipped out through the door, leaving it locked behind her. She could still hear shouting, alarms, and high-pressure water hoses in the distance. She knew that she needed to make the most productive use of this unsupervised time that was possible. Once the fire was contained, Lightner would resume his patrols and no doubt check up on her.

She needed to find Chris Tenner and ask him to show her how she could contact her people. She thought back to the beginning of her tour. Chris worked in the control center, the island's automation hub. She pictured the one-story wooden building with solar panels on the roof.

An empty cardboard box blew by in front of her like a tumbleweed, the wind howling between the solar collectors. Hunching into the invisible force, Tara set out in what she hoped was the general direction of the control center.

THIRTY-SIX

Twenty minutes later, Tara walked up to the building where Chris Tenner worked. She opened the outer door and went through the plastic strips into the dimly lit computer room. *Remember, call him Robert Benson, his Solar Island alias, if other people are around.*

The point was moot, however, because she found Tenner alone at his workstation, a cup of coffee in one hand, and two screens directly in front of him. One displayed some kind of technical data, the other a satellite photo of the approaching cyclone.

"Hi," Tara announced herself, still not certain that someone else might not be within earshot in an adjoining room.

Chris Tenner calmly swung around in his chair. "Hello, Tara."

Tara gave Chris a hard stare. She flashed on the sound-gathering microphones and spoke in a low voice. "Stick with Amanda. Play it safe." Tenner nodded. "All right, *Amanda*, but we're okay here. Dobson, our statistician, is off-duty right now, probably boarding up his quarters. I'm on duty until ten tonight. You heard about the fire?"

"Saw it happen." She recounted her missing laptop and phone, then the whirlwind windmill chase after Lightner.

"He's definitely onto you. Be careful, T—Amanda. Lightner's a dangerous man. You saw what he's capable of."

"That's why I got this," she said, revealing the derringer.

Chris raised his eyebrows, then shook his head. "I guess you didn't get this far in the FBI by being too passive. I'm afraid you're quite a bit outgunned on this island with that little accessory, though. Lightner's got a whole collection, and so do a couple of his Sovereignty Movement people."

"What about you?"

Chris shook his head. "Lightner conducts strict searches of all employees who board. The handful of times I've had shore leave since I came to work here, I've been searched head to toe each time. He controls the arsenal."

"Did he ever give a reason for wanting to arm Solar Island in the first place?"

"Said it was to protect us from pirates. Solar Island is too big to actually dock in a port somewhere, so he doesn't have to worry about declaring weapons. It slows ships down to have to declare weapons when they get to port, so most are unarmed at sea, which makes it easier for pirates. I also heard him say once that if it came down to a confrontation with a navy, say the U.S. Navy, that being able to fight back a little might make them think twice about starting an international incident."

"But it sounds more like he's using them to control his people internally."

"The threat is definitely implied. It's classic Lightner: On the surface of things, the weapons are to protect his citizens from outsiders—pirates, navies, random intruders. But then there's an undercurrent of 'I've got the guns, you don't. I'm the supreme ruler of this place.' I've never seen him shoot anybody—a gunshot would be heard all over this place. But, as you've seen, his preferred method is to push people overboard. Like what happened to Bernie."

Tara sucked in her breath. "I've got some big news for you, Chris." She paused, observing him, assessing his readiness for the bombshell she was about to drop. She didn't have to tell Chris about Bernie still being alive, but she thought that together they could help each other.

"What?"

"Bernie Riley is alive."

"What gives you that idea? Did he float to shore somewhere?" Tenner was clearly excited at the prospect of Riley's survival. He stood from the chair, eagerly awaiting Tara's response.

"No. He's here. On Solar Island."

"*What?!* How—"

"Calm down; let me explain. I did some snooping around in between segments of Lightner's guided tour. I found a below-floor crawlspace area and went down there to check it out."

Tara could see Chris looking at her, taking in her words with rapt attention. She deliberately didn't mention the exact location of the grate until she had had a chance to gauge Tenner's reaction to Riley's deliberate disappearance. Riley had gone against their plan, after all. She didn't want to create further conflict on this island.

"Go on!" Tenner urged.

"I found a man living down there. Introduced himself as Bernard Riley. He didn't think I'd recognize his name."

Tenner frowned. "How do you know it's him? What's he look like?"

Tara pulled her digital camera from her purse and brought up the picture she'd taken of Bernard's back. She showed it to Tenner. "That proof enough for you?"

"My god! He's been here the whole..." Tenner trailed off and handed the camera back to Tara as he eased himself back into his chair.

Tara nodded. "He's been here the whole time, hiding out in this crawlspace area."

"I'm glad he's alive! But how is that possible? How did no one find him? Where is he?"

Tara thought fast. Maybe she ought to mediate the reunion, to ensure that they didn't fight, and to be present to coordinate a resistance effort that would allow her to survive long enough to be...she avoided the term "rescued"...to be *picked up* by her Guam team.

"I can show you. You want to go with me to meet him?"

Tenner shook his head. "I'd like to meet him, but I can't desert my post. If something happened while I was gone and Lightner looked for me...all three of us could be found out."

Tara frowned. "I think I've already been found out." She explained Riley's microphone jammer. Tenner cracked a big smile on hearing the story. "That sure does sound like a gadget Bernie would make."

Tara realized that they'd been talking for a while now. "Listen, Chris, pretty soon the fire will be under control and Lightner will come looking for me. I need to know if you can put me in touch with my people on Guam."

"Whoa, hold on. First of all, you've come to the right place if you want to know what's up with the fire status. That's part of my actual job. Hold on." Tara watched as Chris punched some buttons on a console. Red LED lights were lit up on a panel.

"Still showing ruptured oil lines in some of the solar troughs," he said, moving to a different section of the control panel. "Let me call up the video sector."

Tara recalled their trip to the beach, when she had wondered about them then. "That's right, you said the solar farm has video monitoring?"

"Not most of it, but a couple of small sections. Here it is: Look, they're still working on it."

A dedicated video screen showed the men using the fire carts to battle the blaze that raged in the solar farm. Looking closely, Tara could actually see Lightner himself pointing at something off-screen.

"Okay, thanks. Next question. Is there a way I can make a secure phone call or email to my field station in Guam to coordinate my helicopter pickup?"

Tenner swiveled to look at her with a furrowed brow. "Oh, right, because your sat-phone was stolen earlier today."

"And laptop. Right."

Tenner appeared to concentrate for a moment, stroking the stubble on his chin, swiveling in his chair to look at his console, then back to Tara. "I can't do that. All of my off-island comm channels, including electronic mail, are monitored. That's why I had to go through all that trouble to get a message to you, with the coded sound file and all."

Tara sighed. "I see. I wonder if it would be worth it to send a message anyway, even though Lightner will eventually see it. I can have an FBI team commandeer this place tomorrow with a single message."

Tenner gave her a look that said, *You poor, poor girl. You just don't understand, do you?* He said, "I don't advise that course of action. Here's why. I've been tracking both the cyclone *and* Solar Island's course. The cyclone is getting closer and stronger—I think it's going to actually hit us directly! And what's worse, Lightner has our course—I can't control that—set directly into the storm! It's as if he *wants* to head into it."

Tara nodded. "He does. Claims it's to test the island's strength, but really I think it's only because he doesn't want my chopper to be able to pick me up."

"What I'm getting at is that you can't count on your team being able to rescue you."

Tara bit back a response and let Tenner continue. "Even if they could get here, you'd need a lot more than just the two guys who were with you on the way out here—to subdue Lightner and his forces. He's not going to just surrender at the first sight of a badge. The FBI has no jurisdiction here."

"If I can get through to Guam, I can let them know they need to bring more men. We've been granted special extraterritorial jurisdiction."

"He won't give a rat's ass about that. We're in international waters. You know where he stands on that. You said you talked to your people last night, right? What'd they say?"

"They said they'd try to make the helo trip tomorrow morning, weather permitting."

"Weather will not be permitting."

"So I've heard. Let's think about this a different way."

"I'm all ears."

"Lightner's basically putting everyone on this island at risk by steering the island into a cyclone."

Chris waved her off. "Doesn't matter anymore. Look at this thing," he said, pointing at the weather-satellite image that depicted a tight, white-colored swirl over a blue background. "It's going to hit us, no matter what we do now—probably one or two in the morning. It's small but fast."

"Still, if he had motored the opposite direction early on..."

"Perhaps," Chris said. "What are you getting at?"

"We can use the storm as cover to take over the island. Stage a mutiny."

Tara's sentence hung in the air. Tenner's jaw slacked for a second;

then he recovered. "I thought I just said that your team won't be able to get to us tomorrow."

Tara exuded all the confidence she could muster. "I *am* the team, Mr. Tenner. It's not the optimal situation, but right now it's the way it is. You called the FBI for help, and I'm the one they sent. So you got me. Here I am. I'm doing the best I can. You want to get out from under Lightner's spell, tonight is your chance."

"But how?"

"We dig in and fight. You, me, and the Resistance." Tara could see Tenner's face taking on a look of disbelief, so she continued before he had a chance to close himself off to her proposal. "We skip the call to my field office. They'll know they need to come out here ASAP anyway after I don't make my daily call tonight. But if we can take Lightner prisoner and detain him until—"

"Whoa, whoa! Take him *prisoner*? How?"

"With this." Tara waved her little derringer. "And the element of surprise."

The intercom at Tenner's station crackled. "Benson, shut off oil outflow valve 67B, stat!" Chris Tenner's hands promptly flew over his controls before speaking into the intercom. "Copy that, 67B now shut off. Standing by."

Then, to Tara, he said, "That's why I can't leave my station."

She nodded, then continued. "I'm not suggesting that you abandon your duties. We'll make our move on Lightner in the middle of the night, when his guard is down a little, and when the cyclone will be at its peak."

Tenner looked at Tara as if she'd just sprouted a third arm. "What would we even do with him if we did manage to subdue him? Tie him to your bed? His allies in the Sovereignty Movement will storm wherever you try to keep him and bust him out at gunpoint."

"Not if they don't know where he is."

Tenner cackled. "They know every inch of this island! Some of them literally helped him build it."

"They didn't find Bernie's hiding place, did they?"

THIRTY-SEVEN

"Start a mutiny?" Bernard Riley said, looking up at Tara from his sitting position on a crate. He tipped his head back for a swig of rum while he considered it.

After persuading Chris Tenner to go along with her plan, Tara had left him at his post and crept back down to Riley's hideout beneath the shed.

"Let me hear the plan one more time." Riley set the bottle down and gave her his full attention.

"Tonight sometime after midnight, I'll use my gun to detain Lightner, and you and Chris will help me bring him down here, where we will subdue him. Tie him up, handcuff him, whatever we can do until the cyclone passes and my chopper can get here."

Riley let out a low whistle. "Ain't that the craziest thing I ever heard!" Then he leaned in closer to Tara. "You realize that there are two chances for this to go wrong. One: the capture phase. And two: the detainment phase."

Tara nodded, impressed. "That's how I think of it myself," she said.

"Lightner or his people will *kill* us if they get the chance, once we start this thing up. You understand that, right?"

"I do."

"If they get the chance to fight back when we try to take him at gunpoint, we'll be overwhelmed. It has to stay us against him alone. And once we get him down here, if they find us it'll be like shootin' fish in a barrel." He gesticulated wildly in the small space, his hand nearly hitting the pipework hanging from the ceiling.

"I agree, so I put it to you: Stay here and live in fear, hoping things will improve; or do something about it. I came all the way out here to help you. In my professional opinion, this is our best chance at survival. We're lucky he didn't burn us down to the waterline today."

Riley nodded. "I thought I smelled smoke. Then when my water pipe shut off, I knew it was a fire and they were diverting water to put it out."

"So, are you in?"

Riley looked around at his cave-like dwelling. "I'm tired of living like a prisoner. I'm in."

"Good. I'll come for you a little after midnight. Wear dark clothes if you can. Bring the best weapons you can improvise. All I have is my pistol."

"Yes, ma'am. Believe me, it'll be a pleasure thinkin' up things to beat the crap out of Lightner with."

Tara shot him a disapproving stare. "We're only going to use the minimum force necessary to exert control over him. No more. This is not a revenge mission. You will be aiding the FBI in capturing a suspect wanted by both the FBI and CIA. In return for that cooperation, you will be granted immunity against any possible industrial-espionage charges that could be brought against you by Lightner or Solar Island's investors. Do you understand?"

"I got it. Control him, don't hurt him more than necessary. Okay by me."

"Good. Get ready. I'll see you tonight with Chris."

Bernard appeared to sober up at the mention of his former partner in crime. "He probably wants to kill me."

"He was relieved to find out you're alive. Don't worry about that. Worry about continuing to stay alive."

She gave him a bag of rolls, oranges, apples, and a piece of fish she'd smuggled from the dining hall. Then she turned and left him there, sitting on his crate, looking around his hideout for things that could be used as weapons.

Outside Bernard's lair, Tara watched the weather deteriorate. The sky overhead was not dark and menacing, only a drab shade of gray, with no sun shining. Tara heard a scraping sound and looked back down in time to see a piece of sheet metal blowing across the deck. Leaning into the wind, she decided it was safest to be inside. She set off on foot for her quarters.

One of the fire carts passed her on the way, and she hailed the driver, who pulled over. "How goes the fire?" she asked.

The firefighter, a grungy-looking Caucasian in his fifties, gave her a shrug. "It's out. Who knows what kind of crap will start up next. I'd get inside if I were you, lady. Lotta these structures are just plywood sheets stapled together. Stuff's gonna be flying around, if you ask me." Then his radio erupted with some chatter. He picked it up and drove off.

Tara pressed on until she reached the quarters building. Entering her room, she was pleased to see that her window had been boarded over. *Should also help to soundproof it in here, not that I can call anyone. Nice and dark in here, too.*

Knowing that she had a long night ahead, Tara decided to get a couple of hours of sleep before dinner. She undressed and climbed into bed, and was asleep within minutes.

Tara was surprised to find the dining hall busier than usual—the most crowded she'd seen it yet, in fact. The long tables were occupied for nearly their full length, with Dr. Lightner at the head of one end, flanked by members of his Sovereignty Movement. She looked for Chris Tenner, but then remembered that he was on duty. Most of the other people she'd met were present, though, with the exceptions of Bernard and Spencer.

But something was different. There were no plates, no clinking of silverware. Tara watched as kitchen staff began distributing bagged meals to each person at the table. Then Lightner spoke.

"Let us give thanks to our brave firefighters who contained and extinguished the windmill blaze." Everyone at the table erupted into thunderous applause, even Tara, who truly was thankful for that. Lightner continued.

"We will be reevaluating the need for wind power going forward."

Lightner waited for a smattering of laughter to dissipate, then said, "With the cyclone on the way, we thought it best that everyone take their meals to go and either hunker down for the night in your quarters, or man your stations."

A chorus of agreement swept over the table. "Too much glass in here," someone said, referring to the high windows all around the dining hall.

"I quite agree," Lightner said, "and so once you grab your meal—fried chicken tonight!—please be on your way. The telecom system is working, as is the video alert system—for now, anyway. Be sure to monitor your radio channels: That's the most dependable means of communication. Gentlemen, together we will ride out this cyclone, and when we emerge operational, the world will know that Solar Island is indefatigable—both as an energy provider..." he paused for dramatic effect, holding up a glass of wine "...and as a nation," he finished.

Amidst the applause, Tara took a white paper sack from a passing kitchen worker. Then she rose from the table and exited with the flow of others doing the same.

THIRTY-EIGHT

Tara retreated to her room once again, this time to prepare. She hyperventilated, conscious of the fact that tonight would be one of the most dangerous of her career. She could not afford to overlook anything during this planning stage. She loaded and unloaded her little derringer, checking the action. She changed out of her shorts and halter top and into a pair of black jeans with a black long-sleeved shirt. She was glad that she'd brought the matching black tennis shoes, and she was especially grateful that she'd had the foresight to bring along her black windbreaker. She wished she had a black beanie cap to cover her blond hair—the regular hat she had would be useless in this wind. She'd brought no holster for the derringer, so she opted to simply carry it in her front right pocket. Not the optimal quick-draw situation, but it did afford concealment.

She hoped that Bernard and Chris would be able to come up with some preparations of their own, but she did her best to focus on what she could control herself. Rummaging through her backpack, she retrieved the Swiss Army knife that Lightner had permitted her to carry through customs, pocketing it as well.

As the wind slammed into her boarded window, she did some brisk calisthenics to limber up. While she exercised, she thought about what else she could do to get ready. Would the gun be enough? She knew Bernard had at least a lead pipe. She was counting on Chris to come up with rope and duct tape. She considered taking her backpack, but decided against it—agility would be her best friend on this sortie.

Tara wished she knew so much more. Where would Lightner be tonight? In his quarters? Where did he quarter?

But she doubted he'd be asleep tonight. He'd be steering his island through a Category 5 cyclone. One hundred-seventy-five-mile-per-hour winds. Would she even be able to survive that?

She wasn't sure, but she was Special Agent Tara Shores, and she would die trying if that's what it took.

She stood and jogged lightly in place, listening to the wind worsen outside. She tried to forget that she was on an island, to forget that a construction of Dr. Lightner's own demented mind was the only thing between her and the Pacific Ocean in one of the strongest possible storms.

She sat cross-legged on the floor and meditated, eyes closed, head tilted down, imagining peaceful green valleys and pleasant meadows, far from the sea. She pictured herself walking there, free of worries or trouble. Some time later, she opened her eyes and slowly rose. She checked her watch: 9 p.m. The storm would be hitting soon. It was time.

Tara slipped out of her room and looked up and down the hall. Behind one door she could hear men drinking and playing cards. Cyclone party. She wondered if one of them had been the one to slip into her room and steal her sat-phone. She pulled her door shut with a soft click and crept down the hall to the room Chris Tenner had said was his.

Making sure she was unobserved, Tara knocked on his door in three sets of three, as he had asked. The door opened a crack, and Chris's head appeared. He stepped aside long enough to let Tara enter, then shut the door and locked it.

He was wearing blue jeans with a blue windbreaker. "Ready?" he asked.

"Ready as I'll ever be."

"Your gun?" he asked, looking her up and down. She patted her pocket. He nodded, picking up a small duffel bag from his bed. He unzipped it and removed a small buck knife, a coil of rope, and a roll of duct tape. "Got the line from one of the boats before it got too topsy-turvy down there," he said.

They heard a percussive noise on the plywood sheet covering Chris's window. "Here comes the rain, blowing sideways," he said.

"Where's Lightner's quarters?" Tara asked.

"He's got a private cabin along the perimeter. I don't expect him to be in there tonight, though. He'll be on patrol."

"Is there a good place we can lie in wait? Rather than walking around looking for him?"

Chris nodded thoughtfully. "That would be the best way to go," he said. "It sort of depends on what goes wrong first, but let me think where he will surely have to transit through...."

After some discussion, they had ruled out certain approaches and solidified others, weighing the pros and cons of various options. Tara looked at her watch. It was almost ten o'clock.

"So we get Bernie first," she said.

Tenner nodded. "I'm not doing this without talking to him first. And we'll definitely need his muscle."

Tara thought that Tenner, like most men, was underestimating her fighting abilities. She didn't hold it against him, though. How could he know that she'd been trained in hand-to-hand combat techniques by the FBI; and even if he did know that, that she routinely won the spirited competitions among her fellow agents with the same training? How could he know that she had been forced on previous murder cases to put those very skills to use—with deadly effect—at sea?

Still, Tara reasoned to herself, if there was going to be any bad blood between Chris and Bernard, it would be best to air it out before they had to actually work together to take Lightner down. Having Tenner see the place where they would hold Lightner captive couldn't hurt, either.

They left and made their way to the living-quarters exit door. As Tara pushed the door open, she encountered resistance. It was difficult to open. At first, she thought someone was pushing back on it; then she realized with a cold shock of fear that the wind was doing the pushing. She managed to squeeze through to the outside while Tenner pushed on the door.

Tara was unprepared for the savagery of the storm. Sheets of rain blew sideways, pelting her in the face. She struggled to hold the door open long enough for Tenner to slip through.

Nearby, an electric cart lay overturned on a track. Chris eyed it and looked at Tara, who shook her head.

"We walk." The carts' roofs would catch a lot of air. Tenner pointed to a dark passage between two long solar-collector rows, and they ran to it.

THIRTY-NINE

It would be far too dangerous to remain outside for long. This was quickly apparent, even walking between the rows of solar troughs and heliostats, which themselves were bolted to the deck. The trough passages acted as a buffer against the rain; but when the wind came in as a downdraft, they acted as a wind tunnel, amplifying the gusts. After Tara slipped and fell for a second time, she stayed sitting.

"You okay?" Chris called back to her.

"For now. But listen, it's suicide out here. Worse than I thought."

"You want to give up?"

Tara shook her wet head. "No. We can make it to Bernie."

Suddenly they heard a crash as a loose section of plywood came flying from above and slammed into a heliostat a few yards ahead of them, shattering its mirrors.

Tenner waved for Tara to follow, then started moving down the tunnel of solar collectors in the same direction they'd been traveling. The going was slow and treacherous. Bent to the wind with eyes out for airborne debris, the surface beneath them slick with rainwater, the pair pressed on. As footstep blended into footstep and minute into minute, each turned over different scenarios of their hoped-for confrontation with Lightner in their minds' eyes.

They had almost reached the shed when a chicken half-ran and half-blew past them underneath a solar trough. *Must have escaped from the greenhouse*, Tara thought. She wondered how Dr. Cobb was doing inside his glass fortress. A few yards later, they reached the greenhouse, entirely boarded up. At least he had plenty to eat, she thought.

They took a last look around, and, after being certain that they were unobserved, Tara pulled open the shed's metal door.

Inside the shed it was thankfully dry, but the sound of rain hammering on the metal walls and roof was almost deafening. Tara watched Tenner as he looked all around the shed, a puzzled look on his face. "Where's Bernie?" he asked.

Tara took a few steps and then pointed to the grate in the floor. She knelt down and removed the covering while Tenner looked on in disbelief.

"After you drop down, pull the grate back over the opening," Tara said, shimmying through the entrance as the walls of the shed shook and vibrated.

She stooped her way through the tunnel. Behind her, she heard the sound of the grate sliding back into place, followed by Tenner's labored footsteps.

"Bernie!" Tara called out ahead of her, to warn the man. The last thing she wanted was for him to mistake her as an unknown intruder, and for her to be on the receiving end of his trusty lead pipe.

"I'm here," came Bernie's voice. "You okay, Tara?"

"Yes," she called, stepping into his crawlspace abode. "I've got Chris right behind me."

Bernie crouched in his lair, lead pipe clutched in his right hand, tapping the other end gently into his left. When he saw Chris enter, with no one else behind him, Bernie's face became emotional. He let the pipe drop to the floor. "Chris, I'm sorry. I—"

"It's okay, Bernie. Agent Shores told me. I understand. I'm just glad you're okay, is all." Tenner stepped forward and embraced his friend. He leaned back, holding Bernie by the shoulders. He shook his head. "You coulda just told me you didn't want to go through with it, you dumb oaf! Make everybody think you're dead...."

"That's to our advantage now, though, isn't it?" Bernie asked.

Tara nodded, ready to move things forward. "It certainly is. So, I hate to break up the reunion, but we've got work to do. Bernie, can you get us an update on the cyclone on one of your radios?"

"You bet," Bernie said, picking up a handheld radio and switching it on. A robotic voice gave weather information. Bernie shared the last of the rum bottle with Chris while they listened to the update.

"We'll be in the eye of the storm in one hour!" Bernie said, consulting some charts spread out on the floor. "Storm's been traveling faster than forecast. I've been charting our course as best I could."

"Nice job," Tenner said, looking at the map. "You're very close. It has been moving faster than expected. Judging from our GPS coordinates I plotted earlier today, I'd say you're only about five miles off. That's amazing."

"The eye is calm, right?" Tara asked.

"Right," Chris said. "But this girl's a fast mover, so we might only be in the eye for an hour or so. Also, the eye wall is the strongest part of the cyclone. So just before and after the eye hits..."

"...hold on tight!" Bernie finished for him.

Tara looked at her watch. After eleven now. "So we want to take Lightner down before the eye hits, if possible; otherwise, we'll want to wait until after we're out of the eye again."

Both men nodded. "Be hard to find him for sure in only an hour, though," Tenner said.

"I've got an idea," Tara said.

"Uh-oh," Bernie joked.

Tara went on. "Let's wait for Lightner inside the Control Center. Sooner or later tonight, he'll stop by there, don't you think?"

"I think he will, yeah, but it'll also be staffed by two people—and they're both card-carrying Sovereignty members," Chris said. Bernie nodded in agreement.

"We can say we wanted to get out of the weather but also be of some help. I offered to come along to report when I saw you heading out from the living quarters."

"But then it'll be three on three when we have to deal with Lightner. That's a pretty even fight, which is not exactly what we want."

"Four on three," Tara said, holding up the derringer.

"I wouldn't depend too much on that little peashooter. They might be armed too."

"I think the storm itself is going to be as dangerous as Lightner and his men," Tara said. "Instead of running around outside looking for him, let's lure him to us."

"How?" Bernie asked.

"We go to the Control Center. But instead of waiting for Lightner to show up and then having to fight whoever's there all at once, we take out the two men on duty first."

"Just walk in and storm them?" Tenner asked.

"I think if they see Bernie, they'll be ready to fight, so we can't let them see him. The rest of us just walk in and say we're here to help, can't sleep but don't want to be outside. Then, after a few minutes when they're comfortable with us and their backs are turned, we incapacitate them."

"Knock 'em out, or what?" Bernie asked. "And where will I be?"

"Bernie," Tara said, "I'm afraid you'll need to wait outside until we open the door to let you know it's safe to come in. If they see you come in, they'll never let their guard down."

"Okay," Bernie said. "Makes sense. So, how are you and Chris going to take them down?"

"I'll hold them at gunpoint while Chris ties them up and gags them."

No one said anything for a few seconds. Tenner merely nodded.

Tara continued. "Then, Chris, correct me if I'm wrong, but hopefully a command will come in to the Control Center, which will go unanswered, and Dr. Lightner himself will come to investigate."

Tenner's face lit up. He said, enthusiastically, "I can deliberately set some controls in a way that triggers alarms that will send Lightner running to Control."

"Excellent," Tara said. "So let's go do it before the eye hits."

"When we get Lightner back here," Bernie said, "we tie him up to those two pipes over there." Tara eyeballed the corner of the space, where two large-diameter metal pipes crisscrossed over a corner. She could see that Bernie had moved a lot of junk out of the way to clear a path to the area.

Tara nodded. Then she held up a finger.

"Almost forgot," she said, pulling her Swiss Army knife from her pocket. "Anybody want this?"

Bernie reached out and grabbed the little utility tool.

"The lead pipe's better than that," Tenner pointed out.

"Toss me your duct tape," Bernie said, unfolding the tool's largest blade. Chris tossed him the gray roll. Bernie peeled off a long strip and then held the knife against one end of the pipe. Then he used the tape to wrap the knife in place. When he finished, he held his makeshift spear up for inspection.

"Nice," Chris said.

"Glad to see you two working together again," Tara said before adding, "Just watch where you point that thing. Ready?"

The two men nodded and they filed out of Bernie's lair. Bernie carried a radio and the lead-pipe spear. Chris had a length of rope tied to his belt, the duct tape in his pocket, and a folding buck knife in a belted sheath.

Tara was in the lead as they crouched through the tunnel. But when they reached the grate, she could see that something was wrong. Too much light was coming through the grate. Then, with a start, she realized what had happened.

She called back down the chute: "The shed's gone!"

"Just go for it." She wasn't sure who'd said it, but they were right. It was doubtful anyone was walking around out there.

Tara popped the grate and pulled herself up. Immediately she had to struggle to stand steadily in the cyclone's fury. It was difficult to even look into the wind.

She held her ground as Tenner and Riley emerged from the opening. Riley especially was astounded by the storm's fury, having not been outside much for a week.

Tara had to yell to be heard over the storm. "Which way?"

Tenner pointed to a solar tunnel, and off they went. When they reached the end of the tunnel, they ran hunchbacked across the windswept open space until they reached the relative safety of another trough tunnel. Tara lost track of time as they picked their way across the island. Each of them fell and had to be pulled up by the others several times. Eventually they came to a deserted crossroads, and Tenner signaled for Tara to stop. He pointed across the intersection. The Control Center.

Tara dreaded crossing the open space. Unbelievably, the weather seemed to be intensifying—the wind even faster and more sustained, the rain heavier, the sky darker.

"Gotta be the eye wall!" Bernie shouted. Tara could barely hear him. It was like being in a tornado. She began to fear that she would be hurled into the air and flung overboard, never to be seen again.

"Ready?" Tenner asked. Tara felt her pocket for the derringer. Still there. She nodded.

"Showtime," Tenner yelled over the storm. With that, the unlikely trio took off at a sprint across the chaotic open space. An electronic message screen still hung above one of the cart roads, its display darkened. More electric carts lay on their sides on the path, including one of the red fire carts.

They reached the front of the building without incident. The wooden sign bearing the words "CONTROL CENTER" now hung from a single chain, flapping wildly.

"Bernie, you'll need to wait in this doorway until we come out for you," she said.

He nodded. "Maybe I can find a good use for that chain," he added with a grin.

Tara and Chris Tenner looked at each other. Her eyes said it all: *Ready? Once we open that door, there's no turning back.*

Bernie turned to Tara. "If the eye hits and you still haven't come back out, I'm coming in after you."

She nodded her approval.

Bernie stood out of sight around the corner. Then Chris opened the door to the Control Center.

FORTY

Chris Tenner led the way through the plastic-strip door, Tara right behind. She was surprised to see only one man in the room. Matt Dobson, the statistician, sat in one of the wheeled office chairs at the control console, his back to them.

"Hi, Matt. Came by to see if you need any help," Tenner said.

Dobson spun around in his chair, jittery. "Scared the *crap* outta me, man! You two walk very far?"

Tenner fielded the question. "Yeah, I thought I would see if I could help. Waiting around for my room to blow away was getting boring."

"What's with the reporter?" Dobson said, turning back to the control booth.

"Sorry, I was getting scared in my room by myself; I saw Chris going somewhere and I offered to come with. Report on how Solar Island fights a huge storm. Doing my job keeps my mind off the danger, I guess."

Dobson spoke without turning around. "Well, Chris, Jim Watkins was supposed to be on shift right now, but he radioed me to say it was too risky to leave his quarters and that he wasn't coming on duty. Said he'd maybe try to sneak over during the eye."

Tara and Chris exchanged a glance. Tara now had her derringer out. She nodded. Chris unhooked a length of rope from his belt. Tara raised her pistol and pointed it at Dobson while side-stepping over to him.

"How's everything running?" Tenner asked, hoping to keep Dobson mentally occupied right up until the moment he saw Tara's gun trained on him. Dobson shook his head of shaggy brown hair. "Crappy. Pretty much had to take everything offline.

Backup generators are looking spotty. Not sure we're going to have lights through the night."

Tara was now firmly within Dobson's peripheral vision, standing about ten feet from him on the left end of the control console.

"Mr. Dobson, on behalf of the United States Federal Bureau of Investigation, I need you to put your hands in the air, please." Tara spoke calmly but with firm authority. Even Chris Tenner marveled at the seeming transformation she had undergone from mild-mannered reporter to gun-toting federal agent. She held the derringer rock-steady in a two-handed grip, feet spread apart, pistol aimed at Dobson's chest.

Dobson was still punching buttons on his console, muttering to himself, when he turned to look at Tara. His features took on a surprised but also amused look.

"FBI? With a derringer, is that what that is?" Dobson asked. "Cool, but don't point it at me, please. They're wimpy, but you could still take an eye out with one of those things." He turned back to his control board, saying something about how people get crazy during a cyclone under his breath.

Tara wasn't going to lie to herself. She missed her Glock. No one joked about the Glock. "Let's hope I don't have to do that," she said. "Please put your hands up, Mr. Dobson."

"Do it, Matt." This from Chris, who had crept up five feet behind Dobson. His length of rope was at the ready.

Dobson slowly raised his hands and even more slowly spun in his chair so that he could see Tenner. "What the hell's going on?"

"The less you know, the better, Matt. Don't make us hurt you."

"Crap." Dobson bolted up from his chair and leapt toward Tara. She fired two quick shots from the derringer, one into each of Dobson's kneecaps. The big man toppled instantly, sprawling onto the floor, clutching both knees.

Tenner was on him in a flash, giving Tara a sidelong glance while he tied up Dobson. "Christ, lady, did you have to take out *both* of his kneecaps?"

"He had to be neutralized," Tara said, while reloading the pistol.

"Hopefully there won't be permanent damage."

Tara knew it had been a ruthless move, but she was operating alone on a floating industrial center in the middle of nowhere during a cyclone. If she was threatened, she would not hesitate to defend herself with tactics that put shock and fear into her enemies.

Dobson screamed a mindless, guttural yell while Tenner hog-tied him. "Sorry, mate," he said, stuffing a washcloth into his mouth, "need you to be quiet for a while." Then he duct-taped the cloth in place by wrapping the adhesive strip around Dobson's head several times.

"Tape his eyes, too," Tara commanded.

"Mmmmmph!" Dobson protested.

"Is that necessary?"

"Just do it. He doesn't need to see anything during any of this. The less you know, Mr. Dobson, the safer you'll be."

Tenner slapped a piece of tape across Dobson's eyes, and the man went limp, apparently resigning himself to his fate, whatever that might be.

Tenner and Tara dragged Dobson's immobilized body to the back room, leaving him just behind the console. He was out of sight should anyone come walking into the control room.

Tenner took a seat at the control booth, eyeballing the array of flashing LEDs and digital readouts.

"I'll go get Bernie," Tara said. She darted back to the entrance, where she cautiously opened the door. Bernie was standing there in the partial shelter of the doorway, soaking wet in the rain, a length of chain now wrapped around one arm. Tara waved him in. She was about to shut the door when she saw something unusual.

The sky—full of stars!

Bernie saw her looking at it. "We're about to be in the eye!"

Tara thought about Dobson's partner who'd said he was waiting for the eye to make the trek to the Control Center. "C'mon," she said, running back inside.

Bernie walked into the control room, and Chris quickly led him to the room in back.

"Good work," Bernie said upon seeing the trussed-up Dobson. He turned to Tara. "You shot his kneecaps out?"

Dobson grunted past his gag.

"I told him to put his hands up. He charged me. I neutralized him," Tara summarized.

Bernie raised his eyebrows but said nothing.

"Stay in here with him and watch him," Tara said.

"Yes, ma'am. Guess I better listen to you," Bernie said, taking another glance at Dobson's knees, now bandaged after Tara had found a first aid kit mounted on the wall.

At the control console, Tenner spoke to them without taking his eyes off the instrumentation in front of him: "I think if I shut off the emergency generator—which is what the entire island is running on right now—that Lightner will come to check it out."

Tara eyed the doorway, the derringer dangling at her side. "Maybe we should wait for Dobson's shiftmate. He said he might try to make it here during the eye. I can see stars overhead now—Bernie says the eye is almost on us."

"We shouldn't try to take down Lightner during the eye."

"But now that we've taken over this building, we'll need to maintain that control," Tara said. "This is our stronghold during the eye. It's defensible. There are no other entrances, right?"

"Correct. Unless someone comes through a ventilation duct or something like that, but why would they if they don't know what's going on in here? Let's see if I can get position and weather data." Tenner strode to a pair of LCD monitors and tapped on a keyboard. "It's a miracle we haven't lost our satellite dish yet."

"Where is it?"

"There are two. A big one that gets Internet and television from around the world, on top of the power tower. That one's in Davey Jones's locker right about now. But there's a smaller backup used only for data transmission that's over by the de-sal plant, tucked in there somewhere with all those pipes. That's what probably shields it from the storm. Anyway, I'm still getting data from it. Here's our position, and here's the cyclone."

He fingered the screen, where a red dot representing Solar Island was positioned inside a clear circle surrounded by a massive white circular storm pattern. It took Tara's breath away to see just how enormous the storm was. Living in Hawaii, she'd encountered a couple of hurricane warnings, but never in her life had she been in the middle of anything with as much power as this.

"Unbelievable," was all she could say.

"Sucker's two hundred miles wide. Good news is it's ripping along at a blazing fast clip—almost forty miles an hour!" Then he turned to look at her. "Don't confuse that with the rotational wind speeds, though. That's just the rate at which the whole system is traveling across the ocean. Top wind speeds in this sucker are approaching 175 miles per hour."

"And how wide is the eye?"

Tenner eyeballed the scale at the bottom of the screen. "About forty miles."

"So we've got about an hour to hold down the fort here."

Suddenly they heard the front door open and footsteps trammeling inside, fast.

"Stay here for now; look like you're working," Tara told Tenner. She ran to the wall adjacent to the door and trained her derringer on the entrance. She heard the flapping of the plastic strips.

Then a skinny male figure strode into the room. "Good to see you, Jim," Tenner greeted him, letting Tara know that this was Jim Watkins, Dobson's coworker who had waited for the eye for his chance to make it to his station.

"Hey, Chris, where's—" He froze in mid-sentence as he turned and saw Tara standing against the wall in her two-handed shooter's stance, the derringer pointed at his own chest.

Watkins put his hands up immediately. "I'm cool," he said. "Don't shoot."

She nodded. "FBI. Just stay where you are, keep your hands in the air, and you won't get hurt."

Watkins appeared doubtful. "Let me see your badge."

"I don't have it with me."

He actually smiled a little at that. "What's going on here? Mutiny?"

"Don't worry about it, sir," Tara said. "Just do as I say and I promise that you'll come out of this okay."

"You got it."

Then Bernie came out from the back room, swinging his lead pipe. Watkins's eyes grew large as saucers when he saw him.

"Holy...Bernie! What in the devil's name is going on here?"

"That's what I said, Jim," Bernie said, dropping his pipe and removing a length of rope. Some chatter came over the radio. Then Lightner's voice cut through it all.

"Control, gen line status, over."

Out of habit, Tenner's hands flicked over the controls, but when he started to respond into the radio, he stopped himself and turned to Watkins. "Jim, I need you to tell Lightner that the generator line signal amplifier has been boosted and it's fully operational."

Watkins appeared frozen as he processed what was happening.

"Do it. Walk slow," Tara said, waving the gun from him to the control console. Watkins complied, taking slow and deliberate steps to where Tenner sat at the console. Tenner slid out of the way as Watkins approached.

Watkins picked up the mic and parroted the message Tenner had given him.

"Okay, out," Lightner replied.

Then Tara had Watkins step into the middle of the room while Bernie bound his arms behind his back and tied his ankles together.

"Sorry about this, Jim," Bernie said, "but it has to be done." He blindfolded Watkins in the same way they had done to Dobson. Just before he was fitted with a gag and blindfold, Watkins said, "You're dead if you get caught, you know."

Then Bernie dragged him to the back and laid him down on the floor near Dobson. Tara left Bernie watching their captives, rejoining Tenner at the control console.

"How's the eye looking?" Tara asked.

"Forty more minutes," Tenner said, eyeing the organized weather pattern on screen. "Then I'll take down the genny, ignore Lightner's calls, and it'll be showtime."

"What can we do until then?"

Tenner took a deep breath before answering. He looked around the Control Center, cave-like with its lack of windows and low ceilings.

"Round up some flashlights."

FORTY-ONE

"CONTROL, monitor your generator line, we're getting intermittent blackouts here, over." Dr. Lightner's voice filled the Control Center as Tara and Chris exchanged glances. Bernie emerged from the back room.

"Control? Please respond." Lightner again.

Tenner got up from his chair. "In about five minutes I'll flip it off and leave it off. We don't want to turn it off too early, or we might attract more than just Lightner in here wondering what's happened."

Tara nodded. They didn't need the whole island converging on them. The terrible weather waiting just beyond the eye wall was their cover, but it was still some time away.

"Control? You read me? Stand by," Lightner said over the radio.

Five minutes later, Tenner killed the generator. Solar Island, a place built solely for the purpose of bringing light into the world, was thrust into complete darkness.

Tara flicked on her key chain penlight and Tenner lit up a Streamlight LED flashlight. It was all the light they had. Bernie came out into the main room, clutching his lead pipe.

"Let the mutiny begin," he said.

Tara aimed her light beam on the wall next to the door, near where she'd waited for Watkins. She was about to start verbally strategizing a plan for taking Lightner down when they heard the front door open.

"What the hell is going on?" Lightner yelled. They heard him throw apart the plastic strips. Tara motioned for Bernie to move next to the door. She pantomimed a low swinging motion against her knees. *Hit him with the pipe.*

When Lightner strode into the room, Tara was pointing her derringer at him from mid-floor, Tenner was out of sight in the back room, and Riley was right next to the door. Tara thought her demonstration had been clear, but for some reason Bernie struck Lightner in the chest with his pipe, a blow that Lightner blocked with an arm. Tara heard a sickening crunch as one of the bones in Lightner's forearm broke. Face contorted into a mask of surprise, pain, and fury, Lightner kicked Bernie in the thigh and then the two were grappling in the open room.

"Bernie, enough! Back away," Tara shouted.

Bernard had his pipe raised again, but Lightner kept him at bay with a series of solid punches to the body with his remaining good arm. No single one of them was serious, but together they were devastating. Tara could see that Bernard Riley, who'd been cooped up in a crawl space for a week on a junk diet, was no match for Lightner, who had made daily use of the exercise track during that same time.

Tara circled the fighting pair but didn't dare take a shot. "Chris!" she yelled. Tenner charged from the back room, the beam from his flashlight making a crazy zigzag pattern on the floor and ceiling as he ran. Head down like a bull, he rammed into Lightner, who was about to get the upper hand on Bernie. The impact pitched Lightner into the wall while casting Bernie aside like a billiard ball not meant for the pocket.

Tara could read in Lightner's eyes that he'd had the wind knocked out of him.

"Back off!" she said to Tenner, who sidestepped his opponent's grasp. That left Tara's gun with a direct line of sight to Lightner. She assumed the two-handed shooter's grip and aimed for the pinpoint of light from her penlight on Lightner's chest.

"Freeze, Dr. Lightner! FBI! Don't move."

Tenner directed his Streamlight beam onto Lightner's face. Lightner hyperventilated, his eyes shifting from Tara to Tenner to Riley and back.

"Chris, tie him up," Tara said.

"What is this? What do you want?" Lightner gasped.

"We want out of here," Bernie said. The Swiss Army blade at the end of his pipe passed through Tara's light beam, and she saw that the blade was covered in blood, though she wasn't sure whose.

"Where did you come from?" Lightner asked.

Bernie slugged him in the stomach. "Shut up."

"Bernie!" Tara yelled. "Chris, tie him up. Hurry."

"Mutiny. That's what this is," Lightner gasped.

"Dr. Lightner, I hereby place you under arrest on orders of the Federal Bureau of Investigation. Cooperate and no one will get hurt."

"Except for you," Lightner spat, while Bernie and Chris converged on him with ropes. "Mutiny is punishable by death."

"Put a sock in it, you old bastard," Bernie said. He stuffed a rag in Lightner's mouth and slapped a piece of duct tape across it. Then he spun him around to face the wall and tied his arms behind his back. Lightner grunted as his shoulder blades were pulled together by the bonds and his broken forearm was forced into the bound position.

"Don't do his legs," Tara reminded them as Bernie started to bind his ankles. "We don't want to have to carry him. Blindfold him, though."

At this, Lightner grunted furiously from behind the gag. When a blindfold had been placed, Bernie and Chris backed away from their prisoner. Tara continued to point the derringer at him.

"I've got my pistol trained on you, Dr. Lightner. I'll shoot you if I have to. Don't make me do that." From the back room came the sound of grunting from Dobson and Watkins. Bernie went back to check it out. Tenner moved to the control console. He eyeballed the weather screen.

"Cyclone's still moving even faster than expected. Second eye wall contact coming right up. It's about to get nasty again."

"Then let's move out," Tara commanded. "You ready, Bernie?" Bernie emerged from the back room. "Yeah. Tweedledee and Tweedledumb in there are ready for a nice nap in the dark."

Tara designated roles for the trip to Bernie's hideout. She wanted Bernie, the weakest, not to be involved with corralling Lightner. "Bernie, you walk point and lead us to our destination," she said, not wanting to even tip Lightner off to the fact that there was a secret place to take him to. "Chris and I will guard Lightner behind you."

Bernie nodded and skipped ahead to the exit door. Tara pushed Lightner out the door by the gun barrel in his back, to let him know she had it trained on him, while Tenner stood to his left side, gripping an arm in a vise-like hold.

Tara glanced upward as they stepped outside, marveling at the transformation. The howling winds and lashing precipitation had been replaced by clear skies, with the moon and the stars lighting their way. Knowing that the other side of the eye wall was not far off caused her to jam the gun barrel into Lightner's back a little harder, prodding him to hurry along.

Bernie's head was on a swivel as he walked point. They heard noises not too far away, the sound of a door being pulled shut, perhaps, or a plywood board falling to the deck. They even registered distant voices. But they saw no one. The calm eye weather made for easy traveling, and before long they were staring at the displaced shed, now lying in disarray near the greenhouse.

Tara watched Bernie wrestle the shed back to its upright position. Then he dragged it back over the grate.

Lightner made some noises behind his gag. Tara jabbed him with the gun barrel, and he was quiet. Bernie finished repositioning the shed and waved them over as he ducked inside. Chris dragged Lightner by his good arm as Tara followed behind, derringer aimed at Lightner's back.

Bernie wrestled the grate free and motioned for Chris to descend first. While they waited for him to squeeze down the hole, Tara addressed Lightner.

"You're going to drop down a tight vertical space. We will be right ahead of and behind you. Don't try anything stupid, and you'll be fine. Just let yourself drop down the rabbit hole, Dr. Lightner."

Lightner grunted once in response. Tara had him sit near the opening and then scoot forward until his legs dangled over the side. At the sign of open space, Lightner began whimpering.

"It's a short drop, Dr. Lightner. Maybe four feet." She wondered if he thought they might be pushing him over the side of the island. Would serve him right if they did, she thought, but she didn't want him to launch into a panic.

"Chris, reach up and grab Dr. Lightner's foot to let him know you're down there." Tenner reached up out of the darkness and punched Lightner in the ankle. Lightner grunted again in response.

"Push off, Dr. Lightner, and Chris will make sure you land okay."

Lightner remained still. Tara prodded him with the derringer in his back. He scooted forward until only his arms were holding him over the opening. Then he let go. Tara heard a muffled thump and an exclamation of exertion from Chris. Shining her penlight down the shaft, Tara could see that Lightner had made the drop and was now being led down the tunnel by Tenner.

Tara dropped down after the captor and his captive, while Bernie brought up the rear, pulling the grate cover back into place as he descended.

When the three of them convened in Riley's makeshift home, Bernard indicated for Chris to back Lightner up to the rear of the hideout and the junction of pipes that he had prepared earlier. Once Lightner's arms and legs had been fastened to the pipes, taking care to arrange it so that his broken arm was pinned to his body to eliminate as much movement as possible, Tara asked them to remove Lightner's gag.

Chris gave her a doubting look. "If he shouts while someone happens to be up there within earshot..."

"Just take it off. He's not going to make any noise. Can I trust you on that, Dr. Lightner?"

Lightner grunted emphatically.

"If you do make any noise, I'll shoot you," she said, stepping up to the now-immobilized and blindfolded Lightner. She ripped the tape from his mouth in one swift pull and then plucked out the washcloth.

Lightner exhaled heavily. "Where are we?" he asked softly.

FORTY-TWO

"You're in a safe place, Dr. Lightner," Tara said.

"Nowhere on my island is safe for you three anymore," Lightner said, defiant even in restraint.

"We'll see about that, you old bastard," Bernie said, switching on a battery-powered lantern. Tara shot him a disapproving stare by the bulb's reddish light.

"What do you hope to accomplish by holding me prisoner?"

"On behalf of the FBI, Dr. Jacob Lightner, you are under arrest for one murder which I directly witnessed, as well as numerous other crimes to be detailed later."

Lightner laughed. "I thought you were kind of a lousy reporter. At any rate, you have no jurisdiction here. We're in the middle of international waters."

"Do I look worried about that?"

Chris Tenner cracked a smile at Lightner's ensuing silence. "You finally managed to piss off the wrong people with your pseudo-political shenanigans in the South Pacific, lording your energy over third-world nations like some kind of power-happy despot."

Lightner wrenched his good arm against the pipes, and then his legs, but his bonds held fast. "Treasonous scum! I built an island that brings light to places where before there was only darkness!"

"Only if those places are willing to kowtow to your political demands," Tenner said. "You tell them who they can or cannot do business with in return for agreeing to sell them energy. You've been in talks with North Korea, for God's sake!"

Lightner made them all jump by shouting his reply. "Is a farmer not entitled to the fruits of his labor? I farm the *sun!* I bring its fruit to market. I am an independent entity entitled to make my own decisions regarding to whom I *sell* my commodities. I will not give away the fruit of what I have built to parasites!"

To Tara it was a surreal scene. A bound engineer in a crawl space on a synthetic island in the middle of the Pacific, thrashing around in darkness lit only by flashlights as he raved about economic principles. But something else was bothering her: Her sense of balance was off. Then she realized that even though she was holding her flashlight steady, its beam was rising and falling over Lightner's head. They must be fully back in the throes of the cyclone, and the entire island was now bucking back and forth, she envisioned with a chill.

"Please calm down, Dr. Lightner," Tara said. "When the cyclone passes, I'll be taking you aboard my helicopter back to Guam, where legal counsel will be available to you."

"Shout like that again and you get the gag," Tenner added.

Lightner cackled like a madman but said nothing further. Tara had to put a hand on the wall to hold herself in place as the island continued to sway under the cyclone's powerful gyrations. Bernie passed around some rations—power bars, sardine tins, even a few candy bars he'd squirreled away. Lightner refused all offerings of food.

They had settled in to wait out the rest of the cyclone's fury when suddenly one of the big pipes on the ceiling burst, unleashing a torrent of water. The force of the spray was dangerous, like a fire hose blast; and by the time the three of them had scrambled out of its direct stream, the floor of Bernie's hideout was covered with water.

"What's happening?" Lightner yelled. "What broke?"

"I said shut up, Lightner," Tenner said, but he could no longer move directly in front of their captive without braving the erupting pipe, which seemed to have no letup in sight. Tara watched as Tenner slipped and fell, cursing as he struck an elbow on the hard, wet floor.

Bernie sidled up to Tara and spoke directly into her ear, so that the sound of the rushing water would prevent Lightner from hearing what he said.

"We're not going to be able to fix that. The flow is just too high. That's the seawater intake for the de-sal plant. The only way to stop it is to shut down the de-sal intake pipe, from inside the de-sal plant. I don't know why they didn't do that already. But this whole little room will flood before we can get over there to do that. And the other pipes could burst at any moment too—and believe me, we don't want to be around for that. They don't all carry water, if you get what I'm saying."

For some reason, Tara pictured Spencer in his own little hovel in the de-sal plant, perhaps sleeping through the cyclone, dreaming of better days. "Is there any way we can radio Spencer, get him to do it?" She looked to a handheld radio on the wooden spool used as a table.

Bernie shook his head. "I just use it to monitor what's going on outside. Everyone uses the same channels, so if we use it, Lightner's people will hear. Also, by saying there's a leak in that pipe, they could look at a schematic and trace the pipe's route, possibly locating our hideout that way."

Suddenly another pipe exploded from the wall, unleashing an explosion of cold water that pelted them from the side.

"What's going on?" Lightner demanded.

"Your island's falling apart in the cyclone," Bernie said.

The four of them digested this amid the cascades of water all around them. Tara sloshed toward the exit to escape the onslaught of pounding water. She had to close her eyes to shut out a flashback to her childhood where she'd gone into a Florida canal in a car driven by her parents, and only she'd come out. Vehicle in the water. Water swirling inside. Darkness enveloping her as she went underwater. Her father's hands pushing her up through an open window...

"We have to get out of here," she said.

FORTY-THREE

By the time Bernie and Chris had managed to undo Lightner's restraints, the water in Bernie's lair was knee-deep. Tara had reached the grate and had her derringer aimed up as she looked through it. Bernie was behind her, while Chris brought up the rear with Lightner under his close control. The shed had blown away again, leaving the grate area exposed. Tara could hear only the sounds of the cyclone, so she popped the grate off and looked out.

No signs of people. One of the golf carts lay toppled in an intersection, and a plywood board went sailing by overhead. Never in her life had Tara been direct witness to such brutal weather. She did not want to leave the safety of their crawl space, but the rising water gave her no choice.

"Where should we take him?" she asked Chris and Bernie.

"Take me to my quarters," Lightner said. "Let me go."

Tenner kicked him in the shin. "Shut up!"

Tara could see that Tenner was scared, stressed, wondering how they were going to get through this. Tara thought fast. It didn't matter whether they wanted to go topside in this weather or not: They had no choice. In a few minutes, Bernie's hideout would be submerged. So the only question was where to go. The closest large structure was the greenhouse, with its glass windows boarded over. But would Dr. Cobb even hear them knocking? And there had been a lot of workers in the greenhouse, Tara recalled. Many of them were sympathetic to Lightner. What if they were still there?

Tara looked at the scientist now, firmly in Tenner's vise-like grip. She knew that behind his blindfold, Lightner was seething with hatred. She would have to be very cautious around him from this point forward. She had no doubt that, were the opportunity to arise, Lightner would kill her.

"Let's go to my quarters," Tara said.

No one had any arguments, even Lightner. But when Tara stuck her head up through the grate opening and felt the full force of the cyclone's wind, she wondered if it would even be feasible to travel the short distance to the quarters building. Down below, she heard some kind of scuffle start up and felt water splash onto her legs.

"C'mon, Tara, we gotta get this turkey to market," Tenner said.

She slid the rest of the way out of the grate and rolled away from the entrance, not wanting to stand right away and present a larger profile for the tremendous gusts.

Down below, she could hear shouting. She crawled back to the grate. Lightner was stiff-arming the lip of the grate entrance with his good arm, bellowing about how he couldn't see what he was doing.

"Take his blindfold off. It'll make it easier going for all of us, and we're going to need every advantage we can get out here," she yelled above the storm's fury.

She could see Tenner and Riley contemplating this as the water swirled around their thighs.

"Do it!" Tara prompted. They complied. Now able to see, with his legs free but hands still bound behind his back, Lightner allowed himself to be pushed through the grate opening by Tenner and Riley, who were quick to follow him.

The four of them grimly surveyed their surroundings as the cyclone ravaged Solar Island.

"Still think it was a good idea to head right into this thing, you idiot?" Tenner spat at Lightner, who merely smiled in return as the wind-driven rain pelted his face.

"Let's go," Tara commanded, rising to a crouched position. She led the way toward her quarters. She quickly found that because the wind was at their backs in this direction, they found themselves being tumbled along. Not only that, Tara realized with a start, but something else was different, too. Sometimes they seemed to be trekking *upward*, and then they would be sliding down across the slick deck. The mental picture of their situation struck fear in Tara's heart. Solar Island—the entire disc structure—was riding over colossal ocean swells, floating up over a crest and then riding down into a trough. How big must the waves be for a circle of a square mile in area to be tossed about so? She pushed the thought from her mind. It was too terrifying to contemplate.

Further adding to her stress was the fact that every time Bernie and Chris would go into a slide, Lightner would use the opportunity to try to break from them. Once he actually made it into the cover of a solar tunnel, but Tenner grabbed his ankles and brought him down. Tara had her derringer out, but she really needed both hands to brace herself against her frequent falls. Having the gun out made the going exhausting, but it was her only real protection against Lightner and anyone who might show up to help him.

Tara had no idea how much time had elapsed when they finally managed to travel the short distance to the living quarters. The sight that greeted them was anything but comforting. One entire wall of the quarters building had been sheared away. Tara looked directly into soaked and empty rooms—including her own, which was fully exposed to the cyclone. Tenner and Riley dragged Lightner up to Tara. The four of them stared in silence at the wrecked residence while the cyclone raged around them. The remnants of one of the hanging community monitors were visible lying in the roadway.

"What building is going to be safe?" Tara yelled over the wind.

Tenner shook his head. "If there's a safe building, that's where everyone will be. We bring him in there—" he jerked a thumb at Lightner—"and they'll overpower us."

Lightner's grin was like a beacon lighting a dark night.

"Why not pitch this bastard overboard and be done with it?" Bernie shouted over the weather.

Tenner nodded. "We could say it was an accident—he just slid off in the storm."

Tara frowned at them. She didn't always play perfectly by the book as an agent, but she would never consider doing something like that. She would take her chances with letting Lightner go before she killed him for the sake of convenience and then lied about it.

"Unless he forces us to, we can't hurt him," Tara said.

Then Solar Island began to tilt as it slid down another monster swell, and the four of them scrambled to move out of the path of an overturned golf cart careering toward them. It missed Tara by inches before slamming into the exposed living-quarters building, coming to a rest against someone's bed.

Tenner looked at Tara as he held on to Lightner. "We've got to get inside. Maybe we can hold him hostage. I could hold the gun right to his head to keep his people at bay."

Tara had to admit that she didn't have a better option. To remain out here was to play Russian roulette with the cyclone. It was only a matter of time before they were killed. To enter one of the more structurally sound buildings, where everyone else would likely be, would be to start a battle or a siege. But, as Tara watched a scythe-shaped section of glass from one of the solar troughs skim across the deck, she decided that a sheltered siege was preferable to this exposure.

"Where's the nearest safe building?" Tara asked.

"De-sal," Bernie and Chris said at the same time.

Tara nodded. She knew she at least had an ally with Spencer, who was in charge of de-sal. As the cyclone raged around them, she couldn't think of anywhere else to go.

"Point the way," Tara said, bracing herself against the cyclone's fury.

FORTY-FOUR

Guam

"Sorry to wake you, Rob, but I still haven't heard from her," Dillon said into his phone as he stared out of his hotel window with trepidation at the hard rain and heavy winds that lashed the island.

"Seen what it looks like outside?" Rob asked. If he was groggy from being awakened, he didn't sound it, Dillon thought.

"Looking at it now. Can't even see the beach across the street."

"Lovely night for a helicopter ride, isn't it? Guam International is closed for all takeoffs and landings."

"What about the heliport?" Dillon asked, concerned that local aviation authorities wouldn't even permit them to fly.

"Don't worry, we can take off from the heliport if we're crazy enough to physically try it. I've got a special clearance."

"I don't want to do it, Rob, believe me. But Agent Shores is supposed to be picked up later this morning; and without hearing from her, I have to assume that either the cyclone knocked out all communications on Solar Island, or she's in trouble out there."

"Or both."

Dillon exhaled sharply. "Tell you what," he said; "how about you go get the chopper ready while I beg the analysts in Langley for another satellite fix on Solar Island's position. We should be ready to leave pre-dawn."

Dillon heard Rob's alarm clock shrieking in the background. He'd been planning to be up early even without Dillon's call.

"Let me tell *you* what, Agent in Training Marconi..." Dillon caught the emphasis of his rookie status and correctly guessed that Rob was asserting his Bureau seniority over him. "I'll do a pre-flight, but the final say rests with me. I've got to feel like I can control the aircraft. If I don't think I can do that, then we'll have to wait it out. I'm willing to try, but a cyclone is a cyclone. We can't help Agent Shores if we're dead."

Dillon nodded, even though there was no one else in the room to see him. "Understood. If the weather is this awful here, imagine what it must be like all the way out there on Solar Island, right next to the thing."

FORTY-FIVE

The industrial accoutrements of the de-sal plant loomed ahead of the four bedraggled figures seeking shelter from the staggering forces of nature battering the artificial island. The complex maze of pipes and tanks lifted Tara's spirits. They were going to make it!

Lightner troubled her, though. During the trek he had grown increasingly combative, using the slightest distraction to start a fight. As a result, he had been battered and beaten by Tenner and Riley, who themselves also showed signs of wear. Blood trickled from Lightner's nose and oozed from his hands. But worst was the feral gleam of defiance in his eyes. Tara had seen the look before, in suspects who would not give up without a fight to the death.

She began to wonder if the plan to take Lightner prisoner had been a mistake. Maybe she should have simply waited for helicopter pickup and reported on what she knew about Lightner. But that would be a job incompletely done, leaving the actual apprehension of Lightner for another time. Who knew what other crimes Lightner might have committed by then? And Tara was not an agent who liked to leave things incomplete.

What was done was done, she thought as she led her group into the network of pipes outside the de-sal plant. They felt their way along the smooth, wet metal until they reached the entrance. Tara felt exhausted as she reached up and, derringer still clenched in her right hand, pulled the door with her left.

Locked.

The last time she'd been here, she recalled entering by herself because no one had let her in. But the door had been unlocked.

"Ring the bell," Tenner called from behind her. Tara saw the sign over a caged red light, reading "RING FOR ADMITTANCE."

She pressed the button. A minute passed and then the light changed to green. Tara tried the door again, and this time it opened.

"Give me the gun," Tenner said. Tara peeked inside first. She saw no one. Were she to give the gun to Chris, she would also be giving up her own primary means of self-defense. But she'd rather have Tenner hold on to Lightner than her. So she gave Tenner the derringer. He pressed it to Lightner's temple.

"It may be just a peashooter, old man, but at point-blank it'll put a nice dent in your little pea brain. So don't screw around. Now, walk." He jabbed the barrel into Lightner's temple for emphasis. Lightner allowed himself to be led forward into the desalination plant. Bernie brought up the rear, closing the heavy iron door behind them with a *clang*.

"Hello?" Tara called out. She saw no one. Without looking behind her, she waved on her entourage. They trooped through the main entrance. When they reached the end of the short wing, they made the right turn into the next section. Now they could hear voices. On their left was Spencer's office, unoccupied. They rounded a corner into the main de-sal building, and Tara's heart sank.

About twenty people were lounging in this area, lying on makeshift cots, sitting on metal machinery consoles, and passing bottles of rum, laughing, joking, even smoking. She doubted Spencer would approve, but she didn't see him anywhere. Then the laughing stopped as, one by one, the men in the room saw Chris Tenner with Dr. Lightner in a headlock, pistol pressed firmly to his temple, with none other than the presumed-lost Bernard Riley in tow, holding a piece of lead pipe with a blade taped to one end and a length of chain wrapped around his left hand.

Lightner surprised Tara by reacting before anyone else.

"Overpower these traitors! Suppress this mutiny at once! Great rewards await those who stop this insurrection. Solar Island will not forget you!"

Bernie peppered him with chain-knuckle punches to the gut as soon as he started speaking, but Lightner continued his orders, punctuated as they were by exhalations every time he was hit.

Many of the men in the room got up from their various states of repose and conferred in small knots or huddles. The planning chilled Tara, for she knew that at some point a move would be made against them. Then one of the men, a South Pacific Islander Tara recalled as the man who had pushed the condemned man off the beach, stepped forward and spoke to Tara.

"Let Dr. Lightner go and there will be no further bloodshed."

Tara waited for more, but apparently that was all he had to say.

"No!" Tenner shouted from behind her.

She turned around angrily to address him. "Chris, let me do the negotiating. Concentrate on holding Lightner." She turned back to face the motley crowd.

"We can't do that. Dr. Lightner must be brought to justice for murder and other crimes. He will face a fair judicial process in the United States." She was careful not to use the word *trial* since she couldn't be sure with the CIA involvement that there would be one. "I am duty bound to bring him into custody. Any of you who interfere with that duty will also be held accountable for obstruction of justice under United States law."

This was met with a stony silence. There was no laughter or sarcastic reply; she could see that they understood what she said but they didn't care. Then the man who had spoken to her turned around and pointed to one of his associates.

"Bring him," he said. The words sent Tara's spine tingling.

A couple of tense minutes later, two bearded Caucasian men dressed in dirty rags emerged from around the corner, holding Dr. Spencer Henderson. Tara guessed that even though they couldn't have known yet that Lightner had been taken, Spencer would have protested the takeover of his domain. Knowing that he was a member of the Resistance would only have incensed Lightner's followers.

One of them held a pistol—a real pistol, Tara noted with distaste, a .38—to Spencer's temple. They stopped next to the South Pacific man, who then addressed Tara's group again.

"We are prepared to offer you a fair trade," the man said in his characteristic sing-song lilt.

Tara cringed at the sight of Spencer, who looked like he hadn't slept in a long time. His eyes featured pronounced purple bags under them, and he slumped with the attitude of defeat common to those who had given up all hope.

Tara knew that were they to give up Lightner, there would be nothing to stop them from killing her.

"We can't do that," Tara replied. "It is my duty to bring Mr. Lightner to Guam." She decided to refer to him as "Mr." Lightner rather than "Dr." in order to make him seem more like an ordinary man and less of a deity. Also, she hoped that the mention of Guam—a Pacific Island, sounded better to them than "the United States," a faraway foreign nation. But she was wrong on both counts.

"We kill Spencer Henderson in five seconds if you do not release Dr. Lightner," the Sovereignty Movement spokesman said. He held out a hand, ticking off a count on his fingers. "Five, four..."

"No, please!" Tara realized that she had lost control of the situation. She was only begging for a man's life, no longer negotiating but simply pleading. She felt utterly hopeless. She turned back to Tenner. "Don't shoot him, don't shoot!"

"I won't if I don't have to!" he bellowed.

"...two, one..."

The gunshot literally made Tara jump. Any doubts about the intentions of these men were removed with a single bullet to Spencer's head. The chemical engineer slumped lifelessly to the floor, part of his brain oozing down the side of his face.

Tara felt her gorge rising but forced herself to swallow it back down. She couldn't show any weakness.

"Don't shoot!" she choked out to Tenner, who now had the gun barrel pressed so hard against Lightner's head that a trickle of blood sluiced down his temple from the contact. Bernie was holding out his lead pipe, facing this way, then that, hyperalert.

"Return our leader to us," the spokesman said.

"I cannot do that," Tara insisted, doing her best to keep her voice level. The spokesman snapped his fingers. Two more men stepped forward, each carrying a rifle. They both assumed kneeling sniper positions and trained their weapons on Tenner's head. The man with the pistol who had just shot Spencer also aimed his gun at Tenner.

"You will release him now." the spokesman commanded.

"Don't let him go!" Tara called back to Tenner. She began to walk backward, toward him.

"You shoot me, I'm taking him with me!" Tenner shouted in what was meant to be a defiant statement, but to Tara he just sounded scared as hell. She couldn't blame him.

"These two rifles will explode your skull like a melon dropped from a ten-story building," the spokesman said. "You may not even have time to get off a single shot."

As a group, the four of them began backing toward the entrance wing. Tara could feel the floor shifting beneath her feet as the island continued to ride through the storm. It would make aiming that much more difficult. A tiny factor in their favor, but one she was grateful for nonetheless.

"This is your final chance," the spokesman intoned, his hand thrust into the air once again. "Five, four..."

"I'll take him out!" Tenner said, voice dripping with trepidation.

When the count reached two, the rifles fired. It was a dirty trick that stunned even Tara, although she was running into the entrance wing the second she heard the shots. She would be forever haunted by the sight of Lightner's demonically grinning face splattered with Chris Tenner's blood as she ran past them, and of Bernie Riley swinging his bladed pipe in a blind rage at Lightner's neck, connecting once before being cut down in a hail of bullets.

Tara slipped as she rounded the corner into the entrance wing, but she pushed off the floor with a hand and kept going. She heard shouts behind her as the Sovereignty Movement mobilized after her. She sprinted for the entrance door. As she reached it, she heard the *ping* of a bullet ricocheting off the metal door. She threw her body against the door while lifting the latch and pitched herself headlong into the cyclone raging outside.

FORTY-SIX

Tara skidded on the wet deck surface under some pipework, grateful for any kind of cover. She had a head start of maybe thirty seconds.

She avoided the main path they had come in on and instead ventured through an obstacle course of jumbled equipment adjacent to the de-sal plant. Horrible images of Spencer's execution and Lightner's blood-splattered face flashed inside her skull as she leaped here and crawled there, oblivious to the slashing rain all around her.

She went to leapfrog a large pipe but fell short on the height when the island canted upward, causing her to slam a knee painfully into the steel. Writhing on the wet deck, she choked back a cry as she heard men shouting, looking for her.

It sounded like they had taken the main path but were now also starting to branch out. She picked herself up and forged on, this time low-crawling under the pipe. As she moved, she took a mental inventory of her possessions. She had no weapons. She had the penlight. A PowerBar. She was still wearing the windbreaker.

Then Tara saw the end of the tangle of pipes, and open space beyond. Which way to go? She decided not to stop and think about it. She ran at full sprint for the solar tunnel across the cart track. Her spirits sank as she heard a shout behind her, and then the *clink* of a bullet striking a mirrored heliostat just as she dashed into the tunnel between two collector rows.

She kept up her sprint across the wet deck, conscious that a slip at this speed could be debilitating, perhaps even fatal. Tara was a regular at the FBI gym, hitting the track once a week. She was fast, but not used to running on slick surfaces. But with gunmen close behind, she took her chances that she might fall and ran at top speed, weaving from left to right as quickly as she dared until she reached the end of the trough.

Another cart path crossed in front of her, with yet another array of troughs lined up on the other side of it. She counted three collector rows, then turned right down the fourth and took off again in a full sprint. The rain was coming down so hard now that it cut visibility; she couldn't see to the end of the solar tunnel.

She was maybe a hundred feet from the end when she could see the opening. Exhausted and unsure of where to go next, she stopped at the end of the tunnel and rested with her hands on her knees while she listened for signs of her pursuers. She heard nothing. She assessed her location and was surprised to see that the island's perimeter fence lay just beyond a vehicle track. She had reached the edge of the island.

The view was...sickening, she decided. Tara watched as a crest of white water crashed over the fence and rolled across the cart track, like waves coming up a beach. The salt water greeted her feet as she took in the humbling spectacle before her. Her numbed mind recalled Lightner telling her that Solar Island's deck was two stories high. So these waves were clearing twenty feet. From her vantage point with the island's edge tilted downward, Tara was staring straight into a vision of hell, an angry, boiling sea the likes of which she had never even come close to seeing, and never wanted to again.

The darkness and rain made it difficult to make out much, but somehow one of the perimeter spotlights still shone its beam out to sea, and this illumination afforded Tara glimpses of a shifting cauldron of foamy blackness. It terrified her beyond words, even more than the shooters who now stalked her. The edge of this place was not where she wanted to be.

Tara looked left and saw the unmistakable outline of an empty golf cart, somehow still upright. *Could it still be operational?*

She ran for it. She would not be able to keep up this pace for much longer. The cart would allow her to make steady progress—to where, she didn't know—until she found a suitable hiding spot.

Behind her and to the left she heard a shout. Reaching the cart, her heart stopped when she saw that it was an older model without the push-button start, and the keys weren't in the ignition. She closed her eyes for a moment and brought up a mental image of Lightner walking with her to a cart during her tour. In her mind's eye, he reached up to the visor and pulled the keys down from there. Praying it would be the same way here, she slid her hand over the visor and rejoiced at the feel of cold metal.

She had to use her penlight to see where to put the key. She heard the shouting, closer now. Ideally, she would be away in this cart before they knew she had one. They were looking for her on foot. She turned the ignition. Nothing happened. Forcing her mind to focus, she directed her penlight to the gearshift and saw the problem: The lever was positioned halfway between the reverse and park modes. She threw it into drive, prepared to hunt down the headlights in order to shut them off, but thankfully they didn't come on.

Tara tapped the brakes and saw the red glow of brake lights reflecting off the wet deck behind her. Deciding it was worth a few more seconds, she jumped out of the cart. It was one of the work models, used for carrying maintenance materials, and this one still had a load of PVC pipe as well as a metal toolbox spanning the bed.

Tara lifted the toolbox's lid and removed a pipe wrench. She ran to the brake lights and smashed them out, the noise drowned out by the driving rain. She got back in the driver's seat, wrench still in hand, and slammed the cart into drive, pedal to the floor. The cart fishtailed on the glistening-wet track as she headed away from where she'd last heard her hunters.

FORTY-SEVEN

Tara drove the cart as fast as she dared through the darkness. She felt the island sliding to her right and turned the cart left—up!—between two rows of solar collectors just as a wave slammed into the island and seawater rushed across the roadway. She heard clattering as some of the PVC pipes rolled out of the back of her cart, and for one terrifying moment time came to a standstill when she thought the vehicle was going to slide backward into the rail. But the tires held their grip and Tara accelerated down the straightaway, her mind racing faster than the cart as it searched for a safe place to go.

The gauges on the cart's dashboard provided the only light as Tara sped away from the island's edge. Between the solar collectors it was almost pitch-dark, and Tara relied on the architectural straightness of the rows more than anything else to keep from crashing. Images of the ocean washing over Solar Island's lip still fresh in her mind, she made her way toward the island's center, seeking stability.

Tara shot across an intersection into another solar tunnel. She raced to its end and then the cart rolled over some debris on the track, causing her to veer off and clip the heliostat on her right side. The cart spun out and the tilt of the island was enough to overturn it. As the vehicle toppled, Tara jumped out from it onto the deck, where she slid for a distance before coming to a stop against a pole that had once held overhead lights. She picked herself up off the deck.

She looked around and didn't see anyone, so she went over to the cart. The rain was still coming down in sheets. Using her penlight, she searched around it until she found the pipe wrench. She was standing there trying to figure out which direction to go when she was dropped to her knees by the violent movement of the deck. Solar Island was being tossed around like a rubber duck in a child's bath.

Tara saw the dark silhouette of the power tower looming in the distance. She considered it as a possible place of refuge, but decided against it. Full of glass, tall and exposed, it was probably not the best place to be.

A smaller building, one she didn't recognize, was directly ahead, and she made her way toward it.

Unbelievably, the island was listing at a steep-enough angle that Tara had to drop to her knees and crawl to make forward progress.

Rain slammed into her face while she decided to have a look at the customs building again. It was low-lying. Not made of plywood. Sunken somewhat belowdecks. She ran to it. It would be secure.

As Tara approached the building, she was greeted by a sight that stopped her in her tracks. The deck canted and bucked beneath her. She could only stand and stare. The power tower and customs building were at the very center of the island, where the four main pie-wedge pieces came together to form the huge circular raft.

But something was wrong. Where the wedge-shaped pieces met the island's inner core—the small circle defined by the power tower and customs building—she could see huge gaps where water flowed freely, sluicing back down past her feet. She tried to comprehend what was happening as she struggled to maintain her balance. Then she saw the roughly triangular tip of one of the wedges next to her rip away from the center.

Solar Island was breaking into pieces.

FORTY-EIGHT

Tara scrambled away from the center, not wanting to be near the end of the wedge-shaped piece she was on when it separated. She heard a screeching sound. Looking back, she watched as a second wedge sheared off from the center. Her mind screamed one question.

Would the individual triangular pieces really float on their own as Lightner had told her they would?

She forced herself to hold on to a utility pole in the wind and watch as the separated piece floated away from the island, leaving a Pac-Man–shaped disc with a huge section of ocean where its missing wedge section used to be. The jettisoned piece drifted up the face of a colossal wave, lingered on the summit for a few seconds, and then was lost from sight as it fell down the mountainous trough. Thirty seconds later, Tara saw the piece again, still floating. She wondered how many people were on it.

Then she heard that screeching noise again. *The whole island is splitting apart into the four main sections!* Tara turned and ran from the center. She saw the low plywood building and dashed toward that.

She heard shouting.

Looking past the building, she saw the posse that was chasing her. They, too, had stopped to witness the island's separation. But then she saw one of them point in her direction. They began to run toward her. Tara tightened her grip on the pipe wrench. She would have to hide and lie in wait. A battle in the open against gun-toting adversaries meant death for her.

She crept around one side of the plywood structure. There was an alcove-like feature that housed what looked like a traditional electrical meter. She hid in that space and waited. She heard more screeching of materials as the ocean wrenched Solar Island apart.

She heard a man scream.

She couldn't stand it. She had to see what was going on.

Tara crouched low and poked her head out of the alcove. She was stunned to see two men, both carrying pistols, running her way. *They know where I am*. She was about to run in the opposite direction when the section of island *she* was on parted from the central disc right in front of her pursuers.

One of them had dropped to his knees and desperately crab-walked backward away from the edge. The other man, eyes wide with abject terror, was unable to halt his forward progress in time and skittered over the edge into the ten-foot-wide gap of ocean between his wedge and the one Tara was now floating away on.

Tara saw the power tower recede as her pie-shaped wedge of what used to be Solar Island drifted away from the other two pieces that were still connected. Now on one-fourth the surface area as before, the movement of the deck was much more pronounced than when she had been on the whole island.

She ran for the plywood building.

The only door Tara could find to it was locked. Kneeling on the canting deck, she started to fish around in her pockets for her lockpick, hoping it was still there after all the action. She rejoiced at the feel of the smooth, straight metal. Making sure she had a good grip on the pick before exposing it to the elements, she carefully brought it up to the door lock.

Working with her penlight in one hand, it took some doing to hold the pick steady with the rocking of her quarter-island; but after a couple of minutes she got the pick inserted and felt the familiar and satisfying *snick* as the lock succumbed to her ministrations.

Not knowing who or what might be inside the building, Tara hefted her pipe wrench before opening the door. Then she stepped inside, her penlight cutting a thin swath through the darkness.

"Hello?" she called out, not wanting to startle anyone who might still be inside. "Anyone here?"

There was no reply. She found a wall switch and flipped it on. Then it dawned on her how absurd that action was. Here she was, separated from the main island on a floating pie wedge in the middle of the ocean, and she expected the lights to just turn on. They did not.

From her little penlight, it was hard to tell for sure what this building was, but it seemed not to have the industrial feel of most of the others. For one thing, she was standing on a carpet with some kind of design. Tara shrugged out of her soaked windbreaker and left it on the floor. She was glad to be out of the howling wind and rain. She only hoped that this building would hold together.

She walked cautiously down what seemed to be a hallway. It was pitch-dark in here but for her pathetic little flashlight. Presently, the beam came into contact with an object hanging from the ceiling, just above head height. Inspecting it, she saw that it was a hanging lamp. She was about to dismiss it when she saw the words "COLEMAN CAMPING" painted on the side. She smiled in the darkness. It wasn't a light fixture; it was a lantern. She doubted it would be kerosene-powered since it was indoors, so she looked around for a switch, hoping it ran on batteries and that they were still charged. Her fingers came across a red round button, and she pressed it. White light flickered, then caught, bathing the hallway in steady illumination.

She flicked off her penlight and pocketed it as she looked around at her new surroundings. An oriental rug covered the floor. A small table lay on its side, a tea-service set scattered next to it on the floor. Paintings—oil-on-canvas seascapes—hung on the walls, no doubt bolted in place to have survived the onslaught. One of them depicted a 1700s-era rendering of a many-tentacled sea monster with six large eyes ravishing a sailing ship, pitching men overboard as they screamed in terror.

This seemed to be some kind of entrance area. Ahead, Tara could see that it opened up into another wing off to the right. She followed it and saw that this section was much wider than the entrance wing. It was dark, but ahead she could see another lantern hanging from the ceiling. She went to it and flicked it on.

A living room. She was surprised to find herself standing in the middle of a well-appointed living room. A low-profile coffee table surrounded by overstuffed beanbags occupied one corner. A large photo book titled *The South Pacific from Space* lay open on the floor, where it had slid from the table. A few exotic seashells and coral pieces were strewn about the table and floor. A leather recliner was positioned in front of an empty mount for a flat-screen television. The plasma screen itself lay on the floor beneath its former mount. Its screen had been smashed by a six-foot-tall wooden tiki statue that had toppled onto it from its former position in a corner, its face carved in a menacing expression as it gazed up at Tara from a sea of broken glass. More paintings adorned the walls. In general, Tara could tell that it used to be a comfortable space, if perhaps a bit stuffy. Clearly, someone used this room to relax.

She continued through the living room until it funneled into a narrow hallway that jogged right. This building couldn't be all that large, Tara recalled from her sighting of it outside, so this hallway probably led to the last room. She followed it around a corner until it did in fact open up into another room, this one more square in shape.

She found another lantern and switched it on. Bedroom. A queen-size bed, with full headboard, perfectly made, occupied one wall. A matching dresser took up space on the opposite wall, and an old rolltop desk matched with a toppled modern swivel chair still positioned in one corner.

A reflection over the desk caught Tara's eye. A simple framed print hung there, displaying only the words "The question isn't who is going to let me; it's who is going to stop me."

Tara saw her own face for a moment reflected off the glass. The quote took a second to register; but when it did, she was transported back in time, to her college days at UCLA and a philosophy class where she had been assigned to read selected works from... *What was it?* She struggled to remember...*Ayn Rand. Objectivism...rational self-interest...*

Then it hit her, as she took in a giant carving of yet another sun god adorning the ceiling over the bed.... This could be none other than Dr. Jacob Lightner's house. He certainly fit the mold of an Ayn Rand devotee.

She was inside the home of the sun god himself!

On closer inspection, Tara noticed a laptop computer sitting closed on the desk. She went to it.

Hers!

Tara had no fear that Lightner had been able to gain any confidential information out of the laptop, such as the case file she had on him; but the FBI logo and access warning that launched on the password-protected boot-up screen would have been enough to remove any doubt that she was not a reporter. But in terms of her being able to use it right now to contact Guam, she knew it could no longer be used for Web access at all, since the island's satellite connection no longer existed.

Where was her satellite phone?

She rifled through the desk drawers, finding only an assortment of odd architectural drawings and routine office items. She looked through the rest of the room. Having something to focus on helped to take her mind off the stress of the cyclone. She looked through the dresser, but it contained only clothing and spare bedding. A search beneath the bed with her penlight revealed only a bare floor.

She stood and searched some more around the room, but found nothing. She decided she could do a more thorough search of the rest of the place in daylight. Right now she was beyond exhausted. She detested the thought of lying in the killer's bed, but the sheets looked and smelled as if they had just been changed. She needed rest.

Switching off the lantern hanging from the ceiling, Tara climbed into the bed and let the rocking motion lull her to sleep.

FORTY-NINE

Tara awoke to muted light coming through a single curtained window set high on the wall. She lay still until she recalled how she had ended up in the strange bed. By the time she set both feet on the floor, she knew that something was different.

An odd sensation...

Rising, she walked cautiously out of the bedroom. She looked and listened for signs of others, but detected none. Walking down the hallway to the living room, Tara finally identified the feeling.

Her sense of balance.

It seemed...normal.

She was walking without having to carefully test every step. Without having to hold her arms out for balance. Eager to get outside, she strode faster through Lightner's house until she reached the entrance. She forced herself to listen before opening it.

What if some of her pursuers were trapped on her slice of Solar Island?

But again, she saw or heard no signs of anyone.

She opened the door and stepped outside.

Blue sky!

Before the cyclone, Tara would have found it hard to believe how psychologically uplifting a fresh blue sky could be. But seeing one now lifted her spirits immensely.

And the wind!

Still forceful, but nothing like the oppressive foe it had been hours earlier. Stepping away from the house, she walked toward the rail of what now appeared to be her own private breakaway Solar Island. She made it to the railing along one of the long sides of the pie wedge and looked out on the ocean.

Small whitecaps reared up here and there, but the platform she was on was large enough to keep her from feeling them. Thirty-foot monster waves had been replaced by six-foot seas, navigable even to medium-size sailboats. Tara clutched the cable railing and rejoiced at the change in weather.

The cyclone had passed. She only hoped it wouldn't circle around and come back, as she knew sometimes happened. But for now it had moved on. With the worst of the weather over, she could focus on her predicament.

Tara turned away from the rail and set about the task of assessing her situation. What else was on this slice of Solar Island with her? Who else?

Deciding that whatever it was, none of it could be as important as her satellite phone, Tara went back into Lightner's house and turned it even more upside down than it already was, looking for her phone. She emptied drawers and cabinets, inspected shelves, looked everywhere that might be able to hide a phone. But unlike her laptop, it was not here. Perhaps Lightner had thrown it overboard, worried that it could be used by the CIA to trace his island's position.

Tara went back outside. She looked around, searching for anything that might be of use. Overall, her spirits were high. She was stranded on an incapacitated section of floating island, but it was stable enough, and at some point she would either be spotted by a ship or else be found by an FBI helicopter search. She'd much rather be alone here than on the whole, intact island being pursued by a pack of armed lunatics.

She decided to reconnoiter the mini-island for food and water. Walking around, Tara threaded her way through the wreckage and debris of the cyclone that was strewn about everywhere. It seemed that this section of the island was mostly occupied by solar collectors. There were not many structures on it. Broken pieces of glass from the solar apparatus, plywood boards, leaking 55-gallon drums—all manner of substances and materials lay in a state of upheaval.

Tara was more than a little surprised to see one of the windmills still standing. After Lightner had shut it down, its chances of surviving had increased; but with the violent whipsawing it must have undergone on the separated island piece, she expected it would have snapped off. She continued her walking survey of the island.

Ahead, a forklift lay overturned next to a pile of pallets, and Tara was mortified to see a dead body crushed beneath the machine. She checked the man's pulse, just to be sure, but he was cold, stiff, and long dead. She tried to move the forklift off of the South Pacific man's body, but she was unable to even budge the piece of heavy equipment. Tara found a ripped piece of tarp nearby and used it to cover the body.

Continuing on through the solar farm, Tara noticed that many of the solar collectors were still in one piece, but those that had broken had produced a lot of glass. Also, the deck was slick in spots where the oil had leaked from broken heat-transfer pipes.

Tara advanced cautiously toward the end of her island section. She passed the red gas can still in its Plexiglas cube, now lying on the deck, and walked to the edge of the floating structure. There was no guardrail here, where it had broken free of the main island. She had expected to find a tangle of broken wreckage and snarled metal where the separation had occurred, but she saw nothing like that. It had been a clean break, as if the two pieces had unlocked or decoupled from each other by design, which in fact they had.

Tara backed away from the edge. She was turning around to walk back into the island when she heard a *click* followed by a low hum. A vibration under the deck shuddered through the soles of her shoes. She wheeled back around. A green light in a wire cage at the top of a short pole had lit up.

She looked around the island. Had someone switched this on? She saw no one. But the water beneath the end of the island had begun to boil and churn. And then, slowly at first, almost imperceptibly, the narrow end of the island began to move. Not due to the ocean, but under some kind of power. It swung to the left, and Tara felt the vibrations beneath her feet increase in intensity. Then the island stopped turning and its course straightened out.

The pie-shaped wedge was being dragged through the sea by the narrow end. The forward progress was slow, but undeniable. The island was now under power, moving forward. Tara examined the green light and looked around the edge of the island, but could find no obvious control equipment or machinery that would allow one to operate a motor. Squinting into the roiling bubbles around the island's edge, Tara was unable to see anything. There must be a motor, propeller, some kind of running gear down there, Tara thought.

Then it hit her as she stared into the frothing water. She recalled something Lightner had said shortly after she met him, and now his words bubbled up to her as if with the water displaced by the motor underneath the island.

"*...the four sectional pods that comprise the island's base are designed to separate under extreme stress, such as a major storm. Each is fitted with a GPS locator coupled to a simple propulsion system that will allow them to find each other after they are separated.*"

Tara shivered as it dawned on her that she was now being dragged back to the other pieces of the island, where no doubt Lightner and company awaited her. She tore her gaze from the water below and looked upward. The weather was good now. A helicopter would be coming for her, but they no longer knew her exact position.

At least the island was moving very slowly, not having much in the way of a hydrodynamic hull or sleek form factor. How far away were Solar Island's other pods?

Tara's mind lit on the windmill. It would afford an excellent vantage point. She made her way across the pod to the island's opposite side—to the crust, if the pod was a piece of pie.

She approached the windmill and recalled how the doors on them were locked when she had been looking for Lightner. This one must have been left open, though, because the door had been torn from one of its hinges and dangled into the entrance. She eased past it and climbed the narrow, winding stairs.

Reaching the top, she tried the control-booth door and found it unlocked. She stepped inside. Unbelievably, the acrylic windows were still intact, although a deep scratch now marred the center of one of them. The view they afforded was still first-rate. Tara looked out over a much calmer Pacific as the outer bands of the cyclone receded into the distance, to the west.

She scanned the sea from right to left, looking for the other pods. She examined the view through the right and middle windows without seeing anything man-made on the ocean's surface. Then, at the far edge of the left window's vantage point, almost out of view, she saw it. Far enough away to be only a speck. But it was a speck that didn't belong.

Man-made.

She searched through the cabinets set into the wall and found what she was looking for: a pair of binoculars. She figured it would be silly not to keep a pair up here. Bringing them to her eyes, she focused on the distant object.

Triangular...a pod! Even with the binoculars, it was still far enough away that she couldn't make out much detail, especially with the island's movement, which was amplified this high up. But she was pretty sure that the windmill on that pod had been knocked down. Something else occurred to her, though, as she watched the narrow end of the pod pointing in her direction.

It wasn't simply that her pod was traveling to the other pods. Rather, her pod and the one she could see were moving toward each other at about the same speed. She didn't know where the other two pods were—she suspected they must be out of view behind her somewhere—but what alarmed her was that the time-to-contact until she met the other pod had just been halved.

Tara lowered the binoculars. Solar Island was reassembling.

FIFTY

Tara climbed down from the windmill. She had to prepare herself as best she could for the rejoining of the pods. She surveyed her own pod, walking it up and down, looking for anything she could use as a makeshift weapon. Or as a hiding place. Perhaps she could conceal herself well enough that Lightner would think she'd been swept overboard in the cyclone?

If Lightner was even still alive, that was. Bernie had gotten in a slice to his neck before being felled. But she didn't know for sure and therefore had to assume he was still among the living. If so, she imagined his search would be thorough and exhaustive. She might be able to hide long enough to gain an element of surprise, but doubted she would be able to permanently avoid detection.

So that left weapons. She wasn't finding much among the wreckage littered about her pod. Lightner and his men would be greeting her with guns.

Tara regretted giving her derringer to Chris Tenner, which in the end had not helped him and left her defenseless. She forced the images of Chris and Bernie being slaughtered in the de-sal plant from her mind as she neared Lightner's house.

The house.

She had searched the bedroom reasonably well, but she had been looking for her satellite phone, not a weapon. She considered Lightner as she entered his house once again, this time in full daylight. She thought it likely that he would have some kind of firearm hidden inside. He was a little bit of a pirate, after all, living on the high seas, trading for—and taking—what he wanted from others. After hundreds of investigations over the course of her career, Tara knew the most common techniques people used for hiding guns in their homes.

She walked in and went to the living room. There was a skylight in the ceiling, providing bright daylight. Last night, by the much-dimmer artificial light of the lantern, she had opened the drawers of a display cabinet that held exotic curiosities—seashells, tribal pottery and art objects, even what appeared to be a shrunken head—but she had been focused on her phone and hadn't paid close attention from a weapon-concealment standpoint.

Tara laughed to herself as she laid eyes on an unconventional weapon in the display case. Arranged on a stand was a triangular piece of tropical hardwood about eight inches long with large shark teeth embedded around the edges. Being based in Hawaii, Tara had seen them before and knew them to be made from a rare wood called koa. They had been used hundreds of years ago by Hawaiian warriors in battle. This piece, Tara thought as she opened the case and took the club out, appeared to be a genuine artifact worthy of a museum, not a modern knockoff version like those sold in pricy Hawaiian tourist shops. Lightly running the serrated teeth over the palm of her hand, Tara marveled at how solidly constructed the club was. It was a fine weapon. She stuck it in her back pocket and moved to the large bookcase, a built-in unit stretching from floor to ceiling.

If Tara had learned one thing from executing domestic search warrants, it was that books were popular hiding places for just about anything that would fit in a book. She didn't relish the task of going through every one of these volumes, but with a few hours until the pods neared each other, she had the time and judged it to be worth the effort.

One by one, Tara pulled books from the shelves, opened them, and let them drop to the floor. She had just started in on a third shelf when she opened a gold-leafed hardcover of *The Collected Works of Jules Verne.* As she had seen done many times before, the middle portion of the pages inside had been neatly removed with a blade to create a hollow space within the covers, a hollow filled by a 9-millimeter SIG Sauer pistol.

Tara wondered what Mr. Verne would think of this handgun replacing his words as she removed the weapon from the book. She noted right away that there were no extra rounds stored with the gun, but when she picked it up she could tell by the weight that it contained ammunition. She ejected the magazine and counted fifteen rounds. She spent a couple of minutes going over her new weapon, checking the action, loading a round into the chamber, looking down the sights, until she felt comfortable with it. Tara's spirits were greatly lifted by having a serious means with which to defend herself, and one that she was exceedingly good at.

Not to mention that that's one less gun for Lightner, she thought.

She tucked the SIG into her waistband and continued to plunder Lightner's book collection. Sometimes people placed extra rounds in a book separate from the gun, but in this case she would have to make do with fifteen rounds, because she found no more bullets. She did find one book, *Atlas of the South Pacific*, which had been hollowed out and stuffed with hundred-dollar bills. Tara estimated it was about twenty thousand dollars. She put the cash back in the book and then decided to take the time to put all the books back on the shelves. It would be advantageous to conceal her presence here for as long as possible.

That done, now armed with a loaded 9-millimeter pistol and a shark-tooth war club, Tara left Lightner's abode and went back outside. She tried to picture in her mind the coming together of the two pods, Lightner's men invading her pod, fanning out and searching for her....

She could try to arrange the battlefield to her advantage as best she could. Identify locations that would offer good cover, lines of sight. She could place lanterns in strategic places—the struggle might continue past nightfall; she had no idea. She might as well be as familiar with this place as possible if she was going to have to fight for her life here.

So for the next few hours, Tara went about the pod, stacking objects here, knocking them down there. She was careful to make sure that the place still looked ravaged by a cyclone, but she subtly rearranged it into a theater of war that would give her a slight tactical benefit.

When this was done, Tara revisited the top of the windmill to obtain a visual on the other pod. She felt a rush of adrenaline. She saw it right away, less than half as far away from her as it had been before. Something else was different, too, she thought, reaching for the binoculars.

She focused on the distant object. The pod seemed larger. And then, when she saw one standing windmill and one fallen one, she knew that the single pod had already reunited with another. One-half of Solar Island now chugged toward her.

Lowering the binoculars, Tara scanned the wide swath of ocean for the remaining pod, but could not find it. She looked up. *Maybe three more hours until contact.*

Then a different thought occurred to her. This windmill would make an excellent sniper tower, if only she could knock out one or more of the acrylic panels. She wasn't sure how that was going to happen. The panels were solidly embedded into some kind of polycarbonate frame and had withstood the force of a Category 5 cyclone. She wasn't even sure she would be able to knock one out if she had a sledgehammer.

Still, she thought, making her way back down the stairs, she would keep her eyes open.

Once outside the windmill, Tara walked along the wide edge of her pod. The sea was even calmer now, she noted with relief, and the weather was rapidly returning to some semblance of the iconic South Pacific. After a while, she came across a golf cart—one of the small carts only designed for carrying two people—miraculously still standing on all four wheels, wedged in between two heliostats. Checking the ignition and finding that it still held a charge, Tara set to work extricating the vehicle.

She was glad to drive away in the cart. All the walking and stair-climbing was taking a toll on her, and she needed to be as rested as possible for what was coming. She surveyed her pod from a battle-readiness perspective, making sure everything was as much in her favor as could be. She was considering where to place her golf cart in order to maximize its utility during battle when she came across another building that was still standing.

A small structure about the size of an outhouse, at first Tara thought that's what it might be until she read the stencil across its door: "HEAVY EQUIPMENT."

Tara parked her cart and walked up to the shack. She opened the door and looked in on a jumbled heap of large power tools and other equipment she was not familiar with. While the building itself was still intact, everything inside had been thrown off shelves and wall hooks, and now lay in a jumble on the floor.

She wasn't exactly sure for what yet, but Tara thought that something in here might prove useful. As an improvised weapon, perhaps? A booby trap? She sorted through the confused pile of tools on the floor, untangling them from each other and attempting to assess their purposes. She recognized a jack, and some sort of drill. She briefly considered various macabre applications of the drill, but a power drill with no power was useless. There were brand names she vaguely recognized like DeWalt and Makita, and others she was definitely familiar with: Yamaha, Kawasaki.

Tara was about to leave the shed, not knowing what most of the equipment was even used for, in addition to the fact that most of it required electricity, when she spotted an item underneath a coil of electrical cable. She recognized it as a case for a portable power tool. Opening it, she saw that it was a circular saw with a battery charger. Maybe it had already been charged. She took it out of the box and was relieved to see basic instructions printed on the tool itself. She removed the blade guard and disengaged the safety catch. She noted that the blade was carbide-tipped. She cautiously pulled the trigger and was relieved to see the blade spin to life with a *buzz*. She couldn't help but see the obvious application for this tool: She could use it to cut out sections of the windmill windows for a sniper platform. The saw was heavy, but she would be able to drag the thing up there. The advantage it would afford would be tremendous. She hauled it from the shed and dropped it into the golf cart.

After toting the saw up the last step and into the windmill's access platform, she looked out the windows and spotted the other pods. Much closer now. In fact, she realized, they were close enough to her now that she had to be concerned about being spotted up here through binoculars. She trained her glasses on their lone standing windmill and was relieved to see it empty.

The traveling island had grown too. The other pod had joined the previous two. Tara now rode the missing piece of the puzzle. She saw some kind of activity on one of the pods and trained her binoculars on it.

A heavy lifting crane was being used to pull something from the ocean. Tara adjusted her focus, watching as water lapped over a long, cylindrical object. Steel cables had been wrapped around it, and Tara could see men shouting orders as the object emerged from the sea. Tara recognized it with a start.

The power tower!

Solar Island's circular core itself had also been relocated, and was now being reattached to the pods. She found it amazing that the entire island could be put back together like that, and she wondered in the back of her mind if it would all still work once it was reassembled—but she had no time to dwell on it.

Tara hefted the circular saw. Then she leaned the saw's blade on the window in front of her. She held down the trigger switch and held on for dear life as the carbide-tipped blade chewed away at the acrylic panel. The screeching cacophony was deafening in the small enclosed space. Finally, just as she thought her arms were about to fall off and she was going to drop the thing, she completed a rough square pattern. She laughed to herself at the quality of the cut: It certainly wasn't a neat square, but it would have to do. She set the power tool down on the floor and pressed the cut section with a hand. It budged, but was still wedged in place. Backing up, she executed a high kick to the loose piece with her heel and smiled when it fell away, splashing into the ocean below. She hoped no one had observed the activity from the other pods.

She had removed a section about a square foot in area from the frame. *Perfect!* Tara noted that this was even better than if she had somehow been able to remove the entire window. Her gun would fit through the opening, and she could see around it, but she would also be protected by the thick acrylic.

She repeated the process once more on the right side of the window, to give herself a shooting portal on each side. She slumped onto the floor of the windmill, breathing heavily. She had done it. She now had an operational sniper tower.

FIFTY-ONE

Tara heard a noise and stood up to look from the windmill. She was quick to duck down again. The three-quarter island was only a hundred yards away now, buzzing with activity as personnel scurried about its deck, putting it back in working order while no doubt preparing to hunt Tara down. What's more, the power tower had been raised into position, the tall column once again the island's highest point.

Now without her sunglasses, the solar field of mirrors made it difficult for Tara to look at the island for very long, something she hadn't anticipated when designing her sniper platform.

But she had seen what she needed to see. The fight for her life was at hand. Out here in the middle of the largest expanse of water on the planet, Lightner would attempt to erase her existence.

Standing back from the windows by the door to the access platform, Tara pulled the SIG Sauer from her waistband and checked its action again. It wasn't a sniper rifle, that was for sure, but it was all she had. She adjusted the strap on the binoculars so that they hung around her neck while still allowing her to shoot. Examining the door, she saw it had a lock and engaged it. It would cost her a couple of seconds when it came time to get down off the tower, but in the meantime she wouldn't have to worry about someone sneaking up on her. She took a few deep breaths and briefly closed her eyes. She had done all she could do to avoid this situation in the first place. She'd done all she could to prepare. The 9-millimeter in her right hand and the binoculars in her left, she dropped to her knees and shuffled to her left sniper window.

She could now hear shouts—individual words—drifting across the water. With her eyes just above the bottom window frame, Tara peered down at the activity below. The two tugboats were pulling the three-quarter island toward her pod, guiding it into position. She hadn't counted on that. The additional power of the boats had closed the gap even more quickly than anticipated. There was maybe fifty feet of ocean between the two sections to be joined. A group of men were lined up on the leading edge of the platform, waiting to jump across to her pod when the gap was closed.

Tara tightened her grip on the gun. Slowly she rose until she had line of sight to the men below and scoped them with the binoculars. She didn't want to shoot anyone she knew to be innocent, but she did want to make a point. She scanned the row of men left to right without sighting Lightner himself.

She went back left by two people. There! The man who had thrown the bound man overboard at Lightner's command. The SIG replaced the binoculars at her eye.

Quickly.

It was possible that the windmill was under observation by someone with a rifle. If so, she was an easy target. Meanwhile, she was barely in range with her pistol. She waited until the killer's head was lined up perfectly within her sights. She was now used to the mild rise and fall of her seaborne sniper platform with the ocean swells. She waited...held her breath...and pulled the trigger.

She saw her target slap at his shoulder, as if swatting away a fly. She couldn't tell how serious her hit had been. Deciding that she had better capitalize on the element of surprise while she could, she quickly raised the binoculars again. She recognized two men from the de-sal plant slaughter standing next to each other. She fired off two rounds in quick succession.

Shoot 'n' scoot, she reminded herself, ducking below the window level and crawling to her right-side gun portal.

Three rounds, three hits, she mentally calculated. But now they knew she was here. *Twelve rounds left.* Tara took a deep breath and avoided thinking about her odds in this fight.

She popped up with Lightner's SIG at the ready, forgoing the binoculars. She pumped a shot into the body of a man attempting to throw a rope onto the narrow end of her pod, then ducked again.

It won't be long now, she thought, and then it came.

Crack.

Return fire. A rifle shot, by the sound of it, Tara thought. A bullet smacked high into the wall up by the ceiling.

Four hits. Eleven shots remaining.

Tara decided not to risk taking any more shots from her elevated platform. She was an easy target for a rifleman. If she stayed up here, it was just a matter of time before she would be hit. Better to let them think she was still up here for a few more minutes.

To that end, she stuck the gun out the window without looking and fired toward where she had last seen a group of men standing, quickly pulling her hand back inside. *Ten rounds*, she thought, as she crawled to the door, reached up, and unlocked it. She dropped the binoculars on the floor and slid out of the access platform, closing the door behind her.

She got to her feet and practically flew down the winding staircase, the 9-millimeter held out in her right hand for balance, her left ready to grab the handrail if necessary. She planned as she ran. Her foes probably thought she was still in the tower; she might be able to surprise them again, one last time before her pod was joined to the others.

She exited the windmill and turned for the narrow end of the pod, now being dragged into position with the rest of the island. The sound of a rifle shot connecting with the access platform high above confirmed her suspicions—Lightner's people still thought she was up there.

Tara moved from cover to cover until she reached a formation of empty 55-gallon drums she had intentionally stacked there earlier. Kneeling on deck, she eased out to the right side of the drums and looked over at the docking process.

"Got it, we got it," she heard someone say as the end of her pod penetrated the water space of the main island's open section. The two tugs were now chugging away, probably heading around the island back to the marina. Tara ignored them and focused on the people preparing to come over.

She was stunned to see Lightner's silver-topped head peek around the crane. She didn't think he'd be so close to the action. Raising the SIG, she took the shot. She heard the *ping* of her bullet ricocheting off the crane's metal surface. With her peripheral vision she saw Lightner duck back behind the crane, but she was already sighting another target.

Tara fired at a man who was in mid-leap as he attempted to jump onto her pod while it slid into position with the main island. She shot him high on the chest—almost in the neck—and his body contorted in midair. He fell into the sliver of sea between the two massive floating structures before being crushed between their colliding walls.

Tara ducked back behind the barrels just as she heard the reverberations of return fire bouncing off the metal drums.

Eight rounds left, she thought.

Suddenly, a most unexpected and different sound filled her ears.

FIFTY-TWO

The *whump whump whump* of a helicopter became steadily louder.

Leaning behind the pile of steel drums, Tara cast her gaze skyward. She couldn't see an aircraft. Another shot gonged off one of the drums. She didn't have enough bullets left to waste on random return fire. She heard the helicopter come in lower.

She rolled to the left and risked a glance at the main island. She caught her breath as she watched a Sikorsky S-61R—the same bird she'd flown out on—hover over the resurrected helicopter pad. She had no way to warn them, but they knew from their first trip to Solar Island that Lightner was armed and dangerous. He'd fired warning shots at them then. Why weren't his men shooting at the helicopter now?

Tara rolled back behind the drums. She took one more look, this time from the right side, just long enough to see the helicopter start descending toward the landing pad. The Sikorsky's arrival had temporarily distracted the landing party attempting to cross over to her pod. Some of the men were now running toward the landing platform.

She took the opportunity afforded by the distraction to run from the drums back to the windmill, where her golf cart awaited. She had to somehow get to that chopper.

Tara drove the cart through the cover of the solar collectors. She navigated within the tunnels until she came to the edge of the solar farm, but farther to the right of her 55-gallon drum cover. She was set back from where she had been before, but she could still see what was happening on the edge of her pod.

She counted four men simultaneously taking cover behind heavy objects. She scanned her own pod forward of her position but saw no one. Looking up at the power tower, she could see the helicopter now resting on the landing pad.

And then her heart sank.

She watched as three men took cover positions around the aircraft, weapons aimed at it. Then Dr. Lightner himself—out of range for a reliable pistol shot, Tara saw regretfully—walked, with no visible weapon, to the passenger-side door.

Tara caught her breath as she recognized Dillon's dark hair and lanky frame. She watched while Dillon's and Rob's hands both went skyward as the three gunmen advanced, weapons drawn, converging on the FBI men. Lightner himself stepped back from Dillon and also drew a pistol. Tara slowly exhaled without taking her eyes from the scene.

She had a pistol containing eight rounds against about ten armed men who now held her extraction team prisoner. Still, Tara's mind kept turning over the possibilities, searching for avenues that would not lead to the death of herself or her associates. Once Dillon and Rob were led away, she could try to sneak into the helicopter, where she could use its radio....

But any hope of that was laid to rest by Lightner's voice amplified by a bullhorn pointed Tara's way.

"Attention, Special Agent Tara Shores: You are wanted for crimes against Solar Island, including the murder of six Solar Island residents." Tara wasn't exactly sure how he arrived at six kills. She tallied five, but she didn't allow this flash of arithmetic to keep her from concentrating on Lightner's message.

"We are ordering you to surrender yourself immediately. To ensure your compliance, we are holding a couple of friends of yours from the FBI. I think there's one you may be particularly fond of. He tells me his name is Special Agent Dillon Marconi. Present yourself peacefully, or Dillon's blood will be on your hands."

Lightner's message frightened her, but Tara forced herself to think about it rationally. She didn't see what good it would do if all three of them were in Lightner's custody. She remained silent sitting in her electric vehicle. She kept one eye on the rearview mirror, watching for anyone who dared approach from behind down the solar trough. Up front, she commanded a clear view of the narrow end of the pod, which was now locked into place with the rest of the island.

Then Lightner's amplified voice pierced the air again. "You have five minutes to comply. After that time, if you have not surrendered to us, you will not be pleased with the results. That is all."

Tara watched as Rob's hands were bound behind his back and he was forced into the cargo area of the helicopter by Lightner's Sovereignty disciples. She guessed they would tie him up back there. But what about Dillon? She could see Lightner holding a gun on him with one hand while speaking into a handheld radio in the other. Another man also trained a firearm on Dillon. Then Tara watched as Dillon was marched from the helipad at gunpoint and led down into the power tower itself.

She watched the bottom of the tower carefully, expecting him to be led out onto the main deck; but when a full minute passed without any sign of Dillon or Lightner, Tara made a 180-degree turn in her golf cart and headed back down the solar trough the way she had come. She needed a place from which to observe the rest of the island.

The whole island, she emphasized to herself as she floored the pedal down the straightaway. She could now walk onto the rest of the island, and her attackers could do the same to get to her pod.

She shot out of the solar tunnel and parked behind Lightner's house. With practiced ease, she climbed on top of the cart to gain access to the roof of Lightner's home. On the edge of the roof facing the center of the island, she had arranged a pile of what she hoped look like cyclone-strewn debris—plywood, a 55-gallon drum, a piece of sheet metal, some heavy-gauge PVC pipes—into a configuration that would conceal her as she observed the island's core. Scanning the island from her new vantage point, she was disappointed to see no signs of Dillon or Lightner.

They must still be inside the power tower. What could they be doing in there?

Tara's thoughts were interrupted by Lightner's voice through the bullhorn. She couldn't see him this time, but his words seemed to come from somewhere within the tower.

"Your time is up, Special Agent Shores. Surrender!"

FIFTY-THREE

Peeking through a gap between some sheet metal and plywood, Tara witnessed a sight that left her short of breath. The solar tower was glowing brilliantly, even more than when she'd seen it from the windmill.

It wasn't just natural sunlight reflecting off of it, she thought, but the collector mirrors had been reactivated, their tracking turned back on in time to orient themselves to the late-afternoon tropical sunlight. What's more, Tara realized, from her angle she could *see* the sun's rays hitting the tower like a pyramid of light, the collected energy from the heliostats focusing on a single point near the top of the power tower.

Dillon is in the tower.

Suddenly the light show blinked off. Tara could see the heliostats still moving. They had been rotated downward so their reflected light wouldn't reach the power tower collector.

What is Lightner up to?

Then, in one horrifying instant, Tara had her answer. Lightner and an accomplice appeared in the power tower, with Dillon Marconi, hands bound behind his back, suspended between them. Tara watched, horrified, as Dillon was tied in place to the power tower's collection area—the focal point for all of Solar Island's acres of heliostats.

When the heliostats were readjusted into position, their collective solar energy—enough to power a small city—would fry Dillon like a bug under a magnifying glass on a sunny day.

Lightner's voice through the bullhorn taunted her from the power tower. "In just a few moments, Agent Shores, I will aim the heliostats on the power tower. If you haven't already, take a look up at the tower. See your friend, Dillon? He's about to experience quite the sunburn if you don't give yourself up. So come out, come out, wherever you are, Agent Shores. Time's up!"

Tara was aware that decisions born of desperation had the potential to go very wrong indeed, but she also had a veteran agent's sixth sense about her, and knew that any hesitation now would seal Dillon's fate.

She had to get closer to the power tower. It would be heavily guarded. *I need a distraction. Think, Tara!*

She dropped from the roof into the cart and drove to the heavy-equipment shed. Running inside the shed, she grabbed a power drill and threw it into the front seat of the cart. She drove at the cart's top speed back through the solar tunnels until she reached the fallen Plexiglas cube with the gas can. She stepped from the cart and picked up the cube. A small padlock locked a clasp, keeping the container shut. Tara grabbed the drill from the cart and used it to remove the lock. She took the gas can out of the box and opened its cap. Was it really still gasoline, or would Lightner have replaced it with water?

She sniffed the opening, and the sharp tang burned her nostrils. *Gas!*

Recapping the container, she placed it and the drill in the cart.

She drove to the same spot as before, where she had observed the joining of her pod to the others.

She got out of the cart with the gas can. She opened it and poured the gasoline all over the inside of the cart.

Looks like there's still a need for legacy fuel on Solar Island after all.

Then she dropped the drill onto the accelerator pedal. She took a book of matches she'd found in Lightner's house and used one to light the entire pack. She put the cart into gear and tossed the flaming matchbook into the gas-soaked cart as it sped away. The burning vehicle sped toward the three men who had just worked to join the pods together. They had been huddled down to inspect the coupling mechanism, and Tara savored the look on the face of the first man to look up in time to see the unoccupied flaming golf cart speed toward them. Tara didn't stick around to watch what happened. It didn't matter. She had her distraction.

She could already hear the trammel of footsteps as other men approached the spectacle. The SIG Sauer with its eight rounds remaining in her right hand, Tara ran to the right until she recognized where her pod ended and she had crossed over onto another pod. Lightner and a couple of his men would be guarding the power tower closely. Dillon was the bait, she was the catch. She wouldn't walk right into the trap, but she had to save Dillon.

"Initiate heliostat tracking," Lightner commanded through the bullhorn.

The island seemed so big now that it was back together again. Dillon didn't have long. She had to get to that tower. She flashed on her guided tour of it with Lightner. The main entrance into the power tower was through the customs building, up the ladder from inside that building.

But it was also accessible from a side door set up over the customs building, Tara recalled. She had left it wedged open when she left!

But Lightner and his men must have used that door by now, right?

There was the cyclone...not to mention that the entire structure had been detached from the island and righted again. Was it possible that that little door wedge could have held through all that?

Tara didn't know, and she didn't care. She had no better ideas. She had to deal with the three men she saw in the tower before the others caught up with her after handling her little fire bomb. She ran for the back side of the tower, away from the customs building entrance.

She crouched low behind a pile of scrap wood and debris that had been shoveled into one place. Spying on the tower from behind this pile, she saw the ladder leading to the door set into the side of the power tower, above the customs room. But no people.

Pocketing the 9-millimeter, Tara made a dash for the tower. She jumped onto the ladder and scrambled up to the small metal platform where the door was located. Her heart pounded even faster in her chest when she saw the rubber doorstop still wedged in place. But would there be a guard stationed just inside?

If it was still open, Tara thought that meant they'd assumed it was locked and hadn't noticed. That was the best she could hope for, at any rate.

From this position, she could feel the vibrations of the massive turbines within roaring to life. Lightner was putting Solar Island through its paces, testing its recovery from the cyclone, while planning to fry Dillon in the process. Lightner's next words through the bullhorn actually gave her a glimmer of hope.

"Special Agent Tara Shores: You have chosen to remain in hiding while your associate is sacrificed to our great star. You have made your decision. Matiu, activate solar thermal tracking!"

He doesn't know where I am.

Tara took the gun from her pocket. She eased the door open, the roar from the turbines assaulting her ears as she did so. About ten feet in front of her was a large square block containing machinery with a metal duct leading away from its top. She crept forward, then slunk alongside it until she could peer around the corner. Fifty feet to her left was Dillon, tied to the focal point for the heliostat's thermal energy.

One guard with a pistol stood maybe halfway between Dillon and herself. Lightner and another guard flanked Dillon at the focal point.

It was a bizarre scene, Tara thought, her fellow agent tied to a tower as if in some ancient ritualistic sacrifice. Dillon was about to be incinerated in this solar furnace. She had to act.

That was when she happened to read the label on the metal box she was crouching behind: "STEAM VENT COUPLER."

Her eyes followed the two-foot-diameter metal duct that snaked from the top of the box to the turbine assembly on the right side of the tower platform.

"Goodbye, Agent Marconi," Lightner intoned into the bullhorn. "Let there be light!"

Tara leaned out from behind her cover and fired three shots at the nearest guard.

Two missed, one struck him in the head. As he dropped to the floor, she saw the other guard coming to investigate and squeezed off two more rounds in rapid succession while she ducked back behind the steam-vent box. Neither of her shots found its intended target, but Tara wasted no time cursing her lack of accuracy.

She used her three remaining rounds to blast a close grouping of holes in the steam duct. The room began to fill with the white mist. She stayed behind the box as a volley of return fire was directed her way.

Then she stood and delivered a high kick to the duct where her three bullet holes were. Already weakened, the vent buckled under the force of her blow, the three bullet holes merging into one gaping rip. Tara dodged the ensuing blast of steam, rolling onto the floor.

The room rapidly filled with steam. Because it was open to the air, the temperature in the tower didn't become scalding, but the vapor provided just enough cover for Tara to move toward Dillon without being seen. She wanted to pick up the fallen guard's gun, but his body was in the line of fire from Lightner and the remaining guard.

Tara ran to the front side of the tower, the side where Dillon was being held. She could see Lightner's shadowy form dodging back and forth through the steam, not wanting to remain stationary.

He doesn't know I'm out of ammo, she thought. Then she saw Lightner's guard backpedal away from Dillon. It was Matiu, the islander who had fished Bernie's hat from the water. He was getting out of the way of the solar thermal beam, Tara knew.

She saw her chance.

Charging like a bull, Tara put her head down and sprinted for Matiu, who stood near the edge of the tower platform. She plowed into him at full speed, using her hands to push him away from her body when she made contact.

But her adversary was surprisingly agile, and he gripped her wrists with his hands. The next thing Tara knew, Matiu was spinning her around. Dillon's face, Lightner's shadowy form, and the deck of Solar Island below all whirled in a kaleidoscope of steam-shrouded chaos.

Dillon's bloodcurdling scream cut through the fog of Tara's struggle. "The rays!"

Tara felt something hot flicker over the back of her right hand, which was clenching Matiu's shirt, and then it was Matiu's turn to let loose with a scream.

His body jerked spasmodically, and she knew that the solar thermal beam was now boring into him, searing his flesh. He was barely in control of his own movements.

"Turn him back around! I can *see* the rays!" Tara seemed to hear Dillon from her subconscious. But it was true. Matiu was positioning her so that soon she would be the one in the path of the concentrated energy.

A foul odor reached Tara's nostrils. Her mind didn't want to believe it, yet at the same time she knew that she was smelling the man's burning flesh. Hers was next, if she couldn't get control of Matiu's convulsing body.

But Matiu was twice her size; there was no way she could hope to hold him in place. Tara was locked into a bear hug with her smoldering foe, but he was moving out of position of the energy beam and moving her into it.

Tara knew she would only be able to hold Matiu in position for a few more seconds. Even if he died, there was a limit to how long she could hold up his body as a human heat shield. She had no idea what Lightner was up to, though he seemed to have shrunk back a safe distance from the beam. The steam in the tower was thicker now, making it difficult to see even a few feet.

"Pull him back, pull him back!" Dillon screamed.

Tara used Dillon's voice as a positional reference. She risked her own left arm by wrapping it around Matiu's back, exposing it to the concentrated sunbeam to pull him against her body.

He shrieked as the energy beam seared anew into his flesh. She backed up toward Dillon, dragging Matiu with her.

With her right hand Tara reached back and pulled the shark-tooth war club from her back pocket. She whipped her head back to see how Dillon was tied. One rope around his chest and arms, she saw, before Matiu forced her to turn back around. He spasmodically flailed at her face and neck, wailing incoherently, a last desperate act from someone who has found superhuman strength *in extremis*. Tara felt her left wrist flare with pain, and she moved it out of the beam's path.

She reached back and hooked the shark-tooth weapon under Dillon's rope. She began sawing it back and forth, the serrated edges of the teeth acting as they had been designed to in nature, tearing fibers—manila instead of muscle, but it worked just the same. Dillon lunged at his restraint, putting additional stress on the weakening rope.

With one last effort, before she knew she would have to let go of Matiu's body, Tara ripped at Dillon's rope with the shark teeth. The remaining fibers parted and Dillon let himself drop to the floor just as Tara let go of Matiu. She spun to the right. The solar thermal beam hit the collection point where Dillon had been only seconds before, passing over Matiu's smoldering corpse lying crumpled on the floor.

Only Lightner remained. *But where was he?*

FIFTY-FOUR

Tara watched the solar thermal beam blink out. Then she heard the roaring whine of the turbines drop in pitch. As Tara and Dillon got themselves up off the floor, the steam in the power tower began to dissipate. The energy-generation plant had shut down.

Tara took advantage of the increased visibility to look around the area. She saw no foes. Only two dead bodies—Matiu's, and that of the guard she had shot. Even though the steam had cleared, the air had become a noxious chemical miasma. Tara and Dillon were racked with coughing fits. They made their way to the edge of the power tower, and Tara's face turned ashen as she gazed out.

Solar Island was ablaze.

Not just a simple spot fire, like the one Tara had created with the electric cart—although she supposed that's how it could have started—but a raging conflagration that was consuming the floating structure in its entirety. Black smoke billowed skyward.

As they watched, a massive explosion rocked the island. The fire had reached the battery bank, its molten nitrate salts and volatile chemical cocktail releasing their stored power all at once. The entire island rocked visibly under the detonation. They could feel the vibrations rattle the power tower. One man, wreathed in flames, ran for the edge of the island, pitching himself into the sea twenty feet below.

Tara looked toward the marina. The boats would be the only hope for survivors, but her heart sank when she saw the little harbor already engulfed in fire. She watched aghast as the submersible and its onboard oxygen tanks disintegrated violently before her eyes, creating a vicious shrapnel storm of jagged acrylic and metal that cut down the last man still trying to free the remaining boats.

Dillon pointed at the water, and Tara saw one of the tugboats—the only vessel that had been outside of the marina before the fire—take two swimmers aboard. The remaining survivors of Solar Island were jumping ship to the tugboat—now operating as a lifeboat. The vessel was nearly full to capacity with people, mostly Pacific Islanders, and most of them the peaceful residents of Solar Island who had not waged war against her or anyone else.

Tara clutched Dillon's arm. Their own lifeboat still waited above.

"The helicopter. Let's go."

They ran to the metal ladder and climbed until they emerged on the helipad.

"Hello, big beautiful bird!" Tara exclaimed upon seeing that their helicopter was still there and in one piece.

"Where's Rob?" Dillon asked, voicing Tara's own concern. *Without Rob...*

She didn't want to think about what they would do if something had happened to Rob. Neither of them knew how to pilot the chopper.

Tara broke into a run until she reached the Sikorsky. *Please let him be alive.*

Seeing no one through the front-seat windows, Tara slid the rear bay door back. Rob Tanner lay trussed up inside, tied to some cargo netting.

"Sonofabitch, Shores, am I ever glad to see you. I smell smoke." He glanced at the object still clutched in her hand. "What the hell is that thing?"

"My souvenir from Solar Island." Tara worked her magic with the shark-tooth club on Rob's bindings and quickly freed him. "We need to get out of here, Rob. Right now."

Rob stretched his arms gingerly, wincing as the blood flow returned to normal.

"Rob, I mean it. Come here."

Deciding that having Rob see the situation for himself was worth a thousand words, Tara dragged him out of the helicopter and to the edge of the helipad. From Solar Island's highest point, they watched it burn.

A mere glimpse of the scene was all Rob needed before he was sprinting for his cockpit.

Tara and Dillon stood side by side, looking down on the mayhem. The floating structure was now almost entirely covered in bright orange flames that shot at least ten feet into the air. In one clear area near the perimeter, Tara spotted a silver-haired man shouting commands to men who were in a blind panic, one leaping overboard on fire while another dropped a hose and ran toward the tugboat.

Lightner!

They watched as Lightner continued to spray a fire extinguisher with one hand while raising the bullhorn to his mouth with the other.

"Put it out, put it out—the sovereign nation of Solar Island must be preserved! Any man who leaves now will be tried for desertion!"

Behind them, the helicopter's rotors started to turn.

Soon there were three more men in the water, scratching their way to the tugboat, and it was clear that Dr. Jacob Lightner was alone on Solar Island's main deck.

He aimed his extinguisher at the wall of fire closing in on him, but it was a pitifully small defense against the raging firestorm. As the last of the fire retardant was spent, Lightner let the bottle drop and turned to look up at the helipad.

He looked at Tara, smiling crazily as he shouted into the bullhorn. "Thank you, Tara Shores. You have been the one encounter in my life that can never be repeated."

He then allowed the flames to consume him without a struggle.

Tara felt the tower beneath the helipad begin to wobble. The white surface started to bubble and peel in spots. Rob's tanned arm was waving them over from the cockpit window. Tara and Dillon ran to the Sikorsky and jumped in through the open bay door. Not waiting for them to close it, Rob lifted off as soon as his two passengers were inside. Half of the helipad collapsed to the deck when they took off.

Tara watched the island begin to break apart while Rob gained some altitude above the tricky updrafts created by the fire.

The section where the chemical explosion had occurred was the first to go, fragmenting and floating away from the rest of the island. Then the power tower wobbled precariously and Tara and Dillon watched in disbelief as it toppled to the flaming deck below. The impact eliminated what little structural integrity remained, and soon Solar Island was more of a debris trail littering the ocean's surface than it was a floating island.

Tara told Rob to radio their GPS coordinates to the U.S. Coast Guard Guam station so that assistance would be available to the men in the tugboat if needed. Then Rob radioed the tugboat itself to let them know this had been done.

As the sun sank into the South Pacific, the last pieces of Solar Island sank as well, toward a permanent home on the seafloor in perpetual darkness.

"Ayn Rand," Dillon said, as he and Tara took the jump seats in back.

"What?" Tara said, mind numb as she watched the island burn beneath them.

"Lightner's last words. They're Ayn Rand, from *The Fountainhead.* He wrote about them in a college essay."

Tara nodded as Rob banked the Sikorsky west toward Guam.

"I read that one. Individualism, collectivism."

"I spoke to an old English professor of his, and he sent me the paper Lightner wrote on her books. He was clearly taken with her ideas."

Tara looked back on the remaining fragments of Solar Island as they issued black smoke. For a second she pictured the island in one piece again, flashing on Lightner tied to the pipes in Bernie's crawl space.

I farm the sun! Is a farmer not entitled to the fruits of his labor?

Yes, Tara thought, looking down at the water that became Lightner's final resting place.

Yes, he is.

FOR FURTHER READING

BOOKS

Deffeyes, Kenneth S. *Beyond Oil: The View from Hubbert's Peak.* New York: Hill and Wang, 2006.

Luft, Gal, and Anne Korin. *Turning Oil into Salt: Energy Independence through Fuel Choice.* U.S.: Booksurge Publishing, 2009.

Zubrin, Robert. *Energy Victory: Winning the War on Terror by Breaking Free of Oil.* New York: Prometheus Books, 2007.

SCIENTIFIC LITERATURE

Lewis, Nathan S. 2007. *Powering the Planet.* California Institute of Technology Engineering & Science, No. 2. http://authors.library.caltech.edu/9302/1/LEWmrsb07.pdf

OTHER

Ayn Rand Institute: http://www.aynrand.org

The New York Times | Solar Energy: http://topics.nytimes.com/topics/news/science/topics/solar_energy/index.html

The Seasteading Institute: http://www.seasteading.org/

ABOUT THE AUTHOR

RICK CHESLER holds a Bachelor of Science in marine biology and has had a lifelong interest in the ocean and its creatures. When not at work writing, he can be found scuba-diving or traveling to research his next thriller idea. He currently lives in the Florida Keys with his wife and son. Visit him online at rickchesler.com.